Praise for *Three Nights In Italy*

'A gorgeous, life-affirming helping the people we love become found. Warm, wistful, and wise, *Three Nights In Italy* is a book my heart will treasure'
Laura Jane Williams

'Olivia Beirne writes with such warmth and humour. She just GETS women, and covers both light and serious topics in such relatable, tender ways'
Lucy Vine

'You can feel the warmth of the sun on every single page . . . brilliantly funny and filled with love'
Daisy Buchanan

'A beautiful story about changing your life and taking chances. It had me wanting to hop on a plane to Italy immediately!'
Lorraine Brown

'It was such a fun, pacy read full of colourful characters that will stay with me beyond the page. A story of second chances and taking risks filled with warmth and humour – I loved it'
Caroline Khoury

'A charming, feel-good book that you won't be able to put down. Olivia once again wins you over with her beautifully real and raw characters whose lives you can't help but get invested in! Loved it'
Emily Houghton

'Beirne consistently writes women and their complex, often messy, but tender relationships beautifully'
Pernille Hughes

Olivia Beirne is the bestselling author of *The List That Changed My Life*, *The Accidental Love Letter* and *House Swap* and lives in Buckinghamshire. She has worked as a waitress, a pottery painter and a casting assistant, but being a writer is definitely her favourite job yet.

Also by Olivia Beirne:

The List That Changed My Life
The Accidental Love Letter
House Swap

three nights in italy

olivia beirne

REVIEW

First published in 2023 by Headline Review
An imprint of HEADLINE PUBLISHING GROUP

1

Cataloguing in Publication Data is available from the British Library

ISBN 978 1 4722 8449 5

Typeset in 11.25/14.75pt Bembo Std by Jouve (UK), Milton Keynes

Printed and bound in Great Britain by Clays Ltd, Elcograf S.p.A.

Headline's policy is to use papers that are natural, renewable and recyclable
products and made from wood grown in well-managed forests and other
controlled sources. The logging and manufacturing processes are expected
to conform to the environmental regulations of the country of origin.

HEADLINE PUBLISHING GROUP
An Hachette UK Company
Carmelite House
50 Victoria Embankment
London EC4Y 0DZ

www.headline.co.uk
www.hachette.co.uk

To my Grandma Nain and my Grandma.
Grief is the price you pay for love.

PROLOGUE

ZOE

'Zoe, wake up.'

A familiar voice fills my ears, jolting me from my deep sleep. It's barely a whisper, quiet and scratchy like she hasn't spoken in hours. Which would make sense considering it's the middle of the night. I peel open an eye, adjusting to the darkness around me, except for the sliver of moonlight creeping through the slats of the blinds. Sleeping at Grandma's is like crawling into a cave and closing yourself off from the world. There are no street lights and barely a sound in the Italian mountains where her house nestles. The only thing that can shock you awake is the occasional electrical thunderstorm that snaps and crackles across the midnight sky like a firework display. Well, that and my grandma and her disregard for the time.

I turn my head towards the figure crouching next to me.

Grandma beams back at me, thrilled that her plan has worked. I can smell coffee on her breath, and I scrunch up my face.

'Grandma,' I moan half-heartedly, 'why are you awake? It's the middle of the night.'

I try to close my eyes again, but she gives me a shake.

'I couldn't sleep. I've been up for hours. Come on, get up. I've got something I need to show you.'

I hear the smack of her walking stick as she crosses the wooden floorboards, and I jump as she thwacks it against the door frame, shaking me immediately awake again.

'Okay,' I manage, 'I'm up, I'm up.'

There is very little point me trying to get back to sleep now. Once Grandma has an idea in her head, there is no deterring her. If I don't follow her downstairs in the next five seconds, she'll return with a vengeance. Quite frankly, I wouldn't put it past her to tip a bucket of water over my head.

I drag my legs out from underneath the thin sheet and follow the sound of her shuffling down the corridor. She's like a wind-up toy. She can't walk that easily (to be fair, the woman is in her nineties), but she shuffles with such speed that if you looked away for a second she'd be gone.

Only the moonlight peering through the shutters breaks up the darkness that has swept over the landing. I hold my hands out to try to steady myself as I make my way down the stairs. She clunks down each step and I wince every time she lands. We have spent this entire summer terrified that she's about to fall over and break something, but Grandma goes out of her way to prove that she's made of rubber. Last weekend she tried to get me to compete in a cartwheel race. Considering she can barely walk nowadays without her stick, I'm almost certain she was joking. But she's so furiously against being old that I wouldn't want to challenge her. She'd probably try and forward-roll down the mountain.

'What's going on?'

I turn to look back up the stairs as a beam of light spills over Grandma and me. Mum is standing in her bedroom doorway, arms crossed, frowning down at us. She yawns loudly.

'Oh good, you're up.' Grandma waves her walking stick above her head, not an ounce of remorse on her face at having woken up the whole house. She has at least now reached the bottom of the stairs. 'Come on, Angie. There's something I want to show both of you.'

'Mum!' Exasperation carries Mum's voice. 'What are you doing? Do you have any idea what time it is?'

'Time?' Grandma scoffs. 'What is time? Inspiration knows no time. Magic knows no time, Angie. Time is just a state of mind.' She continue to shuffle into the living room.

Mum rolls her eyes at me, and I shrug. We both know that this is just Grandma – weird yet wonderful, mad but incredible. She's like a child hiding inside the body of an old woman. It's like she doesn't understand rules, or maybe she does and simply refuses to follow the beat of anybody else's drum. But she gets away with it because she's an artist, and that's why everybody loves her.

'Have you been drinking coffee?' Mum asks, pushing her thin hair out of her eyes as she follows her into the living room. 'You shouldn't, it's not good for you.'

'Would you rather I drank brandy?' Grandma challenges.

'Remind me to replace it with decaf tomorrow,' Mum mutters to me as Grandma turns to face us and waves her stick in the air, commanding attention.

'Well?' she cries. 'What do you think?'

'Of what?' I say. 'I can't see.'

'Hang on.' Mum steps back and turns on a lamp. As a warm glow pools around her, she tightens her cotton dressing gown over her floral nightie, her eyes scrunched up like prunes, trying to see without her glasses.

Grandma is wearing soft sunshine-yellow dungarees. Her white hair is wild, falling down her back, with tufts sticking up where she's scratched her head. She has splats of paint across her face and she's clasping a paintbrush. As she waves her hand around, her engagement ring catches the light. That ring has sat proudly on her hand for the past sixty years, and she's always claimed that it's magic. It's how my grandpa speaks to her; she says each glint of the ring is him saying 'hello', or 'go for it!' or – more often than not – 'I love you!' Whenever I catch it glimmering, she gives me a knowing look as though we are sharing a secret.

Now her blue eyes are filled with excitement as they flash between me and her latest creation, and I finally look at what she's woken us up for.

Standing on her easel is a canvas covered in paint. It's messy, with a flurry of colours splattered across it – azure blue and rusted orange, with careful strokes of gold and buttermilk yellow. In the centre is a woman. She is at one with the colours, as though she's created the mess. Her eyes are closed as she embraces the paint speckled across her face.

'Wow,' I breathe. 'Grandma, it's beautiful. I love it.'

'You see, her life is full of colour and madness. It's random and sometimes the colours don't go together, but she's happy. She doesn't care what time it is.'

'Who is she?'

A wise smile pulls at her crinkled lips. She pauses for a moment before exclaiming, 'Who do you think? She's me!'

She holds out her hands, and me and Mum walk towards her. She takes our hands and turns her own so that the ring is facing us.

'She is all of us,' she says. 'She's magic.'

I laugh. 'I'm not magic.'

She raises her eyebrows. 'You don't believe you're magic?'

I grin. I'm twenty-five, but I don't think Grandma will ever not speak to me like I'm the wide-eyed eight-year-old she used to play dragons and knights with.

She squeezes my hand. 'When you're wearing this ring, my love, you believe in everything.'

Chapter One

Angie

Six weeks later

They're everywhere, piles of them stacked up around the village hall. Chicken sandwiches, ham sandwiches, cheese sandwiches, tuna sandwiches. White bread and granary. Neat triangles with their crusts cut off. Little sausage rolls, and bowls of crisps that people continually dip their hands into. They're scooping dollops of hummus or sour cream and chive onto their paper plates, murmuring politely over cups of half-drunk tea and tepid, bitter coffee. It's a sea of drooped shoulders, shrouded in black clothing. And then there are the four of us. Me, Reg, Zoe and Harriet.

It always shocks you, death. Even if you know it's coming, if it's inevitable. You're never ready. Ever since her hand went cold in mine, I've felt as though someone has ripped me from my anchor and now I'm just floating around aimlessly. I'm starved of oxygen; I can barely breathe. But I need to keep moving. It's the only thing I know how to do, and I have no idea what will happen if I stop.

Mum wanted to be buried in Cornwall with my dad. So here we are. A service in the rain, a few polite readings, and now a village-hall wake, full of people I want to shake and scream at in the hope they'll tell me it's not real. That none of this is real.

But it is. I know that better than anyone.

Zoe has been in a corner since the moment she arrived, chatting with her best friend Harriet. Every now and again she glances at me, and I can tell she is about to march over with wide eyes and ask me how I'm doing and whether I'd like to talk. The only thing that could possibly make being at your mother's funeral worse is having your only daughter look at you with eyes full of worry. You're supposed to be worried about them, not the other way around.

Harriet is keeping her busy, chatting and filling her plate high with cake. She's a lifeline, Harriet. She's been a ball of energy ever since she turned up at my door for tea after school, aged eleven, with long, gangly legs and streams of straggly red hair. She's kept her place at our kitchen table ever since.

And then there is my brother, Reggie, the polar opposite of me in every situation. Today is no exception. His is the only laugh to be heard, ricocheting off the walls as he greets family members and old friends with slaps on the back, big, bracing hugs and jostles of shoulders. He seems to be doing a pretty good job of keeping it together.

I'm the fourth piece of the puzzle, and I'm starting to wonder if I could slip out of the door without anybody noticing. I can feel their eyes on me, trying to find the right moment to lay a gentle hand on my arm and tell me how sorry they are for my loss. But I can't have that happen. If a single one of these well-wishing friends even cocks their head in my direction, I'll fall apart.

So instead I focus on the sandwiches, and I'm doing a pretty good job of coping. That is, until the instantly recognisable glissando of ABBA's 'Dancing Queen' slides through the speakers and I rush off to hide in the toilet, where I sob into my sleeve, feeling like I might vomit.

Three minutes of allowing myself to drown. Then a deep breath, a splash of water to the face, and back to the sandwiches. I think it's about time I restocked the coronation chicken.

CHAPTER TWO

ZOE

'Thank you so much for coming, so good to see you!'

I tip another plate of half-eaten sausage rolls into a black bin bag and eye my uncle sceptically. He's been standing by the door of the village hall for the past half an hour saying his good-byes, while Mum, Harriet and I have scurried around sweeping and wiping and unsuccessfully closing various trestle tables. One kicked me in the shins so violently that I nearly gave Mum a stroke with the curse I yelled across the room. I had to promise I'd never say the word again to stop her having a go at me. It wasn't even that bad! All I said was 'pissflaps'.

While all of this has been going on, my uncle has been doing what he does best. Ignoring his responsibilities and smarming up to everyone around him.

I bundle the bin bag into the kitchen and take a deep breath. All day my heart has felt like it's full of lead.

I knew today would be hard, but I also know that this is what Grandma wanted, not that that makes it any easier. It just feels so wrong that this is how we said goodbye to someone so full of life – in a shitty village hall, with rain pummelling the roof. We should have said goodbye to her in Italy, on a mountain somewhere, watching the sunrise. Not like this.

I cringe as my uncle booms his final goodbye: 'Let's not leave it so long next time! Have a safe journey home. God bless.'

He holds his hand up in a wave and then pushes a cigarette in his mouth, pulling the door closed behind him as he steps outside. I look up and see Harriet brandishing a dustpan and brush.

'I think that's everything,' she says, 'but I've got to run. My shift starts in . . . er . . .' she glances up at the clock, 'eight minutes.'

I take the dustpan and brush off her. 'Go!' I say. 'Oh my God, go. You didn't have to help clear up, but thank you.'

She wraps her arms around me and gives me a firm hug. 'I'm going to call you later, okay?'

I nod, feeling a lump in my throat. I've managed to avoid hugs all day.

'I couldn't find your mum,' she says as she lets me go, 'but tell her I said goodbye.'

'I will.'

I look through the hatch of the kitchen, glancing around for Mum, who slipped away the moment people started leaving, mumbling something about sandwiches. We all know she just wanted to get out of saying goodbye.

Uncle Reggie reappears from outside, bringing in a trail of cigarette smoke with him. He flashes his veneers at the empty room, whilst pulling off a pair of sunglasses, even though it's currently raining outside and we haven't seen the sun in three days. His oily hair is slicked over his balding scalp, and he loosens the black tie around his neck, smacking his hands together.

'Right, Ange. Where are ya?'

I step out of the kitchen, dustpan and brush still in hand.

The problem with my uncle is that unfortunately he is incredibly difficult to like.

Well, he has no problem on the dating scene, and was married to my Aunt Fanny for ten years before she left him. He works in property, jetting all over the world selling houses to the rich and pompous (think *Selling Sunset* with more Lynx Africa), and he's very good at charming people into buying luxury homes. So maybe what I should say is: *I* find him impossible to like. He's smarmy and rude and makes no effort to hide how highly he regards himself versus everybody else, but in particular my mum. In his world, he's sitting on top of Everest whilst Mum is in the cereal aisle of Londis.

'That's that all done then,' he says, grinning at me. 'Where's your mum, eh? Ange?' He yells her name across the empty hall, and I bristle.

'I'm sure she's coming,' I mutter, trying my best not to glare at him.

'Ange!'

'Don't shout at her,' I say. 'This is a really hard day. She's not coping well.' My voice catches. I can't bear seeing my mum like this, floating around like a ghost.

'Right,' he says, pulling out his phone. 'Ah. There she is.'

When Mum reappears, she somehow looks even smaller than she did this morning. Much like Grandma, she is a petite woman. She stands at just over five foot, and has thin, mousy hair, which usually covers half her face. Her glasses have square frames, and they're constantly in her hand, being cleaned by the sleeve of whatever cardigan she's wearing. She is soft, with round edges and a quiet, tinkly laugh. She spends her entire life looking after everybody else, but she won't let anyone look after her. She didn't used to be this bad. I remember her laughing when I was a child, going out with friends and dancing round the room with me whenever *Strictly* was on. But fourteen years ago, my aunt – my mum's closest friend – left and our lives were turned upside down, and it's like all Mum's confidence was taken too.

'Sorry,' she says, going straight to one of the few standing trestle tables with a damp cloth, 'I was just sorting out the recycling.'

'Right,' Uncle Reggie says, barely listening, 'great. So I have to run, I'm working in France for the rest of the week. My taxi will be here any second.'

I blink at him. 'Are you not going to help clear up?'

Mum flushes under her fringe, but he doesn't even flinch.

'Well, you've done it all, haven't you? Maybe save me a picture of Mum,' he adds as an afterthought.

Mum glances round at the many photos of Grandma around the hall. 'Which one?'

'Oh, any.'

'Right.'

'Before I go, just a quick update on the will.'

My stomach turns over. I hate talking about all of this. It seems so formal and final. An entire life packed up neatly in a little box, like she wasn't a living, breathing person for ninety years.

'So, we all know that Mum wanted to auction off her art-work and any of her belongings. Her furniture and jewellery and so on.'

Mum nods. 'For charity.'

'And for us,' Uncle Reggie says pointedly. 'Split down the middle.'

Mum continues wiping. No trestle table has ever been so clean.

'I've arranged for the auction to be next week,' he says, not taking his eyes off his phone. 'I'll let you know how it all goes.'

I feel like my heart has dropped through my body. 'Next week?' I repeat. 'That's so fast.'

'Well, no point putting it off, is there?'

'But I wanted to go,' I say, walking over to Mum. 'I was thinking, this doesn't feel like the right way to say goodbye to Grandma. We should do something in Italy too, near her home.'

I try to look at Mum but she's still scrubbing, avoiding my eye.

'You can still do that!' Uncle Reggie says, waving a hand at me. 'Her house will still be there, just without her things.'

'It won't be the same without her things!' I protest. I take a deep breath. 'What about her ring?'

'What about it?' His voice carries an air of impatience.

'Grandma always said it would be mine.'

'I didn't see that in the will.'

His words sting, and for a moment, every word I know falls out of my mind.

'Come on, Reg. You know she promised it to Zoe.' Mum's small voice creeps across the hall.

A car horn beeps outside, and he looks over his shoulder. 'Fine,' he retorts. 'I'll keep a ring aside for you.'

14

'Not just *a* ring,' I say, my heart thumping. 'Her *engagement* ring. The one she never took off.'

I need that ring. It carries her magic. I always knew that one day I'd be wearing it – it's what she always said. I don't want to leave it up to him to keep it aside for me. I don't trust him.

'Why don't we all go?' I blurt the question, panic rising in my voice. 'We could help with the auction and say goodbye properly.'

A shadow passes across Uncle Reggie's face. 'There really is no need.'

'Mum,' I turn to face her, pleading with my eyes, 'what do you think?'

'Oh, I—'

'Zoe, stop it.' I flinch as Uncle Reggie's voice cracks through me like a whip. 'You're upsetting your mum. There is no need for you to come to Italy. I've got it all sorted.'

The car horn honks again, and he places a patronising hand on my arm. 'You just stay here and take care of your mum, okay?'

Heat prickles up my body as he kisses Mum and picks up his bag. 'I'll be in touch!' he calls over his shoulder. The door slams, and seconds later we hear the taxi skid out of the car park.

For a moment we both stay where we are, silent, then I walk over to Mum and place my hand on top of hers, releasing the cloth and halting her frantic scrubbing.

'It's clean, Mum.'

Chapter Three

Harriet

I drum my fingers on the reception desk and start counting again.

I have been sitting behind this desk for four hours. Or two hundred and forty minutes. Or twelve full-length fantasies where I slam my hand on the desk, demand to see my manager, then swan off into the sunset with my winning lottery ticket in hand. One of those fantasies involves a dog, and one features Chris Hemsworth, but they all involve Zoe. Well, except the Chris Hemsworth one. Thor trumps girl code. Sorry, Zoe.

I know pretty much everyone hates their job, but I *really* hate mine. And I hate that I hate it. But no matter how many meditations or sun salutations I do, the rage reappears and bubbles under my skin the second a plumped-up pompous old fart swans to the reception desk and asks me to do . . . well, anything.

And yes, to be fair, I can understand why they think that requesting an extra pillow or more biscuits is a normal thing to ask a hotel receptionist. It's hardly their fault that they only have to convert oxygen into carbon dioxide before I'm beginning to plot their murder. But I don't want to be here. I categorically *do not* want to be here. I want to be anywhere else but here.

Well, apart from my last job as a waitress. Or that hellish job working in a call centre where my manager timed my toilet breaks. How am I supposed to check Instagram when I'm expected to pee at the speed of light? Who am I, Seabiscuit?

I turn over the scratch card next to my phone and scowl at it. I slammed it down in frustration about an hour ago when it gave me lemon, lemon, *heart*.

My phone lights up as Mum sends through another photo of my baby brother. He's a fat little thing, with cute rolls and a smile that takes up half his face. I send a heart back, even though the update makes my own heart turn over.

I'm not proud of this, but I'm not sure I ever expected my mum to have a life outside of me. And yes, I don't like the light that casts me in, but it's the truth. It's not that I don't want her to be happy; it's more that I thought she *was* happy. The two of us were a team. My dad has never been around, and me and Mum have always been thick as thieves. She's a nurse, so worked a lot of night shifts, which led to lots of sleepovers for me at Zoe's, but other than that, we were always together. I toyed with the idea that she might get a boyfriend one day (not that I'd ever really seen her date), but a *baby* as well? That's a whole new family. A whole new family without me in it.

And out of nowhere, it gave me the blinding, striking feeling that this was what she had always wanted, and that maybe she hadn't been as happy as I thought she'd been for all those years. But now she is . . . and I'm still hanging around.

I look up as the bell that hangs above the door tinkles and my manager, Sophie, sashays through reception. I jump to attention like I've been zapped and suddenly bang on my keyboard, pretending to look incredibly busy and not like I was imagining a moonlit walk across the beach with Chris Hemsworth. I can see her out of the corner of my eye, peering at me, and I will my cheeks to stay a normal shade of pink and not give me away.

'Hi, Harriet,' she says as she reaches the desk.

I hit a few more keys for good measure. 'Oh, hello, Sophie. How are you?'

'What are you up to?' She cranes her neck ever so slightly in an attempt to view my screen.

'Oh, you know,' I say lightly. 'Just answering some emails.'

(Nobody emails me.)

'Have you been up to room 201 yet?'

'Hmm?' I try and feign ignorance, even though I received a rather terse call from someone about an hour ago demanding a fresh set of towels. I would have gone up sooner, but they didn't say please. Rude people don't deserve nice towels.

'Oh!' I say, as if the memory has just dropped into my mind. 'Yes. No, not yet. I'm just getting to it.'

She pinches her lips together. 'Okay. And what about the function room? Is it cleared from the wedding?'

Urgh, the function room. I was hoping that if I avoided that for long enough, somebody else would do it.

'I don't think so,' I say carefully. 'I've been on reception today.'

This is my answer for everything, and it's the perfect alibi. You have to have a receptionist on the desk at all times. Nobody can argue with that. And is it my fault that I can't split myself in half and clean the function room and sit on reception at the same time? Of course it's not. Nobody can get annoyed with me for that.

'And how are you getting on with the filing?'

I glance down at the stack of papers that were plonked on my desk two weeks ago.

Ah. Shit.

'I'm just getting to it now,' I say sweetly, leafing through the top pages.

Sophie sighs. 'Look, Harriet. Can I be honest with you?'

Hmm. Can I say no?

'Of course!'

'I don't really get the impression that you enjoy being a hotel receptionist.'

She pauses, and I try and will my face not to move when all I want to do is scream that *of course I don't enjoy being a hotel receptionist.* I haven't enjoyed a single job I've had since I left university. I know I could quit and get a new one, but what's the point? They're all the same. Everything will be the same until I can finally win the lottery, grab Zoe and run away.

'Of course I do,' I say, mustering up some enthusiasm. 'I'll start on the filing now.'

'Actually,' Sophie holds out a hand, 'would you mind taking the fresh towels up? I'll cover reception.'

I push my chair back.

Win the lottery, grab Zoe and run away.

Chapter Four

Zoe

I take a sip of my black coffee, the bitterness biting at my tongue as I try to focus my squared eyes on my flickering computer monitor. It's barely 8 a.m., and I've been sitting here for an hour. I'm two coffees down already, and I'm not supposed to start until nine. But I needed to be here. I couldn't bear the silence of my house any longer.

Not that I've done anything since arriving at work. I can't stop thinking about yesterday. Once Uncle Reggie had skidded off in his taxi, leaving me and Mum with our sad, limp bin bags and our sad, limp smiles, the rest of the day skimmed by in a blur. We cleaned the rest of the hall in near silence, and only left when the caretaker arrived to retrieve the keys. We didn't speak about Italy; we barely spoke at all. I felt as if I was being pulled in two. On one hand, I wanted to ignore Uncle Reggie and book my flight. But whenever I looked at Mum, I could feel my heart turn over. She's barely holding it together, and I have a horrible feeling that the only thing keeping her moving is my constant checking-up on her. If I left her, even for a few days, I don't know what would happen. She's refusing to cry in front of me, or even talk to me. All her energy seems to be funnelled into her constant fussing. Manically cleaning the house, changing my sheets every day, cooking elaborate meals from scratch. God knows what she'd do with all those emotions if she was on her own.

I wiggle my computer mouse and try to focus on the screen.

I work at a small and very intimate wedding planning agency as one of their lead client coordinators, run by my boss, Heidi James. I started here three months after I finished university and have been planning and pitching weddings alongside my colleague, Orla, ever since. Orla's weddings are sexy and wouldn't look out of place on a Kardashian's Instagram feed. Whereas mine are simple and romantic. A lot of the clients I win are couples who want to elope and get married on a Cornish beach at sunrise. Heidi calls what I offer 'a romantic service'. Which I absolutely hate. It makes me sound like I'm available to be an escort who doubles up as the little spoon while watching reruns of *Friends*.

Orla and I each know our own strengths, but that doesn't stop us having to pitch for every client, which means we're constantly fuelled by the knowledge that the winner will walk away with a fatter pay cheque and bragging rights for the rest of the month.

Where Orla has style and perfect hair, I have my own super-power: Kitty, my glorious, real-life-angel assistant. She started about ten months ago and swiftly became one of my favourite people in the world. She's like a human Care Bear, with soft purple hair and big, bright eyes. She swoons over the brides and gushes over stories of how they met their other halves. She loves love. I love love too, but I'm also very happy to tick off another successful wedding and move on to the next one. Kitty asks for updates on the honeymoon and squeals if she sees a social media post six months later about a pregnancy announcement.

Orla hired her own assistant, Saskia. Who is just as poised and perfect, and, much like Orla, never accepts the offer of one of Kitty's Krispy Kremes.

It's not that I don't enjoy my job. I do. In fact, I love it. But there are only so many times you can make other people's dreams come true before the failure of your own starts to sting. Though pathetically, I don't even think I know what my dreams are.

The lights flicker on around me, jolting me from my thoughts. I look up, expecting Heidi, but instead all I can see is what looks like an enormous gift basket on legs stumbling through the office. As it crashes into a desk, I jump to my feet, rushing over to help. That's when I notice the novelty yellow tights and mini skirt.

'Kitty!' I cry, taking the basket out of her hands. 'Are you okay?'

Today she is wearing a white T-shirt with a large glittering heart on the chest, matching her winged eyeliner, which is framed with a dusting of silver shimmer.

She blinks up at me. 'Oh, I was hoping I'd beat you in this morning! I had a whole thing planned!'

I frown. 'Planned?'

'Sit down!' she orders, gesturing me back to my desk. 'Please,' she adds. 'And close your eyes!'

I do as I'm told, feeling my eyes throb as I shut them. They have been dry and scratchy since the funeral, sore from the wash of tears and bloodshot from the force of peering at Mum to try and check she's okay.

'Okay!' Kitty sings. 'You can open them!'

I look at my desk and feel as if I could burst into tears all over again.

'Kitty . . .' I breathe. 'What is all this?'

She's decorated my desk with a large Starbucks coffee, a unicorn bath bomb and an enormous bunch of flowers.

She drops into Orla's empty seat and smiles at me. 'It's just a care package,' she says. 'I know this weekend must have been really hard on you.'

Do you see what I mean? She's a real-life angel. 'Kitty, thank you so much.'

'You don't have to be here,' she adds. 'You need to give yourself time to grieve.'

Her words cue a zap in the pit of my stomach.

I don't want time to grieve. Time to grieve is time to accept what's happened, and I'm not ready to do that.

I force a smile onto my face. 'It's fine!' I say. 'And I *do* have to be here. Libby is coming in tomorrow, remember?' Libby is our newest client, whose rustic wedding is all scheduled for next week.

Kitty claps her hands together. 'Like I'd forget!' she beams. 'I can't wait! I've got all these table-setting ideas. I've found a company that can make custom bows for the back of the chairs, isn't that amazing? Like you can have a special message embroidered inside the bow!' She waves her own Starbucks in the air with such excitement that for a second I'm worried she's about to sprinkle Orla's desk with caramel frappuccino.

'That's cute.'

'But really,' Kitty's eyes are suddenly wide and earnest, 'if you need to take some time out, then let me know. I'll cover for you.'

'I'm fine,' I reply, turning back to my computer as Orla and Saskia walk in. 'But thank you. You really are the best.'

★

I take a final drag of my cigarette, then peel my lips away, the sticky gloss I'm wearing leaving a pink shimmer on the stub, before flicking it to the floor, giving it a quick stamp with my boot and ducking inside Tesco. I only have thirty minutes before I need to get back to the office, and what was once a relaxing lunch break where I would do a quick snoop of the ASOS website, or occasionally stroll around the local park, is now a military operation.

The problem is, I don't like leaving my mum any more. It never used to be like this. When I was a child, we had a fairly normal relationship. But then there were the three of us: me, Mum and my Aunt Fanny, with Grandma only a phone call away. Aunt Fanny was more than just my uncle's wife; she was my mum's best friend. She spent more time with us than she did with my uncle, sweeping us to dinners and taking us on cinema trips. Mum was always laughing, but then overnight everything changed and she hasn't been the same since. It's a horrible moment when you realise your parents are human too. That they can't be happy all the time and constantly make everything better. They feel pain, and the worst part is that often you can't do anything to help.

As time passed, Mum slowly slipped into a new way of life.

She got an admin job locally and became friendly with all the neighbours. Her calls to Grandma went from once a week to every day. She became obsessed with the Marvel franchise, so we saw every single movie together. She *seemed* happy, though she never laughed as much as she did before. I suppose she was coping, and I started to relax and feel like I could leave her again. I went to university, and Harriet and I started talking about going travelling, maybe even living abroad (everyone has a *Sex and the City* New York fantasy in their twenties, right?).

But then Grandma started getting older, and out of nowhere it was suddenly impossible to ignore her age. It was like every time Mum spoke to her, or came back from a week away in Italy, she'd be a little more tense. The opposite of Grandma herself, who I never saw worry about anything. Grandma always barked at us not to bother worrying, because what was the point? We'd all spent years knitted into the fantasy that she would live for ever. Every time we went to Italy to see her, she was the first to open the red wine and the last to go to bed. I guess we were stupid enough to trick ourselves into believing that she was indestructible; she just wasn't like other people's grandmas.

But when she turned ninety and started to lean heavily on her walking stick, she started to not feel so invincible, and as we watched her body shrink and the life pull from her, the tie I felt to my mum tightened. I couldn't leave her. And now that Grandma has died, I'm not sure I'll ever be able to leave her again.

I've lived with Mum since I graduated, and with Grandma gone, I can't stand the idea of her sitting in the house by herself for eight hours a day while I'm at work. So I check on her every day under the guise of a 'nice coffee and catch-up'. There is absolutely no point in actually asking her how she is – all I ever get is a 'fine, darling!' – so in order for me not to incessantly worry that she's about to fall into a pit of depression, I schedule these thirty-minute check-ins throughout the week. And have dinner with her every night, apart from Saturday, when Harriet drags me into town and Mum is left with Ant and Dec for company.

It's fine. I keep telling myself that it won't be for ever. It's just until the light behind Mum's eyes starts to reappear. Although the longer it goes on, the more I feel like it will never end.

I scuttle into Costa, which is inside our local Tesco and always brimming with yummy mummies in sports leggings with enormous prams and plump babies who look like fresh ducklings. The same woman has worked here for the past four or so years, and every time I ask for oat milk, she looks like she wants to kill me.

I scan the room for Mum and spot her immediately. She's standing staring at the coffee board, her eyes glazed over. There is a queue of people behind her, all clasping paninis and nibbling on their lips impatiently, but she hasn't even noticed them. She's in a daze.

I quickly manoeuvre my way through the queue, murmuring apologies at anyone who shoots me a look of disgust at the idea that I might be pushing in.

I gently take Mum's arm, and she jumps, turning to look at me. 'Oh!' She suddenly plasters a smile on her face, even though her eyes are dewy with tears. 'Hello, darling!' She glances around, suddenly noticing the queue snaking behind her.

'What would you like?' I say, pulling out my bank card and

giving the barista my best smile. 'I'll have a large oat latte, please, and . . . a cup of tea, Mum?'

Mum pushes her thin hair off her face, her cheeks reddening. 'Oh yes, that would be lovely. Thanks so much.'

I steer her to a table. I pretend to be looking at my phone as she dabs her eyes and we both sit down. This keeps happening. She can't seem to face even the normal everyday tasks. She'll be in the kitchen, chopping vegetables, or running a bath, and she'll grind to a slow halt and just start staring. Her eyes mist over and her body completely stills.

'How are you?' I ask.

All of a sudden, she snaps out of her trance-like state and it's like nothing has ever happened.

'Oh!' She smiles. 'I'm fine, love!'

She's always fine. And then we start the cycle all over again.

Chapter Five

Zoe

Six hours later, I'm sitting in my car in a dark street behind our local pub, the Queen's Head, sucking on another cigarette. The engine is running, and I've been staring at people going in and out of the pub, trying to stay calm as I think about Grandma's ring.

I don't trust my uncle to find the ring and bring it home for me. I don't trust him to run the auction, and I hate the idea of staying here, carrying on like normal, while all of Grandma's things are being boxed up and sold to the highest bidder. It doesn't feel right.

But I can't leave Mum. I mean, for God's sake, I can't even leave her alone for a working day without checking in on her. Let alone run away to Italy for a week.

Although I'm starting to wonder if there is any point in me checking in on her, considering that she won't talk to me.

I break out of my thoughts as I spot Harriet charging down

the street towards me. Her red hair is flying behind her, and she looks like she's fleeing a murder scene.

I swallow a smile. Harriet was on another Tinder date tonight, and about twenty minutes ago, I received the word 'pineapple', which is our code word for a get away from a bad date. What are best friends for?

To be honest, I'm quite pleased, as I can use this as support for my anti-dating stance. Harriet likes to challenge me on it every so often, but I can't face Tinder. I tried it for a bit after I broke up with my boyfriend from university, but with every swipe, I felt like I was pulling back a layer of my confidence, and after being ghosted for the third time, I started to feel like love didn't even exist. So I deleted the app and focused on work instead. Well, work and being Harriet's personal chauffeur. Better that than turning to writing sad love songs.

'Oh thank God,' Harriet puffs, falling into the car and slamming the door shut. 'Start driving, please. I don't want him to ask for a lift. I told him I had to go because my cat was sick.'

I look up and see a bemused man with floppy hair stumble out of the pub, looking around aimlessly.

She shrinks down into the seat, and I snigger as I push the car into first gear and roll down the high street.

'How was it then?' I ask, grinning.

She shoots me a look. 'Awful.'

'Worse than the first date?'

'So much worse!' she cries. 'The first time we met, he talked non-stop for an hour, but I just thought he was nervous and would ask me some questions the second time. But he was worse! It was like me agreeing to another date fuelled his confidence in his one-man show and tonight was a bloody encore.'

I laugh. 'I don't know why you agreed to see him again.'

She sighs. 'Pickings are slim. Anyway, what have you been doing with yourself?'

I sigh as I flick the indicator on and steer the car around a corner.

'Oh, not a lot,' I say. 'Just obsessing over my grandma's ring and wishing I could go to Italy.'

Harriet looks up from her phone hopefully. 'Are you about to quit your job and run away?'

'No,' I say, steering my way round a roundabout. 'I can't leave Mum. But the idea is tempting.'

'Well I'll come with you in a heartbeat. I am absolutely desperate to get out of this town. I nearly quit my job three times today *and* I think I almost got fired once. Oh!' She suddenly sits up straight as we drive past a KFC. 'Can we stop and get some food? Please? I'll buy you a burger.'

I pull into the car park and wrench my handbrake up. Harriet unclips her seat belt and looks at me expectantly.

'Aren't you coming in?'

'Can't I wait here?'

'No,' she says. 'I'll need your help carrying everything.'

I groan and pull my hood up to try to hide my face, which is raw after the vigorous scrubbing I gave it earlier and shining from the face mask I lathered on moments before Harriet called me.

Harriet clacks across the car park and I totter after her. At five foot eleven, she already towers over me, but in her heels she's almost a foot taller. We've been best friends since school, and there was a blissful time in Year 7 when we were the same height. Then she hit puberty and shot up. But what she gained in height I gained in breast. Which may sound great, but in reality she looks like Jessica Rabbit and I look like Mrs Doubtfire.

'How hungry are you?' I ask as we push through the doors.

'Starving,' she says, 'and I want to eat my feelings of disappointment too. Oh, and anger. So it's going to be a lot of food.'

'You're not really that disappointed, are you?' I ask.

'Of course I am!' she cries. 'I wasted an entire evening and a full face of make-up on this guy, and he didn't even ask me how my day was!'

Well, that's fair enough.

'Right,' she says as we reach the counter, 'can I please have a Zinger Meal, some popcorn chicken and a bargain bucket.' She snaps her fingers. 'Oh! And a cherry pie. Thank you.'

I laugh as she pays and the woman behind the counter gives her a receipt.

'You will never eat all of that,' I say.

'Maybe not on my own.'

'I'm not even that hungry. How are—'

'Oh my God! Harriet Ashton!'

We both turn on the spot to see a gaggle of girls sitting around a table wearing flashing headbands with furry L plates bouncing at the top.

Oh no. It's Jo Ripley from school. Please don't recognise me. Please don't recognise me. Please don't . . .

'And Zoe?'

Urgh, great.

I smile, trying to act normal with my bright purple hood pulled close to my face, like I'm totally cool and put together and don't look like a massive purple condom.

'Hi, Jo,' Harriet says. 'Are you on your hen do?' She glances down at Jo's glittering 'Bride-to-Be!' sash.

Jo springs to her feet and wraps her arms around us both.

'Yeah!' she cries. 'I live in London now, but I wanted to do a hen at home so that all the girls could come.'

She gestures behind her, and my eyes scan the sea of girls, who are smiling awkwardly at me, just like they used to at school.

Oh God. Is it too late to take my hood down? But what is my hair doing? Argh! I don't know which is worse! I can't take it down and then put it back up. Right, no, it's staying as it is. I will just have to be Tinky Winky. The worst Teletubby, even with that fabulous purse.

'I'm getting married next month!'

I force a smile, realising that Jo has been babbling away whilst I've been thinking about which Teletubby I look like.

'I wanted to go abroad, but we couldn't find the time. It is so stressful organising a wedding, you know?'

Harriet nods. 'Oh yeah, Zoe does weddings.'

'Oh!' Jo squeals, and to my alarm, she grabs my hand. 'Congratulations! When's the big day?'

I snatch my hand away, my face burning. 'No, I *work* in weddings,' I say quickly. 'I'm not getting married. I'm very much single!' I add, with a horrible, awkward laugh that nobody joins in with.

Jo pauses, before snapping back into an excited smile. 'Do you both still live down here then?'

'Yeah,' Harriet says, looking over her shoulder as the woman behind the counter calls out her order. 'We can't seem to get away from the place.'

'It is so nice here,' Jo oozes. 'Every time I come down, I think, why did I move to London? But my job is up there, so . . .' She shrugs, and I try to copy her expression.

'Have a great wedding,' I mumble, following Harriet as she waves goodbye to Jo. 'It was lovely to see you.'

'And you!' Jo calls, waving at us both. 'And good luck with the weddings!'

★

'I hate that,' I mutter, as I click my seat belt back on and turn the key in the ignition.

'Hate what?' Harriet replies, slamming the passenger door shut and immediately biting into a piece of chicken.

'*That*,' I say. 'Why don't I have anything to say?'

'To who?'

'To Jo!' I cry, as I start reversing out of the space. 'She had all these things to say about having a job in London and getting married and I just stood there.'

'You could have told her about your job.'

'Yeah, but that isn't interesting, is it?'

'Isn't it?'

'No.'

Harriet fishes in the paper bag and hands me a piece of popcorn chicken. I slot it into my mouth.

'Thanks.'

'They're overrated,' she says, taking another bite. 'Men and all this dating crap. I'm telling you, one more bad date with someone from Cornwall and I'm packing it all in and getting a one-way ticket out of here, with or without you.'

'If you went without me, I'd be really sad,' I mumble, grabbing another piece of chicken from the depths of the paper bag.

She raises her eyebrows at me. 'Well, if we don't go at all, I'll be sadder.'

A glob of mayonnaise splats down her top, and she groans.

'We will go,' I say, 'to Europe and South America and Asia and Australia.'

'When?'

A prickle of heat rises up my face. 'As soon as Mum is okay enough for me to leave her.'

Harriet looks out of the window, and I feel a swell of relief that she doesn't ask me when that might be. Because we both know that I have no idea.

'Can I stay at yours tonight?' she asks, changing the subject.

I pluck another piece of chicken from the paper bag.

'Of course.'

CHAPTER SIX

HARRIET

I splash cold water on my face and look at myself in the mirror. The curls I pulled through my hair last night have flattened, and my skin is slightly tinged grey from the smears of black eyeliner under my eyes. Why is it that no matter how much you scrub, you are never able to fully remove your make-up?

I pick up one of Zoe's cotton pads, dab it with make-up remover and sweep it across my face. I can hear Zoe pottering around in her bedroom, Radio 1 singing through the house. It's a habit she's had since we were teenagers, having the radio on constantly. She doesn't like the silence.

I pick up my hairbrush and drag it through my hair, a dull ache thudding in my chest.

My shift starts in an hour. Another entire day wasted sitting behind that desk. I get this feeling almost every time I wake up and realise it isn't one of my precious days off. At first, I thought it was simply a kind of work blues, the same everyone gets on a Sunday night. But then, as I was staring into space while propped behind the reception desk, I started to bury myself in the feeling. Really pulling it apart, sticking my face in it to try and work out what it was. And the more I did it, the more apparent it became to me. It isn't just a feeling of not wanting to go to work, or a deep feeling of dread about the next eight hours of the day. It's fear. The fear of this feeling being there every day for the rest of my life if I don't work out what will stop it. What will make me want to get out of bed in the morning, excited for the day. What will make this feeling go away.

It's not something I've figured out yet, and the idea that I never will terrifies me.

I take a deep breath and walk out of the bathroom. I can hear Ange clanging around downstairs, no doubt throwing ingredients into her beloved slow cooker or into a big pan to bubble and stew into a thick soup. I skip down the stairs, ready to shout good morning to her, when something makes me stop and peer down into the kitchen. The radio is just as loud downstairs as it is in Zoe's room, and Ange is chopping vegetables. There's a whisk propped on the side, gently dripping cake batter onto the counter. The smell of bread is high in the air. It's barely seven in the morning. How long has she been awake for?

Watching her is like watching a wind-up toy. She's moving from place to place, her arms whizzing and her mouth manically mumbling to herself. Sam Smith's latest song echoes through the kitchen, the slow, sad music making her hysterical movements even more bizarre to watch.

'Morning!' I force myself to say as I reach the kitchen. Her head snaps round to look at me.

'Oh!' she cries. 'Good morning, Harriet! How are you? Would you like tea? I've just made a pot.'

'Oh, yes please. But I can . . .' I trail off as Angie starts to pluck down mugs like I haven't even spoken.

'Have you done all this this morning?' I ask.

'It's not much!' she says at once. 'Just a bit of cooking.'

The oven pings, and billows of steam fill the room as she bends down to pull out a loaf of bread. It's woven together in a thick, lustrous plait and the dough is stretched and cracked under the chestnut-brown glaze.

'Why don't you sit down?' I try and steer her into a seat. 'I'll sort the tea. You can relax or something.'

I'm trying to sound helpful and upbeat, but she turns away from me, slipping from my hands.

'No, no,' she says. 'I have far too much to do.' She starts splashing milk into the mugs.

'It can wait,' I smile. 'Half an hour with a cup of tea and a good book feeds the soul. That's what my mum always said.'

She hands me a tray with two mugs. Her smile is so bright it looks like it's about to snap.

'I don't need to sit down,' she says. 'I'm fine.'

I study her. Her glasses are fogged up, and her small chocolate-brown eyes are crinkled under the force of her smile.

She's not going to listen to me.

'Right,' I say. 'Well, thanks for the tea. And the bread looks great.'

'It's burnt,' she says, and before I can stop her, she picks up the baking tray and drops the loaf straight into the bin.

'Ange!'

'It's all right, love!' she says. 'I'll make another one.'

My heart hammers in my chest as I carry the tray upstairs. My nose crinkles as I walk past the bathroom, getting the distinct smell of Lynx. Zoe is sitting in front of her mirror, staring.

'I think your mum has a teenage boyfriend,' I say, putting the tray down on her bedside table. 'It smells like a teenage boy in this house.'

This snaps her out of her trance. She shoots me a look of disgust.

'That's the worst thing you've ever said,' she says. 'She's fifty-three.'

I shrug. 'Don't be so judgemental, Zo. She's allowed a love life.'

'Not with a teenager.'

'So the teenage boyfriend's yours then?' I smirk, picking up my tea and sitting on the bed.

She raises her eyebrows at me. 'My Uncle Reggie was here at the weekend,' she reminds me. 'For some reason, he loves to smell like an eighteen-year-old.'

I nod. 'I prefer the idea of your mum being a cougar.'

She holds up two fingers and takes a slurp of her tea.

'I need to leave for work in the next fifteen minutes, by the way,' she says. 'You don't have to go yet, do you? Mum would probably love the company.'

Hmm. I'm pretty sure she wouldn't.

'Sure,' I say. 'Listen, I think I have an idea.'

Zoe raises her eyebrows at me in the mirror. Her face is elongated from pushing moisturiser into her skin.

'I've been thinking about what you said about the auction, I think we should go. We can pick up your grandma's ring, give her a proper send off and then finally go travelling.' I point a hairbrush at her. 'Your mum should come too. It'll be fun.'

I see panic flit over her face.

'She won't come,' she says in a small voice, 'and I can't leave her. She thinks it would be disrespectful to Uncle Reggie and that we should leave him to run the auction by himself, like he suggested.'

Her jaw clenches. I know she and Ange have been arguing over this since the funeral, about whether Reggie will keep the ring aside for Zoe.

'What about the ring?' I say.

'What about it?'

'Do you trust your uncle to save it for you?'

She pulls a face. I already know the answer to that question. I hold up a finger as I finish my tea.

'How would you feel if you found out that it had been sold and you hadn't tried to stop it?'

'I'd be devastated,' she says simply.

I shrug, pulling my hair back into a ponytail.

'What about Mum, though?' she asks.

I sigh. 'I agree with you, Zo. She needs to come too.'

'But she won't.'

'Then you'll have to try and convince her.'

Chapter Seven

Angie

I look down at my shopping basket. Sugar, flour, milk, butter. All the basic ingredients for a cake. I promised I'd make one for Jeremy, the elderly man who lives down the road. He always requests the same. A nice lemon drizzle. It's his favourite.

When I saw him in his front garden yesterday, he was crouched down with a trowel, furiously digging. His blue pullover hung over his body and his face was red and blotchy. He told me that one of his plants had died and he wasn't sure why. He wasn't upset – he was more annoyed than anything – but when I looked into his light grey eyes, I felt a shock go right through me. I don't think I've ever been sadder to hear of a plant dying.

So, I offered to make him a cake. Another nice lemon drizzle should do the trick. It's a cake I've made a thousand times, but you'd never have known that this morning, with three sponges discarded in the bin. I mean, thank God I got up at five to start baking! Otherwise I would never have found the time to get everything done!

I can usually make a sponge in my sleep. But one came out burnt, one flat and one with the texture of rubber. I don't know what's wrong with me at the moment, but when Zoe finally came downstairs to grab a piece of toast and head to work, she looked at me as though I'd wrangled my way out of a straitjacket.

Thankfully, the fourth sponge was perfect. But it meant that I had as good as emptied my cupboards, so now I'm back in Tesco, staring at the eggs.

Free-range, corn-fed, organic, omega 3 . . . They're all boxed up in different-coloured cartons, various images of happy chickens on the front.

But are they really happy?

I step a bit closer to the aisle of eggs and focus my eyes into the black circles of a chicken, staring back out at me.

The eggs we eat are unfertilised. We know that, but do the chickens? Are we ripping an egg away from a chicken that thinks there's a baby in there? Are we leaving that poor bird alone and heartbroken?

A lump starts to fill my throat, and I shake my head.

Why have I never thought of this before? How can I have been so selfish my entire life not to give a chicken a second thought?

I start to scan the shelves again, heat prickling at my chest.

How are you supposed to know if any of these eggs were taken ethically? Is there even such a thing? Are all these chickens alone somewhere, madly scrabbling for someone they love who has been snatched away from them without warning, with nobody to explain what has happened or give a reason *why*? *Why* has this happened? *Why has this happened to me?*

'Madam?'

I jerk around in shock as a young man with a trolley piled with boxes of eggs approaches me. I step back so he can restock the shelves, trying to pull myself together.

'Did you want some eggs?' he asks, glancing back at me when I don't leave.

'Oh.' I hold my basket close. 'No. I don't think so. Thank you.'

★

I give three raps on the door and step back. The cake is hiding under one of my favourite tea towels, and the September sun is pooling down on me. I love Jeremy's house, and I admire it every time I walk by. It's a townhouse, with dark red bricks and a gorgeous bay window. His front garden is small but perfectly maintained, and every Christmas he gives me an enormous sprig of his home-grown Brussels sprouts. To Zoe's horror, we eat them for days.

Jeremy pulls the front door open, and I smile. He's wearing a burgundy pullover today, and a baker's hat that hides his wisps of white hair. He steps back, a crooked smile on his face.

'Hello, Angie,' he says. 'How are you doing? You haven't been baking for me again, have you?'

'It's only something small.' I smile, stepping inside. His house is as neat as a pin. The walls are peppered with perfectly framed photographs, and he always puts a lace doily under my cup when I stop by for tea.

'You didn't need to do that,' he says. He picks up the kettle and raises his eyebrows at me. I nod gratefully.

I place the cake down on his kitchen table and remove the tea towel. To my dismay, I notice that the sticky lemon glaze has gooped together under the heat of the sun. It looks like someone has sneezed on it.

'Oh no!' I cry. 'Oh God. Jeremy, I'm so sorry. I'll make you another one. Let me take this one back.'

He turns to face me and frowns. 'What's wrong with it?'

'All the icing has melted and stuck together . . . Oh, it looks horrible. I'm so sorry. This is the last thing you need with everything that happened with your plant yesterday. I can't believe I did this. I . . .'

He holds out a hand. 'You've just apologised more in one breath than I have this entire month. Sit down, Ange.'

He pulls out a chair and gives me a stern look. I sink down into the seat and watch as he carries the periwinkle-blue teapot to the table.

'Now, I'm going to have a piece of this delicious cake,' he says, carving a slice and putting it on a plate, 'and I strongly suggest you do too. I think you need it.'

I take the plate. 'My waistline doesn't need it,' I joke. He gives me a death stare that wipes the smile off my face.

I slot a corner of the slice into my mouth. The tart lemon carries the soft sponge. It is lovely, a carbon copy of all my other lemon drizzles.

'How are you, Ange?' Jeremy asks, pouring streams of tea into dainty teacups. 'How are you coping?'

'Fine, thanks!'

He pauses for a second, and then picks up a little jug of milk. I nod.

'And what about your Zoe? How is she?'

My chest tightens.

Zoe, my beautiful, fiercely intelligent twenty-five-year-old daughter. My daughter who keeps trying to force me to have real, heartfelt conversations with her and snaps at me every time I change the subject. My daughter who is fluttering around me like an anxious butterfly even though we seem to behave more like sniping crocodiles every time we talk to each other. The one who keeps dropping little hints about us going to Mum's house together one last time, even though the thought of seeing her house again and the town she loved so much without her in it makes me feel as though I could die. The crashing reality that she really has left us. That she's left me in this world without a mother. My daughter who I can feel getting angrier and angrier with me every time I refuse to talk about it. That Zoe?

'She's great, thanks!' I say, holding the teacup between my hands. 'Doing very well at her job, which is good.'

Jeremy looks at me like he's waiting for me to say something else.

'She's considering dyeing her hair blonde, but I don't think that's a good idea,' I add. 'Though what do I know?' I pick up a strand of my own thin hair and laugh. He does not mirror me.

'Well, that's good,' he says after a pause. 'And you're sure you're okay?'

I take a deep breath, my whole body filling with air like a balloon.

'Oh yes,' I say, with a wide smile fixed on my face. 'I'm fine.'

CHAPTER EIGHT

ZOE

I look down at my notepad, chewing my pen, as our latest client babbles down the phone. She's on loudspeaker, and Kitty is sitting next to me scribbling notes. Libby is the biggest client we've had in years, and her budget matches the size of her list. Really, she's a client who is more suited to Orla than me. But she was totally swept away at the idea of an intimate, romantic wedding. Which would be great if she didn't then immediately invite two hundred guests and ask us to research manor houses in the south-west.

I take a deep breath and try to focus, the stress in Libby's voice carrying across the meeting room. Ever since my conversation with Harriet, I haven't been able to concentrate on anything. I nearly approved Kitty ordering a £20,000 pink disco floor as an 'office investment', and when I changed my mind at the last second, she thought I was spooked so went through her entire sales pitch *twice*.

Harriet's idea has been swirling around my mind since I left the house this morning. She said it so simply, like it was the most obvious thing in the world. Why wouldn't we go? What was stopping us? She was my grandma. What was there to think about?

And she's right. That's the worst part. Of course I want to go, of course I should be there. How can I just sit here and act normal when all Grandma's artwork and belongings are being auctioned off to the highest bidder? But it's Mum. No matter how much I talk to her, argue with her, she won't listen. Nothing will snap her out of this infuriating bubble that she's trapped in, frantically making soup and cake and endless amounts of bread.

And then, about an hour ago, a message from Uncle Reggie buzzed through onto my phone. It was the flyer he'd designed for the auction, and the date was screaming up at me.

Tuesday 13 September.

Six days. In less than a week, it would be over. And I'd be sitting here waiting to hear how it all went? Hoping that Uncle Reggie would return with Grandma's ring so I could keep one small part of her with me at all times. I'd never see her house again as it was when she lived in it. And I was supposed to just sit here and let it pass me by.

It hit me like a lightning bolt, and suddenly it felt as though I'd been snapped out of a dream.

With or without Mum, I needed to go to Italy. I needed to find the ring and say goodbye to my grandma properly before everything was gone.

Kitty gives me a look, and suddenly I realise that Libby is waiting for me to say something.

'Sounds wonderful!' I say. Thank God for Kitty's notes.

'Okay, well, lovely to talk to you, Libby!' Kitty says. 'I'll send you a follow-up email and let you know when the mixologist gets back to me about the signature cocktail. I've made a note about tequila.'

I lean closer to the phone. 'Thanks so much, Libby!' I say. 'Chat to you soon.'

I let out a whistle of air and smile at Kitty. Her hair held in a high, springy ponytail in a sparkly scrunchie and her big eyelashes flap at me. Today they're purple, matching her hair.

'Gosh,' she grins, 'this wedding keeps getting bigger and bigger! You'd never guess that the key word on my mood board at the start of all of this was "intimate".' She gets up and then turns to face me. 'Fancy a tea?'

'Er . . . in a second,' I say, closing my notebook, deciding it's now or never. 'Kitty, can I talk to you for a second?' I glance around, making sure Heidi isn't about to burst in.

Kitty's eyes are wide. 'Sure!' she says. 'You're not about to fire me, are you? I mean, if you do, it's totally fine, but I absolutely love this job and I—'

'Kitty!' I interrupt her, laughing. 'Of course I'm not about to fire you. God, I couldn't survive without you. You make the world go round in this place.'

Little patches of pink form on her cheeks. 'That's what my mum says.'

I hook one leg over the other. 'No. I need to ask you a favour.'

'Anything,' she says immediately, suddenly looking very sincere. I honestly think that if I asked her to give me a kidney, she'd do it. Though to be fair, I'd totally give her one back.

'I think I might go to Italy. I need to convince my mum to come, so I'm not one hundred per cent sure, but I think I might go.'

Her hands fly to her chest. 'For your grandma?'

'Yeah,' I say, trying to control my racing heart. 'Her things are being auctioned and I want to be there. But the thing is,' I eye Orla as she marches past the glass office, chatting busily to Saskia, 'the auction is quite close to Libby's wedding.'

'How close?'

'Two days before.'

She bites her lip. 'Right.'

It is absolutely unheard of for myself or Orla to go away just before one of our clients' weddings. Our service costs thousands, and brides expect us to be there for every moment in the lead-up to the big day. If I had told Heidi I needed to be in Italy the week before, she would have given the wedding to Orla.

'But,' I say quickly, 'it's fine, because I've got a plan.'

Kitty brightens up again. 'Okay.'

'I'm going to go Friday after work and be back by Tuesday. I won't stay for the auction, just to get my grandma's ring and say goodbye to her. I'll fly home late Monday and be back in the office on Tuesday morning.'

Although she keeps smiling at me, her face looks like she's trying to work out the square root of three hundred and six.

'And Libby's wedding is . . . next Thursday.'

'Exactly,' I say, 'so I'll be back in time no problem, and if you have any issues you can just call me. But we can't tell Heidi.'

A look of worry flashes across her face. 'Why? I'm sure she'd let you take a day off. Especially given the circumstances.'

Heidi's loud laugh rolls across the office, and I wince. 'It's not worth the drama when I'll be back in plenty of time. If I ask for Monday off, she'll get stressed and try and reassign the wedding to Orla.'

Kitty gasps. 'She can't! We've worked so hard!'

'Exactly.'

Kitty nods solemnly. 'Okay,' she says, 'you can trust me. Is your mum going too?'

Just as I open my mouth to reply, a message from Mum flashes up on my phone. Guilt pricks under my skin.

'I hope so.'

CHAPTER NINE

HARRIET

Zoe puts down two half-pints of Guinness in front of us, and I frown.

'Why have you got us Guinness?'

We're in the Queen's Head, our local pub. It has low ceilings and a weird spirally carpet with splats of colour that I'm not totally sure are intentional. It's always filled with the same people, propped up against the bar drinking the same drinks and telling the same stories to each other. Zoe and I stick out like a sore thumb.

And now we're drinking Guinness.

'I don't know,' she says defeatedly. 'I didn't mean to. I asked for wine, but I think Andy behind the bar got confused.'

'Got confused?' I repeat. 'Between a glass of wine and a *Guinness*?'

'I didn't want to correct him. It felt awkward. It isn't that bad, is it?' She takes a sip and immediately winces. 'Oh wow.'

'I'm ordering next time,' I say, holding my glass up in a 'cheers' motion and taking a sip of the bitter liquid.

'How was your day?' she asks.

I pause. My day consisted of a mind-numbingly boring shift at the hotel, followed by three hours by myself at home while Mum was on a play date with the baby, and now I'm in the pub sipping a drink I hate.

'Fine,' I say.

'Did you see your mum today?'

'Nope.'

Zoe nods, forcing herself to take another sip. 'Have you spoken to her?'

'Nope,' I say again. 'She's too busy with the baby. Anyway,' I lean my elbows on the table, 'I've got a surprise for you.'

She raises her eyebrows. 'Oh?'

'I started looking at flights to Italy, to go see your grandma. Or, well, her house,' I add, feeling myself redden.

Nice one, you idiot.

Zoe looks surprised. 'Oh, wow.'

'Yeah,' I continue. 'We can fly from Cornwall to Rome! I never knew that! Some of the flights are only about fifty quid, and I don't get paid until Friday but I got a scratch card today, so hopefully I might win something on that.' I grin at her, but Zoe just looks wordlessly down at the table.

'What is it?' I ask.

She catches my eye and forces a smile onto her face. 'Oh, nothing.'

'Zoe . . .'

'I just haven't spoken to my mum about this yet,' she says. 'Not since I mentioned it at the funeral and she, you know, shut it down. I can't book tickets without speaking to her. It's not like I can run away without her noticing.'

She laughs, and I feel a light stab within my chest.

Not being able to run away without your mum noticing, wouldn't that be nice?

'Okay,' I say, forcing myself to stay bright, 'well, maybe once you've spoken to her, I can book it. They have quite a few seats spare at the moment. Would you go without her?'

She gives a non-committal shrug. 'I don't know.'

'You do want to go, though, right?'

I give her my biggest smile, but she looks down at her hands.

'Yeah,' she says in a small voice. 'Of course, just maybe let's wait until I've spoken to my mum?'

'Well, these flights are for tomorrow. So if you want me to book them this evening, let me know,' I say.

She takes another sip of Guinness and flinches.

'God, this really is disgusting.'

'I know,' I say, taking the drink off her. 'I don't care how nice you are, I'm complaining to Andy. We cannot drink this.'

Chapter Ten

Zoe

It turns out it's easy enough to say that you're going to Italy. It's a nice idea, bubbling in your mind, but the reality is a bit more stressful.

My phone vibrates on the table as a message from Harriet pops onto the screen:

Have you spoken to your mum yet? I'm about to start work, so can try and book the flights on my break, if I get one!

I quickly type back a reply, *I'm on it*, and then slip my phone back into my pocket.

Mum smiles at me over her glass of water and I smile back, guilt sloshing around my body as though my intentions are flashing above my head like a neon sign.

I'M GOING TO ITALY TOMORROW.

WE'RE BOOKING FLIGHTS IN THE NEXT HOUR.

ALSO, I'VE NEVER REALLY LIKED YOUR SPAGHETTI.

I've never lied to my mum. Sure, there are things I haven't told her, but I don't go out of my way to lie. Going to Grandma's would involve me booking flights and leaving the country without her knowing, let alone reappearing with the ring dazzling on my finger (with any luck). And what if something happens to me while I'm out there? What if I get abducted by a gang and they ask my mum for a ransom she can't afford to pay? Or, much worse, she *can* afford to pay but refuses to because she's so cross with me?

That would be a very dramatic way to die. At least if there was some form of afterlife, I think Grandma would be quite impressed. Assuming they just chopped my head off in one swift motion and didn't spend hours torturing me.

Argh! Why am I even thinking about this? What is wrong with my brain?

I twirl another string of pasta around my fork.

I know that I need to start by getting a plane to Rome, which is easy enough. Then I would need to get to Sulmona, which is about an hour outside Rome. Grandma also loved to tell me how the national park next to her house was home to several bears. I always hoped this was something she just said to scare me, but I could never be quite sure. She had a weird sense of humour, in the best way, of course.

'Oh,' Mum says, finally breaking the silence that has been filling our kitchen for the past ten minutes, 'before I forget, your uncle called today.'

A stray piece of spaghetti splats against my chin.

'He wanted to ask if there was anything we wanted put aside before the auction.'

I raise my eyebrows. 'That's uncharacteristically thoughtful of him.'

'Obviously he knows you'd like the ring if it shows up,' she continues, as though I haven't said anything, 'but did you want any of her paintings? They're probably all worth quite a bit.'

I stuff another forkful of pasta into my mouth.

That's the understatement of the century. One of Grandma's paintings once sold for thirty thousand pounds.

'I'd need to see them again,' I say. 'She has so many.'

Mum nods, neatly cutting up her pasta. 'I'll ask him to send some photos.'

We fall back into a deathly silence.

'Or we could go,' I say quietly, not daring to take my eyes off my plate, 'and see Grandma's things ourselves.'

'We don't need to,' Mum says evenly. 'Reggie is taking care of it all.'

She's not angry (Mum never gets angry; she is far too composed for that), but she is rattled. It's as if I've snuck up behind her and ruffled her hair and then hidden her hairbrush. She's trying to act as if everything is normal, but I can tell there is something gnawing at her brain.

'But it would be good to check if the ring is there myself,' I press on, 'and then we get to say a proper goodbye to Grandma.'

'We're not going to Italy, Zoe.'

After another eight minutes of nothing but the gentle ticking of the wall clock, there is a polite knock at the door. As Mum gets up, I twirl some more pasta around my fork, waiting to hear the light murmur of conversation between Mum and one of the neighbours, or an Amazon delivery driver. But when a cold silence seeps through the room, I feel a twinge in the pit of my stomach. I push my chair back and step towards the hallway, a gust of wind whistling round the house from the open front door. Mum is standing facing someone in the shadow of the porch. No one is speaking.

'Mum? Is everything . . .' The words die in my throat as I reach her side, my eyes meeting the bright, beady gaze of a woman I haven't seen in fourteen years.

It's my Aunt Fanny.

CHAPTER ELEVEN

ZOE

The September wind is surprisingly icy, nipping at my bare arms. I fold them across my body, gripping onto my elbows and trying to stop myself from shaking.

I don't think I've ever properly understood the word speechless until this moment. But that's what we are. All three of us just stand there staring at each other. It's like looking at an old photograph. The image is the same – you can recognise the person captured – but it's faded and the corners are curling under years of harsh sunlight. It's aged. It's been worn down.

Her signature ice-blonde bob is exactly how it's always been. Tucked under her chin, not a single strand moving in the wind. Her pointed, perfectly bronzed chin is slightly lifted, and her lips, which are now stretched with silicon, are pursed tightly. Her eyes are the same pools of inky blue, framed by thick dark lashes that sag slightly under the layers of mascara. The only giveaway sign that any time has passed is her skin. Once pillowy and smooth, it's now marked with deep lines that run across her forehead and make an indent in an innocent half-moon shape either side of her mouth.

She's like a tiny bird, teetering on the highest heels with her bony knees jutting out under the tightly tanned skin of her legs. Her red-lacquered nails glimmer under the light and a shock runs down my spine as I meet her eye and can't look away.

It's like seeing a ghost.

I'm not sure how long the three of us stand there in silence. It could have been five minutes or five seconds, but eventually Mum speaks.

'Fanny.'

It's like she's said the code word that snaps us all out of our trance, and Aunt Fanny springs into life. Her spindly arms are thrown into the air and her lips part to show a set of dazzling teeth.

'Ange!' she cries, pulling Mum into a hug, and looking up at me. 'Zoe! God, I've missed your faces. My girls!' Her Liverpudlian accent has thickened since we last saw her. I guess that's where she's been hiding. She reaches a hand out to squeeze my arm.

Before I can move out of the way, she steps away from Mum and pulls me into a hug, her thin arms coiling around my neck like skinny planks of wood. She smells the same. Sugary sweet with an air of roses. It's the type of fragrance you'd get from an aerosol you've picked up for three quid at the till in Superdrug. As I smell it, I feel ten years old again, and for a split second my chest swells with a warm, fuzzy feeling. It only lasts a second, though, as a fury storms through me. The feeling of being eleven and having her leave without so much as a goodbye comes over me. I shove her off.

'What are you doing here?' I manage. 'Are you okay?'

My eyes skim up and down her body, as though I might be able to spot some obvious sign as to why she's shown up unannounced. She doesn't look as though she needs anything, though, so why is she here?

'Well,' she lowers her chin as though she's about to tell me a secret, 'I will be once I get in and have a nice cuppa.' She turns to Mum. 'You've still got my mug, right, Ange? I've never had a better cup of tea than from that mug.'

It's only then that I notice a shiny suitcase propped behind her, and my mouth drops open. I look at Mum, but as soon as Aunt Fanny mentioned a cup of tea, Mum's polite, perfect-host inner monster burst out. The one that squashes all her real feelings and lets Janet from number 40 tell her that she'd be much better off if she lost some weight, all for the sake of another request to pop the kettle on.

She practically springs backwards, ushering Aunt Fanny inside.

'Of course!' she cries. 'Come on in!'

I watch agog as they both move into our small kitchen, Mum leading the way in her fluffy slippers, Aunt Fanny's pointy heels click-clacking their way after her. Her suitcase winks at me on the porch, and I fight the urge to kick it over. It's like watching a pantomime. Or a forced interaction while they've both got a gun held to their backs. They're acting as if Aunt Fanny had just popped to the shops to get some milk. Am I going mad?

I reluctantly lug her suitcase inside and slam the door shut, ignoring Mum's customary small shriek as the window panes rattle. (It's the same sort of vibe she gives when I swear in front of her and she burbles, 'Language!' like a startled hen.)

'Do you still take sugar?' Mum asks.

'Yes, of course. Although only one now.'

'Oh, aren't you good.'

I gape at them both.

'We haven't seen you in, like, fourteen years,' I manage, interrupting Mum, who has started babbling about the benefits of sweeteners. 'Why are you here? Is everything okay?'

Aunt Fanny flaps a hand at me. 'Oh yes, I'm fine. The train down was a nightmare, though. Nobody respects first class any more.' She rolls her eyes and I feel like I'm going to burst.

My voice tightens. 'You literally disappeared, you totally ignored us! It was like you were dead!'

She flinches as if I've whipped her and Mum turns her back to us both, plucking down mugs from the cabinets. 'I'm here, Zoe, because I wanted to see you both.'

'But why now? What—'

'I heard about Clarice.' She turns to face Mum and takes her hand. 'I read about it online,' she says, 'and I had to come. I am so sorry, Ange.'

'That's quite all right,' Mum mumbles, pulling her hand away and sploshing milk into mugs.

'I'm here to look after you both. When's the funeral? How can I help?'

The look of serenity on Fanny's face makes me snap.

'The funeral was last week. We don't need you to look after us.'

She shrugs. 'Well then, I'm here for a holiday, how's that?'

'Zoe,' Mum turns to face me, the steam of the kettle tingeing her cheeks pink, 'why don't you go and find some fresh towels for your aunt?'

'Oh, fresh towels!' Fanny hooks one bony leg over the other and shoots Mum a simpering smile. 'What a treat.'

I turn on my heel wordlessly and start to walk up the stairs. As I reach the airing cupboard, her laugh trips through the house and I feel my entire body tense.

One thing's for sure: she's not back here because of my grandma. I don't care what she says.

Chapter Twelve

Fanny

I sit on a small wooden chair. It's the same one that has always been here. Slightly rickety, with one leg shorter than the rest, and a chipped dent in the base that Ange spent one weekend sanding over to make sure that nobody got scratched on the protruding daggers of wood. I run my hand over the top of the dressing table, my back aching from the hours of travelling. I'm never comfortable any more. I'm sure it's to do with ageing; another part of life cruelly snatched away from you with no warning. My looks, the ability to slip into a deep sleep and not snap awake at four o'clock each morning, and now the simple luxury of sitting on a wooden chair. Perhaps I am about to be one of those women who insists on carrying around a paisley cushion, just in case.

I think I'd rather be dead.

A slice of moonlight is pooling through the window, casting

a milky shadow over my reflection. I have to force myself to look these days. I always loved looking in the mirror; it gave me confidence. But as the years have ticked by, my skin has sagged. Ugly lines have been carved into my face by time, and my eyebrows have started to droop, hooding across my eyes. Some days I barely recognise myself. I don't like this woman, but then I haven't for a while.

I push my spine straight and lift my hairbrush, gently pulling it through my ice-white hair. It's the one thing about myself that has always stayed perfect. The brush glides through, and I lift my chin at my reflection. The last time I sat here, there wasn't even a whisper of these lines, not the faintest clue of what was lurking over the horizon with its spindly, ugly claws. That was fourteen years ago. I was thirty-eight, barely an adult myself. Completely, painfully unaware of what was to come.

A new light fills the room, and I turn my head to see my phone, shouting at me next to my pot of moisturiser. A cool sense fills my body as I read the name.

It's Jon.

In one smooth motion, I switch the phone off and drop it into my handbag.

He must have found my note and realised I've gone.

But he can't find me. He can't tell them what I'm doing, why I'm here.

Not yet.

CHAPTER THIRTEEN

ANGIE

I pound my feet into the pavement, sucking in short, sharp inhalations of breath as my arms pump alongside my body. Up, down; up, down.

I was doing just fine. I was coping. I was doing what everyone tells you to do and taking each day as it came, and I was surviving.

A stray September leaf falls in front of my face and I brush it aside, trying to silence my mum's voice floating into my mind.

Nature's beauty, fiery copper and inky black. Let's take it home.

The sun is still high in the sky, peeping through a wisp of cloud, and there is a gentle breeze teasing the weaker leaves away from their branches to pepper the pavements. Burnt amber and gold, rusted brown and brick red. Mum loved the change in seasons; she always made us stop and admire it all. But I'm not stopping. I'm a woman on a mission.

The mission is simple: to get my heart rate up to a level where it is racing because I've been power walking, and not because of the adrenaline that has been coursing through my veins since the moment I opened the door last night and saw her – Fanny.

I didn't know what to say. I still don't. It felt as though my fragile body had been suddenly pushed to its limits as a new wave of emotions stormed through me. It was like a whirlwind, shaking my bones. How can one person deal with all of those emotions? I couldn't even tell you what they were. In a flash, I took a deep breath and smiled, and they were silenced. Squashed down inside my body, gladly welcomed by all the other horrible emotions that I'm trying to figure out.

I hold up a hand to wave at Mr Granger from number 42. He's dragging his bin back up the garden path, like he always does moments after the bin men chug back down the lane. Perks of working from home, I guess.

My chest spikes in pain and I narrow my eyes, focusing on the thirty-mile-an-hour sign at the end of the street.

I want to lean my head back and scream at the sky. Can't I just be left alone for one week? Let me curl up into a quiet ball and stay there? What else am I going to have thrown at me?

I didn't know how to deal with Fanny. Zoe was standing right next to me, waiting for me to do something. And I couldn't. Another burning emotion to add to the load: guilt.

So this morning I put on my trainers and I started to walk. If I keep moving, then eventually this will all stop. Everything will go back to normal. I won't have to fight these feelings any more.

Finally I'll be left alone.

CHAPTER FOURTEEN

ZOE

'The thing is, Ange, you get what you pay for. If you buy five-pound red wine from Lidl, then it will *taste* like five-pound red wine from Lidl. If you're having a drink, you must do it properly. Do you remember my friend Robert? He's a sommelier. Fantastic man, so intelligent.'

Aunt Fanny leans back in her chair, her wine glass dangling in her right hand and her eyes shut, like she's trying to conjure up Robert to pop up in front of her with a full case of Rioja.

I narrow my eyes. It's been just under twenty-four hours since she arrived, and the most she has done to help Mum is carry her cup of coffee into the living room, where she immediately plonked herself down on the sofa. Since then, I've been to work, to the shops and to the pub to have a drink with Harriet, who was floored at my news of our unsolicited guest. I've driven home to find she's *still sitting down*. While Mum, the person she's apparently here to help, scurries around her endlessly.

Our kitchen is small and L-shaped, with room for a little table, which is propped up against the wall. When Harriet comes over, we have to play musical chairs. One of us will eat while another starts the washing-up, and then we'll swap. We always try and guide Mum into one of the chairs, as she will have always done the cooking, but she never lets us.

But now the three of us are wedged at the table. Our knees are knocking together and we're all politely using our cutlery with our elbows tucked in as carefully as possible. Aunt Fanny's large bowl of pasta has barely been touched. I'm opposite her, and Mum is squashed in between us, with her back inches away from the cooker. I did try and swap with her, but she wouldn't hear of it. Aunt Fanny didn't offer.

'He sounds lovely,' Mum says politely, cutting up her tagliatelle into little squares.

'He's the best,' Aunt Fanny gushes. 'Oh! I know!' She slams her hand on the table and leans forward, her charcoal eyes sparking at me. 'We should take a trip! All of us, to the South of France! I'll give him a call and see if he could give us a tour of his vineyard! Can you imagine? The weather this time of year would be beautiful. It's always so gorgeous there in September.'

Her eyes close again as a smile creeps across her face. I take this moment to roll my eyes at Mum, but she ignores me and keeps her stare fixed on her pasta.

This is Aunt Fanny all over. She has no sense of responsibility and never stops to think about the consequences. She used to whisk us off at the last minute whenever and wherever she fancied. Mum once got called into my headmaster's office for a telling-off after Fanny had scooped me up one Friday and taken me to Thorpe Park. After a stern talking-to, a pale-faced Mum returned home, and Aunt Fanny (who had been none the wiser that the meeting was even happening) was outraged. The following Monday, she marched into school and demanded to speak to the head *in the middle of assembly.* I was mortified, but even the unfriendly letter that landed on our doormat a week later couldn't derail her. Three months after that, she took me out of school to watch the latest Harry Potter film, claiming that it was an 'essential educational trip' to learn about 'great literature'. After that, we went to Pizza Express, and when I told her that I was missing science, she taught me how to make the perfect martini.

'That sounds lovely,' Mum says, in the same polite voice.

'So let's do it!' Aunt Fanny cries, her eyes snapping open again. 'What do you say? How are you fixed for tomorrow?'

I can feel a weird energy bouncing off her skin, like she's suddenly become radioactive. It makes me want to slouch in my seat and hide under the table.

Mum laughs. 'Tomorrow? I don't know about that.'

'Why not?' Fanny says. 'I'll pay! It'll be my treat. Zoe?' She turns to me. 'Are you in?'

I continue to cut my pasta.

'No thank you,' I say pointedly.

I will myself to keep staring down at my dinner, knowing that the second I meet Aunt Fanny's bold eyes, my stern grown-up face will break and my cheeks will flame pink for daring to defy her.

'Oh come on!' she jostles. 'Are you telling me that you're

being offered a free trip to the South of France and you're turn-ing it down?'

'Yes.'

'Why?'

'I don't want to go.' My face is practically on fire now, and I've cut my pasta so many times it's looking up at me like sad little strings.

I steal a glance at Aunt Fanny, who is raising her eyebrows at me. The energy zipping off her has dimmed. After a pause, she claps her hands together.

'Fine!' she says. 'Where *do* you want to go?'

Finally I look up at her, making full eye contact this time. 'What?'

'If not France, then where?' she says challengingly. 'I'm offer-ing you a free holiday. Where do you want to go?'

I look at Mum. She's sipping her wine and avoiding my gaze.

It's like I'm being offered a golden ticket. A wave of nerves ripple through my body and I lift my chin.

'Italy,' I say calmly. 'I'd like to go to Italy.'

Aunt Fanny, none the wiser, grins at me.

'Oh, I love Italy! We spent so much time there when you were a child, going to visit Clarice in her bloody mansion in the mountains!'

My eyes widen. 'Yes,' I say, 'exactly.'

'No.' Mum's voice quivers as she attempts to sound authori-tative, putting down her wine glass firmly. Her thin hair falls in front of her face like lank curtains, but underneath it I can see her cheeks are flaming.

'No?' Aunt Fanny repeats. 'Why not, Ange? You love Italy.'

Mum opens her mouth, but the words shoot out of me before she even has the chance to take a breath.

'Mum doesn't want us to go because Uncle Reggie has told us not to.'

'Zoe,' Mum warns.

Aunt Fanny raises her eyebrows at me. 'Has he now?'

'Grandma wanted us to auction off all of her things and he's insisted on taking charge of it and I think he's going to rig it or something and try to steal the ring so he can sell it and make loads of money. I don't trust him and I think we should be there.' I'm desperate to get the words out before Mum can stop me.

Mum is glaring at me from under her strands of wispy hair, but I ignore her.

'Ring?' Aunt Fanny repeats.

'Grandma's engagement ring,' I explain. 'The one she never took off. It's the only thing I want, and she always promised I could have it. We used to talk about it all the time . . .' I trail off as a sudden lump appears in my throat.

'Ah,' Aunt Fanny nods, 'yes, I remember that ring. It's beautiful. It'll be worth a lot of money.'

'Your grandma won't be there, Zoe,' Mum says in a small yet defiant voice. 'She's not waiting for us in the house.'

'I know!' I snap, swallowing the lump. 'I know she won't be there.' My voice cracks.

Aunt Fanny hooks one spindly leg over the other and leans forward onto her elbows. 'You don't want to go, Ange? Why?'

Mum snatches my bowl from under my hands and gets to her feet, turning her back on us.

'Because it's a long way and Reg has everything under

control! We just need to stay here and carry on as normal. It's disloyal for us to go; he said he would deal with the auction.'

'How kind of him,' Aunt Fanny mutters into her wine glass, sarcasm dripping off her tongue

Mum turns back to us, plucking Aunt Fanny's bowl away and tipping its contents into the bin. I wince as she clatters the empty bowls into the sink and roughly turns on the taps.

'I want to go,' I say. 'I want to say goodbye to Grandma, and before you say anything, I know she's not there!' I take a deep breath as Mum starts scrubbing aggressively. 'I want to say goodbye to her paintings and her house too, and I want to look for the ring. I wouldn't forgive myself if it was sold or lost or something. So if you're offering an all-expenses-paid trip somewhere,' I turn back to face Aunt Fanny, who is swirling her wine, 'then that's where I'd like to go, please.' I try to steady my breathing as my heart races in my chest.

'Zoe,' Mum mutters in a strained voice, 'we are *not* going.'

'I'm an adult, Mum,' I snap again, indignation taking over. 'I can do what I like.'

The last bit fires out before I can stop myself, and although Mum's face is hidden, I see her body flinch. It's like I've hit her.

Aunt Fanny is leaning back in her chair, sipping her wine.

God, what's happening? We never argue.

A long silence radiates around the room, until the rough scrubbing of the scourer against the pan starts up again. The noise scratches in my ears. Aunt Fanny, who seems unfazed by the bristling heat in the room, tips the remainder of her wine down her throat, looks between Mum and me, then smiles mischievously.

'Okay,' she says. 'Let's go.'

'What?' Mum whips round, her face now scarlet.

'I agree with Zoe. I think we should go. I'll book us flights. Ange, do you still have your passport?' She whips out her phone and starts tapping. 'Oh look, we can fly from Cornwall airport tomorrow evening. Perfect.'

'Fanny,' Mum says, her voice shaking, 'we are not going behind Reggie's back. This is a hard enough time as it is. It's not like before, we can't just pick everything up and gallivant off.'

'But if we tell him we're going, he'll hide the ring! He knows I want it!' I gabble.

Aunt Fanny waves her hand in the air. 'Just sleep on it, Ange.'

'I don't need to sleep on it,' Mum says darkly. 'I am not going.'

Guilt turns my stomach over as I look at Mum's stricken face. I don't want to make her do something she doesn't want to, but she needs to be there. We can't go without her.

'Mum, I—'

'There!' Aunt Fanny puts her phone down and picks up the bottle of wine, pouring the final dribble into her tulip shaped glass. 'All booked. Oh, Ange?' She gives the bottle a little shake. 'You don't have any more of this wine, do you? It's actually quite nice.'

Chapter Fifteen

Fanny

It's perfect. I can't believe I didn't think of it sooner. Showing up in Cornwall unannounced wasn't my best plan, but I didn't have much time. Let's be honest, whenever I've run away spontaneously before, it's always worked out rather well. But having the two of them to myself in Italy, things will be much easier. Zoe will have to get over her strop sooner or later, and Ange will relax once she's back in Sulmona with a glass of wine in hand.

I take a deep drag of my cigarette, sinking into my body as the fumes weave their way into my lungs. The sun set hours ago, but the air is still warm, even though it's the middle of the night. It carries the scent of forgotten barbecues and half-finished lawns that started the day with the intention of being mowed. Before another bottle was popped and a can of lager flicked open and everyone ended up dancing on the tables to Take That.

I feel a pang of yearning in the pit of my stomach.

I haven't done that in years. I should be doing it right now. Look at me! I'm not supposed to ferret my days away in a boxy house, striding towards my grave in Kurt Geiger heels.

I glance up at the window as Angie's bedroom light flickers on. I don't know who she thought she was kidding when she announced that she was going to bed at ten. We're the same age, and us women can't sleep once we tick over to a certain side of fifty. But what is she doing up there? Pacing? Thinking? Plotting? It certainly won't be a beauty regime, considering she's had nobody for the last fourteen years to badger her into moisturising and advise her on the importance of a good cleanser. Slipping it into her make-up bag when she argued that she could never afford the brands I pressed upon her.

I puff another strand of smoke into the inky sky. The stars wink down at me. I'd forgotten how loud the stars were down here. You hardly see them in Liverpool.

There is no point me knocking on her door and asking her what the matter is. I know Angie too well. She's stubborn, just like Zoe. So I'm doing what I always did, I'm ignoring them both and doing what I know is best. I'm always right; aside from my hair, it's my best quality. Which is why I booked Italy. I know Angie; there is no way she'd stay behind. She might be annoyed now, but she'll thank me later.

Or maybe she'll thank me in years to come, after they've forgiven me once I've finally told them the truth.

I take a final suck of the cigarette and drop it on the floor, squashing it under my pointed heel.

But for now, limoncello. Nobody does limoncello like the Italians.

Chapter Sixteen

Harriet

Standing at the fire exit, I quickly look left and right to make sure there is no sign of Sophie, before ducking out into the darkness for my late-night cigarette break. Technically it isn't authorised or classed as a proper break, but Sophie told me that through a mouthful of bacon sandwich, so I'm going to pretend I didn't fully understand her. I stick an unlit cigarette in my mouth and pull out my phone to see that Zoe has called me eight times. It's been buzzing on my thigh for the past half an hour while I've been waving off hen parties and groups of giggling girls as they skip off into the night, assuring older couples arriving back at the hotel at the same time that they absolutely won't cause a disturbance later and I will absolutely make sure of it.

The cigarette sizzles under the flame and I press the phone to my ear. Zoe answers after the first ring.

'Harriet!' she gabbles. 'Finally! What have you been doing?'

'I'm at work!' I say indignantly. Occasionally I like to pretend that I take my job as seriously as Zoe does hers. 'Sophie is on shift tonight,' I add. 'She's been watching me like a bloody hawk.'

'Can't you just lock her in the spa?'

'I'd much rather lock myself in there. Although I did win fifty quid on that scratch card I got yesterday, so that was pretty good. What's up?' I take a drag of my cigarette as an ambulance skirts past on the main road.

'Er . . .' Zoe falters. 'My aunt has just booked us flights to Italy for tomorrow.'

I almost choke. 'Sorry?'

'I can't go just with her, and there is no way Mum is going to come. So would you do me a huge favour and come to Italy with us for the weekend?'

I raise my eyebrows. 'You want me to do you a favour . . . by coming to Italy?'

'Yeah, if you can. If Sophie will let you take the time off work. I mean, Aunt Fanny has booked Mum a flight, but you might need to book your own just in case a miracle happens and she decides to come.'

I thumb the scratch card, which is sticking out of my back pocket.

'I'm coming. I'm booking my flight right now.'

CHAPTER SEVENTEEN

ZOE

'Good morning, my darling!' I jump as Aunt Fanny springs out of the bathroom. 'What's your email? I need to forward you the plane tickets. We've got three seats on the six o'clock flight to Rome! The *only* flight to Rome, I'll add. The airport here is *useless.*'

I nod slightly, slipping past her into the bathroom and squirting a line of toothpaste onto my toothbrush. 'Have you persuaded Mum to come?'

Mum spent the rest of yesterday evening in near silence. She can't bear confrontation, and she'd never tell Aunt Fanny what she really thought. She barely told me off when I was a teenager and she used to catch me going to school with cigarettes hidden in my waistband. So she stayed silent, occasionally closing a cupboard a little too roughly or exhaling slightly louder than usual. But she wouldn't look at me, and when she said goodnight and gave me a quick peck on the cheek, I noticed her eyes were wet.

'Not yet,' Aunt Fanny says, 'but I will. Now,' she spins to face me as I start to whizz the toothbrush round my mouth, 'do you have any nice sundresses to pack?'

Her bright, playful eyes make me bristle, and I feel as though by agreeing to this trip, we've crossed a line I wasn't intending to cross. We're not friends. Paying for the tickets doesn't make everything okay.

'This is a trip to say goodbye to my grandma,' I say, spitting out my toothpaste. 'It's not a holiday. I'm going to get the ring.'

She looks back at me innocently. 'And you can't do that in a nice sundress?'

I shoot her a look and slip past her, running downstairs to the hallway, which is glowing in greens and pinks as the early-morning sun pours through the stained-glass window in the front door. As I enter the kitchen, I can hear Mum clattering about, a forced hum following her around the room, and guilt curls in my chest again.

'Morning, Mum.'

She doesn't look up. 'Morning, love. Would you like a tea?'

'I don't think I have time.'

'Okay then.'

We drift back into silence and I chew the inside of my cheek. We've been having a lot of these silences since Grandma died, and now the elephant in the room has got that much bigger. I hate it.

'I'm going to come with you.'

Her words shoot through me and my mouth falls open. Her back is still firmly turned towards me as she continues to bustle around, chopping something.

'Oh!' I cry, my voice high-pitched. 'Really? That's great! I'm so happy! I think it'll be really good for us all.' I hold out my arms stupidly, expecting Mum to at least look at me so I can envelop her in a hug and push away this horrible tension. But she keeps chopping.

The tinkle of the radio fills the silence and the hope drains from my body. When I realise she's not going to respond, I turn on my heel and leave to go to work.

'Well, have a nice day,' I mumble.

One thing's for sure: nothing can make her worse than she is now. She's like a ghost, and I need my mum back.

★

I rush home after work and immediately go upstairs, pulling my backpack down from the top of my wardrobe and flinging it open. We need to leave in thirty minutes, and I usually require at least five working days to pack, so this is wildly out of character for me.

I pull open my drawers and start chucking things into the bag mindlessly. Pants, pants, pants. All the pants. I can't go wrong if I have enough pants. I take out a pair of jeans and a nice top and throw them on top of the mound of clothes. It's the only outfit I ever wear if I go anywhere outside of Tesco. If I'm feeling really fancy – a rare date or a birthday – I'll add a boot, but as we're going to Italy, I throw a whimsical pair of sandals onto the growing pile.

I rub the back of my hand against my forehead. Do I need to pack a jumper, or will it be too warm for that?

I turn on my heel and jump down the stairs. Mum will know; she knows everything about packing. I feel like it's something all mums do. It's like the moment they have a child, they lose the ability to send a text message without three emojis but gain the knowledge of which essential items to take on holiday.

I knock gently on her door. 'Mum?' I call out, pushing my way into her room. She looks around at me, startled, and my heart jumps into my throat. Her eyes are red and slightly puffy, her hair static against her face. She is leaning over an open suitcase, with neat piles of clothes carefully placed inside.

She quickly forces a smile, but it's too big. It pushes her eyes too far up her face, like small prunes.

'Hello, love,' she says. 'Are you okay?'

I hover for a moment, mentally playing out a scene where I ask her what's wrong. But I know what she'll say, so I decide against it.

'Yeah,' I say after a beat. 'I'm fine.'

She turns back to her suitcase. 'Good.'

I walk over. Her bed is perfectly made, the floral sheets stretched out into each corner and the throw pillows plumped and stacked neatly. I notice a small Polaroid photo on her bed-side table and frown, trying to make out the smiling faces. I've never seen the photo before. But before I can get a closer look, she removes it and slips it into her suitcase under a towel. Maybe it was a photo of Grandma.

She folds another pair of socks into the suitcase, and I raise my eyebrows. There's already a small pile of socks sandwiched between a towel and her washbag. She must have at least eight pairs in there.

'That's a lot of socks,' I say stupidly.

She picks up another pair. 'Is it?'

We fall into silence as I watch her.

'I'm so sorry about all of this,' I blurt out. 'I know you didn't want to go to Italy, but I really do think it will be good for you – for both of us. We need to talk about Grandma, and maybe seeing her house and her things one last time might help us, you know . . . process it all. Harriet is going to come too. She's so excited to finally see Grandma's house after how much we've spoken about it. I thought we could take her to that bar by the piazza . . .'

I break off, watching the side of Mum's face, desperate for her to look at me. But her curtain of hair hides her eyes and she continues to fold her socks.

'You don't have to come,' I mumble, heat pinching at my face. 'You can stay here if you want to.'

A small laugh makes Mum's shoulders shudder. 'You know I can't do that.'

'I don't want to force you to do something you don't want to do.'

This time the silence pulls between us, and I feel the tension snake up my neck and curl around my throat.

'Mum, I—'

'Ten pairs,' she says to herself, almost totally unaware that she's interrupted me. 'Yes, I think that'll be enough socks.'

I go to reply when the doorbell rings. I look out the window and see Harriet grinning and waving up at me. She managed to book a seat on the same flight as us, though God knows where she'll be sitting.

'I'll go let Harriet in.' I turn to leave the room, pausing as I reach the door. 'Mum,' I say, making eye contact with the back of her head, 'I'm really glad you're coming. I wouldn't want to do this without you.'

She doesn't even look up.

Chapter Eighteen

Fanny

I love that photo. It's one of the few photos I still have of me and Angie. We didn't have camera phones when we were younger. Everything was captured on the bulky Polaroid camera, which was often slung around Angie's neck even though it was mine. I didn't want that unsightly thing ruining my outfit every time we went out.

Anyway, I may feel like I don't know the version of Angie that has been pacing around the house since I arrived, but I know the real her. Once you peel back the layers of pristine, unbearable chirpiness and neat, freshly ironed cardigans, the same woman is still there. My Ange. The woman who used to eat my dessert and once skinny-dipped in the sea, then laughed when we came back and found all of our clothes had been stolen. The woman who I know is hurting from the loss of her mum and would rather give everyone the middle finger instead of offering them a cup of tea. The woman who, somewhere beneath that perfect façade, is pretty damn angry at her best friend for ditching her without saying goodbye. So I took the photo out of my purse and left it on her pillow, as a little reminder. Like a mirror to who she was before, who I know she really is.

The photo was taken in Sulmona, in a wine bar close to where Clarice lived. We had been drinking red wine all evening, and when Angie noticed our mouths were both stained black, she turned to the waiter and asked him whether she had anything stuck in her teeth. We're both grinning widely in that picture.

It's the photo of the old Angie, the woman I left behind.

CHAPTER NINETEEN

ZOE

I think it's fair to say that my trust in Aunt Fanny is tenuous at the best of times. But waiting to go through security at the airport, it's hanging by a thread. I'm ready to grab her cigarettes, chuck them over the barrier and make a run for it as soon as her back is turned.

I mean, she still hasn't told us where she's been for the past fourteen years. She could have been doing anything! And now she's paid for last-minute tickets to Rome, *and* she's paying for our accommodation. She didn't even bat an eye when I said Harriet was coming too; she just booked another room and asked if Harriet was the 'loud friend with red hair'. How can she afford it?

She's always been like this with money, handing over her credit card to waiters and shopkeepers without even glancing at the bill. She claims to have invented a nail file in the eighties that set her up for life. As a child, I didn't even question it. But now, looking at the woman who has popped back into our lives without so much as an explanation, let alone an apology, I'm not so sure.

So, while I'm standing in the queue waiting for Aunt Fanny to place her bag on the conveyor belt and walk through the scanner, it seems entirely plausible that the reason that she's back and is able to fund the trip is because she's a major drug dealer. That she's on the run from the police, or, much worse, a gang, and has shown up on our doorstep with a bag crammed full of class A drugs. Maybe this trip is an elaborate way of her ensuring she has some company in prison.

Coming back into the real world, I realise I've been staring at the security guard this whole time.

God, he's giving me a stern look. The guilt must be written all over my face. Well, I won't keep your secrets for you, Aunt Fanny, when I'm put on the stand. I'll sing like a canary! I wouldn't last a second in prison. They'd take one look at me and my stupid chubby cheeks and I'd be instantly taken in as somebody's bitch, and *then* . . .

'Zoe?' I jump as Harriet nudges me in the ribs. 'Are you okay?'

It takes me a second to realise that I am goggling at her. Aunt Fanny hooks her bag over her shoulder and laughs loudly at something Mum has said.

For God's sake, get a grip, Zoe. Your aunt is not here because she's a major drug dealer; if she was, she wouldn't be willingly strolling through airport security. Unless it's in my bag and she's going to frame me and . . .

'Zoe?' Harriet urges.

'Sorry.' I blink, forcing myself out of my thoughts, where I'm quivering on the stand with cameras in my face, ready to swear on the Bible. 'Yeah, I'm fine. A bit weirded out. This has just all happened so fast.'

Harriet follows my gaze to Aunt Fanny, who is patting Mum on the shoulder.

'Yeah,' she says, 'it is weird.'

'Like, I haven't seen her in fourteen years, and then she just pops up and now we're all going on holiday together.'

We shuffle forward in the queue.

'Do you know where she's been all this time?'

'Nope.'

'Or why she's here?'

'Nope. Well,' I correct myself, 'apparently it's because she heard that Grandma died, but, like, wouldn't you call first if that was the case? Like, hello, are you okay, shall I come and stay?'

Aunt Fanny lets out another loud cackle, and a man in a business suit shoots a disapproving look at her over his shoulder. His tie is so tight under his chin he looks like a balloon that's about to pop.

'You don't believe her then?' Harriet says.

I pluck a clear plastic bag from the dispenser and start dropping my make-up into it.

'Do you?'

She cocks her head and surveys Aunt Fanny, who's got three clear bags propped up on the counter. One looks as if it's entirely filled with lipsticks.

How has she managed to get *three* through security?

'I don't know,' Harriet says eventually, sealing her own

plastic bag and moving forward with the queue, 'I can't work her out. I do like her, though, there's something about her . . .'

I scowl at the back of Fanny's perfect blonde head. She's like a flickering light, and we're the little moths, zooming towards her as she beckons us nearer. But once we get too close, too comfortable, that's when we get burnt.

★

'Right, what we need is a proper plan.'

I look up at Mum and nod.

Miraculously, we all made it through security in one piece, even though I seriously thought Aunt Fanny was going to be arrested at one point. Not because she was smuggling bags of cocaine. Oh no. Rather because she refused to take off her high heels. She eventually gave in and strode through the body scanner like she was on the catwalk at London Fashion Week. When she put her shoes back on, I'm sure I heard her mutter to Mum that she'd been 'violated'.

Now we're all squashed around a tiny table at Shake Shack, with four flat burgers sitting on identical squares of tin foil. Mum has moved the cutlery pot and jars of sauce to the side as if she's about to launch a military action plan.

Our flight leaves in an hour, and as soon as Aunt Fanny almost squared up to the six-foot-four security guard, Mum snapped out of her daze and went into 'travel mum' mode. The mode that consists of packed lunches and first aid kits and emergency cagoules. It was as though she looked at Fanny and saw her for what she is – another child – and suddenly knew that she had to take charge.

I'm actually quite relieved. It's a comfort to see her in any mode that isn't this weird half a person that she's been since Grandma died. And if I play my cards right, she might buy me a packet of Rolos.

'So,' she says, 'our flight leaves in one hour, which will get us to Rome at nine thirty. We'll get a taxi to our hotel, which Aunt Fanny has kindly booked . . .'

'You have booked it, haven't you?' I say, more severely than I mean to.

Fanny clicks her tongue at me. 'Yes, yes.'

'. . . then tomorrow we will need to get the train to Bugnara,' Mum continues, ignoring us. 'It takes about an hour, so we need to be on the train at ten a.m. at the latest to allow for delays.' She pauses, eyeballing each of us in turn, as if daring us to challenge her plan. We nod back at her sheepishly. Well, me and Harriet do. Aunt Fanny is playing Candy Crush.

'We will need to get a taxi from Bugnara and should be at Grandma's house by the afternoon. We will then have all of Saturday evening and Sunday to look for the ring and anything else we'd like to hold back from the auction,' she shoots me a meaningful look, and I blush, 'and then we will leave Bugnara at nine a.m. on Monday morning to return to Rome for our flight at four thirty. That will get us back to Cornwall airport by seven p.m. and we can be back home by nine.' She breathes a sigh of relief.

'Gosh,' Harriet chimes in, 'so we're going to Italy and back in, like, three days? Isn't that what people from *The Bachelor* do when they want a nice pizza?'

'You're thinking of *Friends*,' Aunt Fanny quips, not looking up from her phone.

'Am I?'

'Yes. The billionaire guy Monica goes out with flies her to Italy for their first date. Think he's called Patrick, or Paul.'

'It's Pete. Anyway,' I turn back to Mum, 'that all sounds great. Thanks, Mum. This time tomorrow we'll be sitting around Grandma's table.' I beam at her and take her hand, hoping she might smile back or squeeze mine excitedly. But it stays on the table, limp, and she looks away.

'Oh, before I forget, I must get some Werther's for the plane.' She jumps to her feet, pulling her hand back from mine.

Aunt Fanny mimics her, leaping out of her seat too. 'Oh yes, I want a copy of *Heat*.'

I take a deep breath as they walk away, resting my head in my hands. Harriet puts an arm around my shoulders.

'You're just like her, you know.'

'Please don't say I'm like my aunt,' I mumble into my hands.

'No,' she smiles, removing her arm. 'Your mum, with all her planning and stuff. She's a control freak like you are.'

I push my hair out of my face and sit up straight. 'Well, I do like a plan. It's very unlike me to spontaneously jump on a plane.'

'I know. It's quite fun, isn't it?'

I look up at her. Her flaming red hair is in a pile on top of her head and her black eyeliner is smudged. Out of nowhere, I feel a sudden pang of guilt as I look at her wide eyes. She's dropped everything for this trip, put up with my lukewarm mood for the past six months while Grandma was unwell and my constant requests to just stay in and watch a film instead of going out. And what have I done to her? Plopped her right in the middle of my weird family dynamics. I didn't even buy her burger.

'I'm sorry,' I say.

'What for?'

'Well, we've wanted to do this for ages, but I kept putting it off. Now you've had to take annual leave for a measly three-day trip to Italy. This is the closest we've come to travelling, and I've brought my bloody mum and weird aunt with us, and—'

'Zoe,' she holds up a hand, 'there is a lot wrong with that list.'

'Like what?'

'Well to start with, I didn't take annual leave. I quit.'

Chapter Twenty

Harriet

I will myself to keep a straight face as I watch Zoe's reaction to the bomb I just dropped. Sensible, organised Zoe who spent three weeks penning her letter of resignation for her teenage paper round.

I wasn't planning on quitting. Well, obviously every time Sophie opened her mouth and didn't ask me what I was up to at the weekend, I began fantasising about handing in my notice and storming off into the sunset. But when Zoe called me and asked me to go with her to Italy, I felt this burning sensation in the pit of my stomach. It was like a physical ache, that's how much I wanted to go with her. I couldn't sit behind this stupid reception desk for a moment longer, especially not while my best friend hopped on a plane for an impromptu adventure. Something we had been talking about since we graduated. She almost sounded guilty when she asked if I'd come with her. I mean, what else was I going to do? Sit at home with my mum, her boyfriend and the baby like the enormous third wheel I have become?

I needed to get out. I've known that for ages. But this was the first time I'd been offered a lifeline.

So I grabbed my scratch card, cashed in my winnings and took it.

And when Sophie asked if I would go and speak to the man upstairs who was screaming down the phone about finding a stray hair on his pillow, I told her I'd rather stick pins in my eyes and walked out.

Then I went to the pub, ordered myself an espresso martini (something the barman had absolutely no idea how to make) and sat at the bar channelling my inner Carrie Bradshaw.

Zoe gapes at me, and when I raise my eyebrows at her, she bursts out laughing.

'I can't believe you did that. What are you going to do now?'

There she is again, sensible Zoe, scrabbling around for a plan.

I shrug. 'Who knows. But right now, I'm going on an Italian adventure.'

'With my mum and weird aunt.'

'To meet a sex god Italian stallion,' I correct her, 'and eat my body weight in pasta with my best mate. Really, Zo, it was a no-brainer.'

★

I was so pleased with myself last night. It's not often that you actually go through with one of the fantasies you've been playing out in your head. I've quit jobs before (and been fired a few times too), but that's always been behind a snivelling, apologetic email where I've made up some stupid excuse and claimed it had absolutely nothing to do with the job, which I *of course love* and was absolutely *devastated to leave*.

But this time I was so pumped up on adrenaline from Zoe's sudden burst of spontaneity that I practically sprinted to find Sophie as soon as I hung up the phone. I told her I had to leave *immediately* as I was going travelling and my flight was booked for tomorrow. I was trying to mask my underlying fear that she might brandish my contract in my face and demand I work my week's notice, but she actually looked quite relieved. If I hadn't been so excited, I'd have been almost offended.

I stayed until the end of my shift, although the last twenty minutes of that consisted of sharing a cigarette with Sophie (turns out the reason she was so anal about my smoke breaks was because she'd been trying to quit for three years and almost passed out with jealousy every time I returned in a cloud of nicotine). I told her that life was too short not to do what you loved. I mean, look at me. I've just quit my job to go *travelling*! *Que* bloody *sera sera*.

I didn't tell her that I was essentially crashing quite an important family trip rather than skipping off to Thailand to dance the night away at a Full Moon party. But that's just a detail! I figured that if I can get Zoe on international soil, I can convince her to stay. I'll get her drunk and put her on a flight or something.

I was so excited to tell my mum. Mainly because I felt like I finally had something to say to her. We'd turned into passing ships in the night, with me working shifts and her out at various baby groups or fast asleep by nine each night. In the rare moments I did see her, she'd ask how my day was and I'd grumble something about hating work and doing the same thing every weekend, and I'd see this look in her eye that I could never quite place. But a part of me thought it might be disappointment, and I hated that more than I hated any job. So the thought of bursting through the door and telling her that I was about to do something I was really excited about filled my whole body like a hot-air balloon.

I tripped over one of Daniel's toys as I stumbled in. It was after 3 a.m. (goodbye, night shifts!), but I was too excited to go to sleep. Without really thinking, I ran upstairs and crashed straight into Mum's room.

'Mum,' I whispered, dropping to my knees by her bed, 'Mum, it's me.'

She scrunched up her face. Her hair was screwed into a messy bun and there was a splat of something crusted on her top.

'What?' she managed. 'Are you okay?'

Next to her, Darren grunted.

'Yeah!' I cried. 'I—'

But at that moment, right on cue, Daniel opened his tiny mouth and started to scream. Darren cursed loudly next to Mum and switched on the light. My stomach turned over.

'Sorry,' I mumbled. 'Was that me?'

'It's fine,' Mum said in a strained voice. 'Darren, I'll go.' She pushed him back down onto his pillow, which he hit like he was made of lead. 'You have work in the morning.'

She stumbled out of bed. She looked like a little mole who was allergic to light.

'Sorry,' I whispered, guilt and embarrassment rolling up my body. 'I didn't think . . .'

94

Before Darren and baby Daniel came along, I didn't even have to think about whether Mum would want to chat to me about my day. Now I find it hard to work out where I fit in. I'm like a piece of the puzzle that is slightly too big. If you lean all your weight on it, you might be able to cram it into place. But it'll split open and pop back out, and it never looked right there anyway. Anyone would be able to tell it was an odd piece. The one that didn't belong.

I followed her out of the bedroom and stood uselessly as she staggered into Daniel's room. I waited for a minute after the screams died down for her to come out again, and when she didn't, I just went to bed.

The next morning, I woke up to an empty house, so I left.

CHAPTER TWENTY-ONE

ZOE

I smile as a small elderly lady with an electric-pink suitcase marches through the airport. She's hunched over, but nothing is slowing her down. I'd like to think she's off to Vegas.

I watch her, thinking of how Grandma used to behave in an airport. She was a cocktail of 'woman on a mission' and 'away with the fairies'. It drove Mum mad.

Grandma's hair was a sheet of white that swung down to her waist in wispy strands. She always wore it down, fiercely tucked behind her ears when she needed to concentrate, and very rarely brushed it. It was always a bit ratty and wild, but that never made it any less beautiful. Her skin was slightly leathered from the years of Italian sun, but her eyes, an icy blue, sparked ferociously under the hoods of her ageing eyelids. She always wore a set of dungarees, that hung off her tiny frame and were rolled up around her ankles, with a bright T-shirt underneath and paintbrushes sticking out of the breast pocket. Quite often still glistening under a layer of fresh paint. She was a tiny woman, even smaller than Mum, standing at just under five foot, with spindly arms and jutting collarbones. She didn't care much about food, and would get so engrossed in her art that she wouldn't eat for hours. When we went to stay, we'd all go out to dinner and she'd marvel at the menu like she'd never seen one before. She'd gush at the waiters and order us anything we wanted. Once we spent a whole summer there and I had gelato every day.

She was different to Mum, fiery and spontaneous where Mum is polite and controlled. Mum always told me that she was more like my grandpa, who passed away when I was small. But when she and Grandma were together, they just slotted into each other like identical halves of the same stone.

Her house in Sulmona was my happy place. We'd often fly over after school broke up for the holidays. It would start as me, Mum, Uncle Reggie and Aunt Fanny, but Reggie would often leave after a week claiming 'important work'. Then it was just the four of us, and that was when the real fun began.

I lean back in my seat as another flight is announced over the tannoy. Just being here in the airport is lighting the little fire that sparked in the pit of my stomach every time I went to Italy to see Grandma. It's like my body craves it, the excitement seeping in from my bones and filling my heart.

I'm finding it hard to correct my muscle memory while I'm sitting here, so I'm allowing myself to bathe in the feeling that the most magical week with Grandma is about to start. In my imagination, she's still at the house in Sulmona. Nobody can take that away from me.

I take a deep breath and look around. We've been waiting for about twenty minutes for Mum and Aunt Fanny to resurface from W H Smith.

Harriet glances up at me when my phone buzzes.

'Anyone interesting?'

I sigh, opening an email from Kitty. 'No, just work. Kitty is sending over wedding information.'

'When's the wedding?'

'Not until Thursday.' I bite my lip as I scan the message. 'Everything is organised, but apparently the bride has started acting a bit . . . weird.'

Harriet arches her eyebrows. 'Uh oh, cold feet?'

I bite the top of my thumb. The email is a stream of words detailing a conversation that Kitty had with Libby on the phone. The only punctuation is several exclamation marks.

'I don't know,' I say eventually. 'I'm not sure what's going on.'

'Ah.'

'And I should,' I add, trying to ignore the feeling that my stomach is shuffling up my body. 'Kitty shouldn't be the one dealing with the bride, it should be me. Really I shouldn't be going on this trip, I should be spending the weekend prepping. I haven't even told Heidi that I'm going away; we're not really allowed to take time off before a wedding. Kitty has done loads, and I've been so stressed with all of this,' I wave my hand above my head, 'that I've barely been able to concentrate. I literally have no idea what—ARGH!'

I shriek as a pint of lager falls to the floor and splatters up the side of my leg. I look round in disgust to see a group of guys laughing. One turns to me and picks up the plastic glass.

'God, I'm so sorry, did it get you?'

He meets my eye. He has freckled skin and short auburn hair

that swishes over his forehead in a textured shiny fringe. His eyes are hazel with flecks of gold, and although his lips are curved apologetically, there is a slight smirk playing on them. He's so close to my feet he's practically kissing them, and for a horrible second I think he's going to pick up a napkin and offer to wipe them clean.

I quickly tuck my legs back under the table, silently thanking the Lord that I shaved them this morning.

'No,' I babble. 'I mean, yes, it did. But it's fine. Don't worry.'

He gets to his feet and looks at me. I move my body away, willing him to leave.

'Okay,' he says eventually, before turning on his heels and rejoining his group of friends. There are three of them, all with backpacks so big they look like a collection of youthful tortoises.

'Urgh,' I mutter, unlocking my phone.

'What?'

'Them.' I shoot them a glare out of the corner of my eye. 'Who gets drunk at an airport at this time?'

I look up from my phone and notice Harriet gesturing at our two shandies.

'Well that's different! We're not throwing them all over people. I bet they're off on a stag do or something.'

'You're very flustered by this,' Harriet says in a horrible superior tone. 'Fancy a slice of Ron Weasley, do we?'

I raise my eyebrows at her. 'Really? That's the best ginger reference you could think of?'

She grins and waves at Mum and Aunt Fanny, who are gliding up the escalator, both sporting brand-new sunglasses and pashminas.

★

99

Mum agreed to this trip on the proviso that it would be perfectly organised and stick to a strict plan. Which is fine. Or it would be if the flight wasn't delayed. By three hours.

I push my lips together, trying to zone out Mum's increasingly heavy breathing next to me. I'm shrinking away from her in an attempt not to catch the stress that is spitting from her pores. She's been practising her 'meditative breathing' for the past forty minutes. Either it's not working, or she needs to ask for a refund from her yoga instructor. It's so intense, she's about to sprout a third nostril and take off.

Aunt Fanny is on her third Chardonnay, jabbering to Harriet about Saint-Tropez and her time in Monaco, and Harriet is lapping up every word. Of course she's been completely swept up in Aunt Fanny's spell; she's intoxicating. But I know better, which has left me trying not to get sucked in by Mum's stress cloud whilst maintaining my composure as Fanny shares sparkly anecdote after sparkly anecdote, making Harriet giggle tipsily. Fanny keeps looking at me hopefully, but I refuse to join in. At first I just avoided her gaze, but then Harriet started looking at me too, so now I'm pretending to be having a power nap.

I suddenly notice that my breathing has fallen in time with Mum's, and I glance over at Harriet and Aunt Fanny, who are laughing and comparing tattoos. Mum's fists are curled into little balls, and I give her arm a poke. She jerks out of her breathing rhythm gruffly, her eyes wide and panicked.

'Would you like a tea?' I say quietly. 'I'm going to nip over to one of those coffee shops.'

She visibly shrinks in relief and nods. 'Decaf, please.'

I squeeze her arm and get to my feet. 'I'm going to go to Starbucks,' I announce. 'Do either of you want anything?'

'I'd love a latte,' Harriet beams, her face pink from all the laughing. I feel a pang of envy.

'An espresso for me, please, darling,' Aunt Fanny says, sticking her hand in her tiny handbag and whipping out a credit card. 'My treat. Maybe some muffins or something too.'

I take the card off her and join the queue, rolling my shoulders to try and relieve my tense muscles.

I don't like seeing Mum feeling uneasy, but, even more, I don't like that we seem to have split into two groups: Fanny and Harriet having fun and laughing through the whole thing, and me and Mum silently panicking in the corner. Why can't we *all* be having fun?

It's Fanny's fault. If she wasn't here and it was just the three of us, we'd all be feeling the same, and maybe even talking about everything and calming each other down. Aunt Fanny knows Mum better than anyone – or she did before she left – so she must be able to see how difficult she's finding all of this, and she's barely even asked if she's okay. Instead she's busy showing off to Harriet with her ridiculous stories about jetting around the world and hopping from one yacht to the next. Lies threaded through each one, like they always are.

But then if she wasn't here, I'm not sure I would ever have been able to persuade Mum to come, and I know I wouldn't have gone if it meant leaving her behind.

I step forward in the queue.

Why is she here? Why now? What does she want?

Uncle Reggie has done a good job of publicising the auction.

Grandma's work used to sell for thousands. Maybe that's why Fanny is here. She's hoping for a cut of the money.

As I reach the front of the queue, a smiley woman in a branded cap beams at me.

'Hi,' I smile back, 'can I please have a decaf tea, two lattes, an espresso and four chocolate muffins?'

She nods and gestures to the card machine, which is already loaded with the amount due, before turning her back on me as she begins frothing milk. I pull out Aunt Fanny's card from my pocket and my eyes are drawn to the name on it.

Mr Jon Harrow.

My throat tightens. Jon. That's the man Aunt Fanny left my uncle for, supposedly. They must be still together then. Or she's stolen his credit card.

I catch the eye of the waiting barista and gingerly tap the card on the machine. It dings happily back at me, and I take the bag of muffins and the tray of cups.

Is this how she's paying for everything?

The thought makes me feel hot under my jumper.

Does Jon know she has his card? She hasn't mentioned him since she arrived, and I—

'Whoa!' I nearly walk straight into another customer. I look up, flustered, about to apologise, when I realise that it's Ron Weasley from earlier. No, *not* Ron Weasley. The red-headed man with the nice eyes and the absurdly big backpack.

Bollocks.

'Is this payback for the pint?' He grins. 'I did apologise for that.'

I blush. 'No, sorry,' I mumble. 'It was an accident. I . . . er . . . didn't see you. I was in a world of my own. Sorry.'

God, what is the matter with me? A fit guy starts talking to me and I can't even string a sentence together!

He smiles at me. 'No worries at all. But watch where you're going. If this is the game you're playing, who knows what I'll be carrying next. It might be a Mr Whippy, and if I lose an ice cream, you're buying me another one.'

I blink.

Don't just stare at him! Say something back! Anything! Say something cool!

'I love ice cream.'

Oh for God's sake, not that. You sound like a greedy five-year-old.

He laughs, but before he has a chance to answer, I bustle past him, my face burning.

I've never thought of myself as a Casanova but I also didn't realise I was *that* bad at flirting! It must be down to the stress of the flight and Aunt Fanny. At least I'll never have to see him again.

I put the coffees down as I reach Aunt Fanny and Harriet. Mum's eyes are still pressed shut, and Aunt Fanny is showing Harriet photos on her phone.

'And here is *your card* back,' I say pointedly, giving her my best Miss Marple stare. To my annoyance, she takes it off me brazenly and slips it back into her bag.

'Thank you, darling.'

I sit down and hand Mum her tea. She opens her eyes and is about to take it when her phone starts to ring. As she pulls it out of her bag, I catch the name on the screen and my heart turns over. It's Uncle Reggie.

'Don't tell him we're going to Grandma's,' I blurt before I can stop myself, quickly adding, 'Please. I want to go to the house before he has a chance to—'

Mum gives me a warning stare. 'Zoe . . .'

'You haven't told him I'm here, have you?' Aunt Fanny says idly.

'I haven't spoken to him since you arrived.'

'Good. Let's keep it that way.'

Mum turns back to me, her phone still vibrating in her hand. 'Zoe, I am not lying to your uncle.'

'If you tell him, he'll only get in a huff and ruin our girls' weekend,' Aunt Fanny interjects. 'He's good at that.'

I am about to retort that this isn't a 'girls' weekend', but then stop myself. She is on my side, I suppose.

'I have agreed to come on this trip,' Mum says evenly, 'even though I am not happy about it, but I am not lying to Reg too.'

Aunt Fanny waves a hand. 'He'll throw a strop whether you tell him now or in a week. We may as well have some fun first.'

I jump in. 'It's not lying it's just waiting until we're there! If he knows we're coming, he might hide the ring so he can sell it at the auction. You know that's what he's like.'

A shadow passes over her face and his name fades off the screen. 'Is that what you really think?'

'Yes.'

I look round as Aunt Fanny answers in unison with me.

I stare at Mum, willing her to understand, but her face is expressionless.

'Passengers for the delayed flight to Rome, we are now boarding . . .'

She gets to her feet, taking her tea off me.

'Come on,' she says. 'Let's get on this flight.'

Chapter Twenty-Two

Angie

'Here you are, madam.'

I look up as the flight attendant hands me a plastic glass of clear liquid. Before I can respond, Fanny leans across me and takes a second glass, tapping her card lightly on the machine.

'Thank you, darling,' she says, giving me a wink.

Have you ever done something that feels so unnatural it makes your entire body shake? Ever since I shut my front door this morning, I've felt it in my bones. Something bad is going to happen. I shouldn't be here, none of us should be. Something under my skin has been jittering, twitching, convulsing. I know it's my body trying to send me a message, and I don't know what it is, but it's not going to end well.

'Are you a nervous flyer?'

I look up at the flight attendant's kind eyes and shake my head, putting the glass to my lips.

'No,' I say in a small voice.

I take a sip of the drink, barely wincing as the neat vodka singes the back of my throat. The acidity pulls me out of my thoughts for a moment. I haven't drunk a straight vodka in years. It makes my tastebuds burst.

Next to me, Fanny is scrolling on her phone, looking at an article about face yoga in the digital version of *Vogue*.

'Everything is going to be fine, Ange,' she says, reading my thoughts.

I take a deep breath and close my eyes. With my eyes shut, I'm back in my kitchen, making a loaf of bread. Where I'm safe, where nothing bad happens.

Where I should be.

Chapter Twenty-Three

Zoe

Harriet nestles in next to me, holding an open bag of Minstrels in my direction. Harriet had managed to book a solo window seat, and the man next to me was only too happy to swap with her if it meant not being squashed between me and a mother with her six-month-old baby. I take a Minstrel and pop it in my mouth, exhaling loudly and sinking into my seat. Aunt Fanny steered Mum straight into the seat next to her on the flight, which meant I could finally peel Harriet away from her.

'How are you feeling?' Harriet asks.

'Fine.'

She raises her eyebrows at me. 'Let's try that again. How are you feeling?'

'Fine.'

'Zoe . . .'

I sigh and lower my voice. 'I'm feeling stressed, upset, annoyed.

Stressed that I'm away from work so close to a wedding, stressed that our flight has been delayed, upset that Mum can't see my point of view and is angry with me. Actually, just upset that she's constantly sad and won't talk to me and has turned into this weird robot. She'd rather just sit in silence, breathing heavily and pretending everything is fine. I basically forced her to come on this trip and she hasn't even raised her voice at me once! I mean, I'd prefer it if she just yelled at me or challenged me or something; at least it would be something real. *Anything* is better than silence. Oh, and I'm annoyed that Aunt Fanny has just appeared and taken over. Like nothing ever happened and she's not sorry at all! It's *infuriating*. I don't want her here. I wish she'd never shown up.'

I stuff another Minstrel in my mouth and Harriet cocks her head.

'I think she's just lonely.'

I scoff. 'Lonely?'

'Yeah. All those stories she was telling me about her life, she's on her own for all of them. She talks about 'old friends' but they're different in every story.'

'Well, it serves her right,' I say bitterly, a wave of guilt washing over me as soon as I say it. 'She can't just turn up because she's lonely after ditching us for fourteen years.'

'I know.'

'Anyway,' I add, plucking a third Minstrel from the bag, 'there's more to it than that. She's here because she wants something.'

'Wants something?' Harriet repeats. 'Like what?'

'I don't know. Money?'

Her brows knit together. 'Money? But she's paid for everything so far. Anyway, no offence, but it's not like you or your mum has a load of cash going spare.'

'Grandma did,' I say.

'No way. Is that what you really think?'

I catch her eye and feel another pang of guilt.

'I don't know,' I say eventually, 'but something is going on. She's not just here for a holiday.'

She lets out a whistle of breath and unclips her seat belt. 'I need a wee, be right back.'

I take the packet of Minstrels off her and shrink down into my seat. Mum and Aunt Fanny are sitting at the other end of the plane. I was expecting to hear Aunt Fanny's squawking laughter and constant chatter, but to my surprise, I haven't heard her once. About half an hour ago I craned my neck to try and spot them, and I saw their heads bent together in conversation. Probably Aunt Fanny lecturing Mum on the best place to buy shoes or something equally materialistic, even though she can see that she's hurting. We can all see it.

'Oh my God! Guess who's on the flight.' I look up as Harriet drops back into the seat next to me.

'Barack Obama?'

'What? No.'

'Katie Price?'

'These are weird guesses.'

'Okay, fine, who?'

Her eyes glint at me. 'Ron.'

It takes me a second to work out who she means, but then I feel a wave of dread.

'You're joking,' I groan. The last thing I want to do is bump into him for a *third* time and warble through another awkward conversation. I was quite set on never seeing him again.

'Yeah!' she cries. 'Him and all his mates! They must be going to Italy.'

'Great.' I guess I won't be going to the toilet for the entire flight. No more water for me.

'Do you think they're going travelling?' Harriet says wistfully. 'Imagine if they're going round Europe.'

I feel a pang of longing. 'You reckon?'

'One of his mates is really fit,' Harriet says after a pause. 'I didn't see him when we met Ron.'

'I saw him earlier.'

'His mate?'

'No, Ron. *Not* Ron,' I correct myself quickly. 'Whatever his name is. I bumped into him when I went to get the coffee. Literally.' I cringe at the memory and Harriet slaps my arm. 'Ow!'

'Why didn't you tell me?'

'It wasn't important.'

'Look at you, keeping secrets from me about a rendezvous with your new boyfriend.'

'There are so many things wrong with that sentence. He is literally a stranger. The only thing we have in common is that we're both a bit clumsy.'

'And love coffee, and are going to Italy, and fancy each other . . .'

I shut my eyes. 'I'm going to have a nap now. Goodnight, Harriet.'

★

It feels like only five minutes has passed before we're landing in Rome. The plane skims the landing strip with a light bump and the baby sitting next to us wails in protest.

Even though it's gone midnight, the Italian air is still warm, and the heat hits the back of my throat as I step off the plane. Taking a deep breath, I instantly feel myself relax, and as we make our way through the airport, I even allow myself to feel excited. For a moment, the possibilities feel endless, as if this could be the start of my very own impromptu adventure. That is until the last suitcase has been claimed, and it dawns on me that I'll be wearing the same knickers for the next seventy-two hours.

'I'm sure it's just coming,' Mum says for the fourth time, as we stare hopelessly at the empty conveyor belt.

'I can't believe they've lost my luggage,' I murmur. 'I thought this sort of thing only happened in films. What do we do?'

Aunt Fanny has had an unlit cigarette in her mouth for the past ten minutes.

She raises her eyebrows at me. 'It's lost, Zo. This is why I only take hand luggage. It's probably stuck back in Cornwall, or having a lovely time in the hands of a woman in Peru.'

'*Peru?*'

'She's just joking,' Mum says quickly. 'It will turn up soon, love, I'm sure.'

'Well we can't just stand here waiting,' Aunt Fanny says. 'Let's report it to the airline and find the hotel. We can always come back in the morning. Besides, I'm sure there's nothing in there that you can't live without for a night. You can borrow my make-up.' She gestures to the snakeskin handbag slung over her shoulder, and I shudder. I think it's fair to say that I will be going nowhere near her make-up bag.

'She's right, Zo,' Harriet says. 'I don't think it's here. You can borrow my stuff.'

I link my arm through hers and we make our way to the information desk. A stern Italian woman with a tight bun greets us with a thin-lipped smile. I open my mouth, before remembering that I don't speak Italian. Grandma always did the talking when we visited, the romantic language rolling off her tongue with ease. She didn't speak a word of it until she moved out here. Then, aged fifty-six, her brain seemed to absorb the language like she'd spent her entire life starved of it. She made friends with everyone she met, and would often throw her arms around the Italians who ran the restaurants and cafés that we'd visit, gushing at their stories and cupping their faces in her hands. She'd then turn to the three of us, brandishing one waif-like arm in our direction and launching into a big speech about us. I couldn't understand a word of it, but I knew that whatever she was saying, it was laced with pride. Grandma loved everyone. She didn't just see the good in people, she saw the best.

'Er . . . hello!' I say, feeling my cheeks immediately flush red. 'Er . . . sorry, *ciao*!' Why did I never learn Italian? I should have asked Grandma to teach me. I spent months out here as a child, and the only word I can remember is *banàna*, and that's because it's the same in English. I don't even like bananas!

The woman looks up at me, giving no indication as to whether she can speak English.

'We've just landed on the flight from Cornwall and I think my luggage is lost. Well, it isn't here . . .' I trail off. Her expression still doesn't alter. 'It's a black backpack,' I press on, 'with a pink stripe and a white tie on the handle. If you find it, please could you call me? We're staying in Rome until tomorrow, but then we're travelling to Sulmona.'

Without moving her face, she pushes a piece of paper and a pen towards me. I stare at it.

'Write your number down,' Harriet whispers to me.

Oh, of course.

I scribble it down and then hand the paper back. The woman takes it silently and nods. I pause, waiting for her to say something, but she turns back to her computer and starts tapping. After a few more moments of us standing there like lost tourists, Aunt Fanny sighs loudly.

'Listen, I need this cigarette. She's got the details and your number; she isn't going to pull your bag out of her arse.'

'Fanny!' Mum cries. It's the most animated she has sounded since we left Cornwall.

'Let's *go*!' Fanny all but pushes us towards the exit, like we're a flock of confused sheep, and I momentarily glance back at the woman, my piece of paper sitting next to a discarded coffee cup on her desk.

We step out of the airport, and Aunt Fanny lets out a groan as the orange flame flickers at the end of her cigarette. She takes a long drag and then holds the open packet towards the three of us. We all hover, and she sighs loudly. 'For God's sake, if you want one, just take one.'

Harriet looks sheepishly at Aunt Fanny, before sliding one out of the packet.

I would like nothing more than a cigarette right now. Some people are smokers, others are social smokers. I'm a stressed smoker. One cigarette after an intense meeting with Heidi or a particularly bad date, and that does me lovely. But if I take one, Aunt Fanny might see it as some form of forgiveness and acceptance of her being here, and I do *not* want to do anything to give her that impression.

Eventually she flicks the packet shut and slips it into her pocket. Then she leans her head back and blows a string of silky

113

smoke into the inky sky. I wrap my arms around my body, tiredness creeping up on me.

'Come on,' I say, 'let's get in one of these taxis. Aunt Fanny, do you have the details of the hotel?'

She takes a final drag and then flicks the cigarette to the ground, squashing it under the ball of her stilettoed shoe.

'Sure, honey. Let's go.'

I climb inside a taxi and clip my seat belt on. We hit the motorway, cars zipping in and out of lanes and the blur of street lights shooting past us. As we come closer to the city, the place starts to buzz. People with arms flung around each other hang out of bars, laughing and jostling. The ancient carved buildings are high, impressively beautiful.

I rest my head against the window. I haven't told anyone about Aunt Fanny having Jon's credit card, because I don't know who to tell. Mum isn't in the right mindset to hear it, and Harriet seems to be totally under Aunt Fanny's spell. I don't want to tell anyone until I'm sure of what she's up to. There is no point confronting her either, as she'll just laugh or try and brush it aside.

I also don't fully understand what it means. A part of me is ready to shrug it off. Plenty of couples share credit cards all the time – what's mine is yours and all that jazz. But there is a niggle in the pit of my stomach that I can't ignore. Aunt Fanny has been aloof ever since she arrived. Every time I've tried to ask her what she's been up to for the past fourteen years, she's expertly steered the conversation in another direction. If you blinked, you wouldn't even notice that she'd done it. But now that I've picked up on it, I feel like a starved dog with a hunk of meat dangling in front of my nose. I'm fixated on it, and as we pull up to the St Regis, a grand five-star hotel in the centre of Rome, I feel as though I could burst with questions.

Harriet gasps as we walk into the foyer. The three of us are alarmingly out of place, in our baggy T-shirts, our shabby suitcases rattling behind us. The smattering of preened men and women glance at us from behind their martinis with an air of discretion you only learn if you were brought up in a certain part of society. It's one that me, Mum and Harriet couldn't fit into if we tried, but Aunt Fanny lifts her chin and strides through reception, soaking up the raised eyebrows and daring anyone to challenge us.

An enormous, achingly exquisite chandelier hangs in the centre of the room, covering us in an expensive champagne-gold light. It draws my eye up to the grand ceiling, which is a painted blue sky and wispy clouds. There are large trees in each corner of the room, looking in equal measure too perfect to be real, yet too flourishing and healthy to possibly be fake.

Aunt Fanny clacks up to the desk like she comes here every day, leaving the three of us standing in the middle of the room, mouths gaping.

'Oh my God,' Harriet whispers to me. 'This place is incredible. I can't let your aunt pay for my room. It must be hundreds per night, not that I can afford that. I'll go stay in a hostel or something.'

'It's fine,' I say quietly. 'It was her choice to book this place. We could have easily stayed in an Airbnb.'

'But I—'

'Just buy her a glass of wine when we're out for dinner,' I interrupt. 'Honestly, this is what she's like. She has more money than sense.'

Fanny reaches the reception desk, leaning her angular elbows on the counter and rearranging a strand of her ice-blonde bob with a manicured hand. The receptionist, a good-looking Italian man with shiny slicked-back hair, bounces to attention. He is clearly dazzled by her. Most people are.

She smiles. '*Salve, abbiamo prenotato tre camera per questa sera. Il nome é* Fenella Winters.'

I gape at her.

'You speak Italian?' I cry, walking over to stand next to her. 'Why didn't you help me at the airport with my bag?'

She turns to face me. 'You made it quite clear that you didn't want my help, love, so I thought it best to leave you to it. Ah,' she turns back to face the man, who hands her three keys, '*grazie, amore mio.*'

He flushes, allowing himself a small smile before glancing back at his computer. '*Certo, vostre camera sono undici, dodici e tredici. Goditi la permanenza.*'

She flashes him another dazzling smile. 'Come on, girls, first floor. We're in rooms eleven to thirteen.'

She clops off and we scuttle after her, Mum and Harriet dragging their suitcases behind them.

'Do we have our own rooms?' I ask.

'I do,' Fanny says, 'and your mum does, but I thought you and Harriet would like to share. Do you remember that, Ange?' She leans back and scoops her arm through Mum's. 'When we used to share a room wherever we went?' Turning to Harriet and me, she adds, 'We once shared a single bed, which was absolute hell!' She throws back her head and laughs. 'Ah, those were the days.'

Mum offers up a small giggle.

'Don't worry, girls,' Aunt Fanny says as two men step forward

116

and pluck our suitcases out of our hands as we approach the stairs, 'you haven't got a single bed tonight.'

*

She wasn't kidding. It's the most enormous room I have ever seen. The walls are lined with a textured camel-coloured wallpaper, and the crisp white ceiling has pearly wooden edging. The thick silk curtains are heavy, with swirly embroidery snaking up the fabric, and the wall above the bed is peppered with expensive line drawings of the female form. We even have our own living room, with a plush L-shaped sofa and a flat-screen TV. There are two showers in the bathroom and a bath big enough to require armbands.

The centrepiece, however, is the bed, which is by far the grandest I have ever seen. All four of us could easily fit in it, with room to spare. There are plump feather pillows piled in front of the headboard and a pristine porcelain-white bedspread without a single crease. Before another thought can enter my mind, I throw myself on top of it like a stretched-out starfish. It's as though the bed is hugging me back, and as I sink into the soft mattress, I feel as though I could cry with relief. After the stress of the last few days, it seems almost unimaginable that we're here. That we made it. And tomorrow we will be on our way to Sulmona and one step closer to finding Grandma's ring. For now, all I have to worry about is the heavenly ten-hour sleep that's awaiting me. It's enough to make me—

'Zoe!'

I jump as the bed ripples under Harriet's weight.

'What are you doing?'

Olivia Beirne

I keep my eyes closed. 'Sleeping.'

Harriet makes the kind of sound a TV host might make when a contestant gives an incorrect answer. 'Wrong! We're going out. Get up.'

It's here that I make a stupid mistake: I open my eyes.

Harriet is like the Medusa of spontaneity. All it takes is one look in her eyes, and instead of turning into stone, you'll be in a push-up bra downing a shot of tequila quicker than you can say 'But what about my soothing sleep playlist?'

'No,' I whine. 'I'm so tired. It's like one in the morning.'

She folds her arms. 'Zoe. We are not spending our first night abroad having herbal tea and a sensible early night.'

'That sounds quite nice,' I mumble.

She clambers off the bed, and just when I think I might have won, a dress lands on my face.

'You can wear this. I'm going to wear that jumpsuit you lent me the other day.'

I scrunch up my face, looking at the sparkling dress and trying to work out which of the several straps are the armholes.

'I can't wear this,' I say. 'Not without a bra.'

'Nobody wears a bra in Italy,' she says matter-of-factly, peeling her T-shirt off and stepping into the jumpsuit.

I'm pretty certain that isn't true. Although my only experience of women in Italy is my grandma, and if she's anything to go by, then maybe it is.

Harriet pulls her long hair out of her ponytail and eyeballs me.

'Get up,' she says firmly, but there is a glint in her eye that makes me grin. 'We're going out.'

Chapter Twenty-Four

Fanny

Thank God I took charge of this trip. Lord only knows what type of place Zoe would have booked. I heard her speaking to Harriet earlier about Interrailing and hostels. Ugh, can you imagine?

I take a sip of the glass of wine I ordered from the bar downstairs. Clear and crisp and icy cold. It has just the bite I need.

Zoe is more like Ange than I could have ever imagined. She has the same dark hair and a chest you could park a car on, and the same scowl too. I've seen it on Ange plenty of times. But now that I've seen it on Zoe, and it's directed at me, it's quite a lot to take in. She used to look at me as though I was the most exciting person in the world.

As I move towards my hotel door, a high-pitched giggle dances down the corridor. I lean against the oak, cradling my wine and tuning into their conversation.

'Have you got the room key?'

'Of course!'

I smile. It's Zoe. Again, just like Ange, always the sensible one.

'Okay, let's go.'

'Where are we even going?'

'I don't care! Let's ask the barman downstairs. We need to do some shots anyway. There's no way I'm going out sober.'

'Maybe if we drink enough, we'll start speaking Italian. *Speaka Italiano?*'

'*Parlez Italian?*'

They're desperately trying to keep each other quiet, but little squeals of laughter burst out.

'That's French, you idiot.'

Their laughter fades down the corridor and I smile to myself. In another world, me and Angie would be sitting on the bed together, listening to the girls go out and reminiscing about all the nights out we used to have. But I know better than to knock on her door now. She barely said two words on the flight.

I sigh. Then I pick up the phone and order two bottles of water, two packets of crisps and some paracetamol to be delivered to their room for when they come back.

Chapter Twenty-Five

Zoe

As soon as we step into the warm night air, a spark fizzes in the pit of my stomach. The cobbled streets are narrow, housing tiny secrets in every corner. People from all over the world spill out of bars and restaurants, leaving a trail of foreign words behind them as they skirt past us, laughing and chatting. It would be so easy to get lost in these winding streets, but as we turn down another lane, following the swell of noise, I start to feel as though I *want* to get lost.

Harriet is practically bouncing next to me. Her arm is linked firmly with mine and her nose is high in the air, like a bloodhound following a scent. I patter beside her obediently.

After several shots of vodka, each burning my throat as they slid down into my stomach like a wave of fire, the barman gave us the name of a wine bar. We're following his directions, which Harriet listened to intently while I worried about whether or not I should go upstairs and put on a bra. What was I thinking, letting her persuade me that I didn't need one?

'Oh!' She lets out a squeal. 'It must be this one here.'

The bar is on the corner of the street, with a throng of people standing outside, all clasping wine glasses and gossiping. I catch the loose threads of their sentences as we get nearer and pick up the odd Italian word I recognise. It makes my heart glow.

If Grandma was here, she'd be straight in. Buying everyone drinks and insisting on topping up strangers' glasses in exchange for a seat part in their conversation. She loved people. I'm not sure where my introverted mum and awkward self came from.

Harriet and I slink inside. The place is tiny, with a dinky bar carved into the corner of the room, a tall, thin man with a dark moustache standing behind it. The bustling room is humming with conversation.

'What shall we have?' Harriet mutters in my ear. 'I think I'd better ask for wine.'

I shoot her a look and laugh. I'm sure we'd be asked to leave and never return if we ordered our usual Jägerbomb and double Archers and lemonade.

The man behind the bar looks up at us as we move towards him. His cool stare meets our childish grins, and for a second I think he's going to ask us for ID, but then he gestures to the array of wine stacked behind him like bowling pins.

I pretend to look, even though the most I know about wine is that it comes in red, white or pink and that Lambrini doesn't count.

Harriet does the same, eventually pointing to a bottle on the middle shelf and smiling graciously. I tip my head in agreement, feeling quite sophisticated, even though I have absolutely no idea what she's asked for. I mean, for all anyone here knows, we could be two top sommeliers. I could be the Delia Smith of wine.

I pull a few notes from my purse and place them on the bar while Harriet takes the bottle and two glasses.

'Wine, madam?' She begins to pour the red liquid into my glass, and I doff an imaginary hat.

'Can you believe we're drinking wine in Italy?' I say, chinking my glass against hers.

'This time last week, we were listening to awful Barbara sing "All That Jazz" at karaoke.'

Urgh. Unfortunately, a weekly occurrence.

I take a sip of the wine and it swills around my mouth like silk.

'Go on then.' Harriet grins at me. 'What can you taste?'

I mime twiddling a moustache and take another sip, realising that I'm actually quite drunk. 'This is a delicate wine,' I answer, gently swaying on the spot. Shit. It would be a very bad show to throw up all over the ankles of these sophisticated Italians.

'Delicate?' she scoffs. 'Like a fair maiden?'

'Oh, the fairest!' I put on my most pompous voice. 'The wine has a rich quality and undertones of . . .' I step back and bump shoulders with the man standing behind me. When I turn to apologise, I realise to my horror that I've just bumped straight into . . .

'Ron?' I blurt, suddenly noticing that in knocking into him, I've caused his own red wine to splash all over his shirt. 'Oh my God!' I gabble. 'I'm so sorry! Let me get you a tea towel.' I scrabble around mindlessly, inwardly cursing myself for offering a grown man a *tea towel* in the middle of a sexy wine bar in Rome.

A tea towel, Zoe? Really? You're not Mrs Tiggy-Winkle!

'It's fine, don't worry.' He laughs, even though the red stain is still spreading across his white shirt.

'I don't think they have tea towels here,' Harriet hisses in my ear, grabbing hold of my arm as I turn towards the bar.

And just when I think I could die of embarrassment, he asks his next question. 'Did you call me Ron?'

Oh shit. As if this moment could get any worse.

'No!' I say, my face burning. 'I called you . . .'

Argh! What rhymes with Ron? Bomb? Could I say that I think he is the bomb? Like a sex bomb? Whatever you do, just don't say thong, Zoe.

After what feels like four years of silence, my woozy mind finally offers up a reasonable option. 'I called you Tom!'

He stares at me. 'How did you know my name is Tom?'

I open and close my mouth like a stupid, useless fish.

Great. The one time I actually haven't stalked a guy on social media, and now I look like I'm about to ask him if he enjoyed the trip he took with his family to Tenerife circa 2014, or whether his granny has recovered from her hip replacement last autumn.

I force myself not to look at Harriet, who is staring aghast next to me.

'You . . . you just look like a Tom . . .'

Please don't ask me what a Tom looks like.

A grin spreads across his face. 'I'm joking. My name's Sam.'

'Oh!' I want the ground to swallow me up. 'Ha ha, that's . . . funny.'

Harriet coughs, taking a large gulp of her wine.

'I'm really sorry,' I add, glancing at his shirt. 'I don't know

124

how that happened.' My frantic eyes fly up to his, looking for anger or impatience, but there's none.

After a pause, he shrugs. 'Honestly, no worries. We're even now. Have a good night.' He winks at me before slipping into the crowd and out of the door.

I stand and stare after him, my heart racing. Harriet snorts, and I thwack her on the arm.

'That's your fault!' I cry as she continues to laugh. 'You got in my head by calling him Ron! God, that was so embarrassing.' I cringe, flapping a hand at my armpit. 'I'm sweating so much. How's my face? Am I bright red?'

She peers at me. 'Er . . . nope. You're not red.'

'Okay, good, that's something at least.'

'But you have got red wine stains on your teeth.'

Great.

★

The wine in England is nothing compared to the wine in Rome. Grandma used to push a glass in my direction from the age of twelve, and I'd take small sips to try and fit in with the grown-ups, but I never really appreciated it. Not like I did last night. Harriet and I guzzled almost three bottles between us, taking whatever the barman recommended from the rack. The bar was buzzing with swarms of people. Couples and groups of friends, older folk and teenagers. It felt as if we were all in on this big secret together, that this tiny bar tucked away on a side street in Rome was the place to be on a Friday night.

We somehow managed to find our way home in the early

hours of the morning, praying the whole way back that there would be some sort of fast-food place open so we could attempt to soak up the bucket of wine that was sloshing around our stomachs. Unfortunately, Rome is far too cultural for a King Kev's Chicken.

But we did find two packets of crisps and two bottles of water waiting outside our door. I could have cried.

In my drunken state, I thought one of the Roman gods had been listening to my incessant whining. But this morning, I knew it must have been that delightful barman from downstairs. I'll tell you what, you wouldn't get this sort of service from the Happy Hotel in Truro. The most they'd leave outside your door is a used plaster.

I roll over in bed, basking in the warm, soft sheets and the fluffy pillows. Unlike my room at home, which seems to have been dropped inside a furnace every time I wake up hung-over, this room is the perfect temperature. A light summer breeze is wafting through the open window, and a dash of sunlight peeks through the silk curtains, gently brushing the edge of the bed. I smile over at Harriet, who is cocooned in the duvet like a happy cinnamon bun.

'Can we stay here for ever?' she mumbles, not opening her eyes.

'In Rome?'

'In this bed. I never want to get out of it. I don't even feel hung-over in this bed.'

'Did you see what that nice barman left us?'

I beat Harriet to our door last night, and scooped up the crisps and the water without giving it much thought.

Well, enough thought to open the crisps *immediately* and

throw them down my gullet like a starved penguin. I'm not an idiot.

She peels open one eye as I hand her a bottle of water. She cracks open the lid and gives me a knowing look. 'See. That's what happens when you don't wear a bra.'

I twist round and pick up my phone, checking the time. Mum was very clear that she wanted to be on the 10 a.m. train out of Rome at the very latest. It is currently creeping up towards ten past eight. Knowing her, she's probably already fully dressed and has been pacing up and down her room for the past forty minutes.

'I'm going to go check on Mum,' I say, forcing myself out of bed. 'I think she'll want us to leave soon.' I turn to look at Harriet as she picks up her phone. 'Have you heard from your mum at all?'

She pulls a face, mid scroll. 'Of course not. Why would I?'

I pause. My mum and I speak every day. Even when I was at university, we'd send messages back and forth and have an evening catch-up whilst I waited for my pasta to cook.

'I'll get in the shower then,' Harriet says, stretching her arms in the air and giving a loud groan. 'We are having breakfast before we leave, right?' She picks up the room-service menu and wafts it in my face. 'I mean, look at this pastry. If I don't have one, I'll spend the rest of my life thinking about it.'

My mouth immediately fills with saliva as I take in the fat, buttery-looking pastry, the sticky pool of yellow cream oozing from its middle, and the drizzle of white icing.

Okay, I definitely need to eat one of those.

'I'll speak to Mum,' I say, plucking a fluffy white robe out of the wardrobe and wrapping it round my body. It's like being hugged by an angel.

I pad out of the room, gently closing the door behind me. The hallway is filled with light, which bounces off the chestnut-coloured wooden floorboards and the large paintings on the walls. Curling my fingers into a tight fist, I rap my knuckles against a door boasting a shiny number 11.

I pause as silence greets me. I knock again.

'Mum? Are you awake? It's Zoe.'

Still nothing. I keep knocking.

'Mum? I just wanted to talk to you about timings for today.'

A cocktail of last night's alcohol with a dash of fear sweeps through my body.

Shit. What if she's not okay? I shouldn't have gone out last night. I should have stayed here and made sure she was all right.

'Mum?' I start knocking more frantically. 'Please let me in. Mum?'

'Oh for God's sake, *what*?'

I jump as Aunt Fanny's bristled voice shoots under the door frame, and it dawns on me that I've been banging on the wrong door.

'Oh! Morning, Aunt Fanny. Sorry, I thought Mum was in this room. Can I come in?'

I push down the door handle and it immediately snaps back up.

'No.'

I let go. Well, that's a bit rude.

'Morning, love.' I spin on the spot as I hear Mum's calm voice. She's wearing a pair of linen trousers and a loose white top. I immediately throw my arms around her as guilt threatens to swallow me whole.

'Are you okay?' I gush. 'I was worried. I couldn't find you!'

'I was in my room, Zo. I'm fine.' She frees herself and peers at my face. 'Are you okay?'

I blink. Of course she's fine. She was just in her room, probably having a lovely relaxing bath.

Maybe I need a lovely relaxing bath.

'Late night, was it?' she adds, a knowing smile creeping onto her lips.

'Er . . . yes,' I say, running my fingers through my hair to try and compose myself. 'Me and Harriet went out to a bar. I just wanted to speak to you about timings for today. It would be nice to have breakfast here.'

'Breakfast!'

We both jump as Aunt Fanny's door flies open. She's standing there in her signature toe-curling high heels, with a leather mini skirt showcasing her bandy, tanned legs. She has a golden pashmina swooshed around her neck, her new sunglasses taking up half her face.

'Great idea, Zoe,' she continues, closing her door behind her and swinging the key between her jewelled fingers. 'I would love a mimosa.'

'Fanny, it's not even nine in the morning,' Mum laughs.

'Darling, *mimosa* is Italian for breakfast.'

I frown. I mean, it definitely isn't.

'We'll meet you downstairs,' she says airily, linking her arm through Mum's. As they move down the hall, I hear Aunt Fanny saying, 'Oh Ange, why do you wear that top? I thought I'd binned all your high-necked tops years ago.'

★

After a sinfully quick shower in the perfect bathroom, Harriet and I arrive downstairs twenty minutes later. I'm wearing the same jeans I flew here in and have just about been able to get away with the same top. I've also turned my pants inside out. Not that I've told anyone this, but it feels like a silent agreement between us all. Nobody ask about Zoe's pants.

The breakfast room is sweeping, with more high ceilings and curved architecture. There's a gentle floral pattern carved into the arches. Like the rest of the hotel, the room is lit with twinkling chandeliers, fresh flowers perfectly poised on every surface.

In the far corner, Aunt Fanny is leaning back on her chair legs, laughing loudly, and Mum is bent over a plate of fruit. But she's smiling.

'Morning!' Harriet sings as we reach the table. 'What's everyone having?'

As I go to pick up a menu, a bright, freshly pressed waiter pops up in front of us.

'*Buongiorno, ragazze, posso offrirvi un caffè?*'

Ah. *Caffè* definitely means coffee.

'Er . . . cappuccino?' I smile at him, then notice Harriet holding her hand up to me. 'Two? Please?' I add quickly, holding up two fingers.

He ducks his head in acknowledgement and sweeps across the room.

'Have anything you want, girls,' Aunt Fanny says. 'It's on me.'

'Have you heard anything from the airport, Zo?' Mum asks.

I sigh and unlock my phone, as if they could be ringing me at this very second.

'No,' I huff. 'Nothing.'

'It probably won't show up until we're on our way home,'
Aunt Fanny says, leaning over and sticking her fork into a slice
of Mum's melon. 'That's what usually happens.'

'Great.'

She looks up at me. 'Darling, we're in *Rome*! We can buy you
some clothes to tide you over.'

'It's not just clothes I need. It's my make-up and my phone
charger and—'

She waves her fork at me. 'Whatever you need, we'll get it.
Just try to relax.'

She flashes me a perfect smile as the waiter reappears with two
mugs filled with frothy milk, and a plate of plump pastries.

Mum gazes at them as we each take one off the plate. She
keeps her hands gripped around her coffee cup.

Aunt Fanny follows her gaze and clicks her tongue.

'For God's sake, Ange. Just have one.'

Little circles of pink form on Mum's cheeks. 'No thank you.
I'm not hungry.'

'What's the plan for today then?' Harriet says, licking the tip
of her finger and using it to dab any stray sugar off her plate.

Mum snaps to attention. 'Well, there are two direct trains
from Rome to Bugnara, and the first one leaves in an hour.'

Aunt Fanny pulls a face, reaching for her mimosa. 'And that's
the one we want to get?'

'Yes.'

'You might have to settle for an I HEART ROME T-shirt
then, I'm afraid, Zo,' she says, and despite myself, I laugh. As I
do, I notice her chest rise a little.

'We could get you the whole outfit,' Harriet grins. 'I'm sure
you can get caps too, and bum bags.'

Aunt Fanny pretends to retch. 'No god–daughter of mine is being seen dead in a bum bag.'

Harriet laughs, but my brow creases. 'I didn't know you were my godmother,' I say, turning to Mum.

'Self-appointed.' She smiles at Aunt Fanny.

Fanny shoots her a knowing look and takes her third pastry. 'But it stuck.'

Chapter Twenty-Six

Harriet

An hour later, we're standing on the platform at Rome's train station. I don't know what I was expecting, but compared to the grandeur of the St Regis, the station is actually pretty normal, making Zoe look even *less* normal. I almost burst with excitement when I saw an actual I HEART ROME stall and bought a T-shirt for us both, but while mine is stuffed in my backpack, Zoe had no choice but to wear hers. She couldn't look more like a tourist if she tried.

Fanny tips her wrist towards me, flashing an open packet of cigarettes. She catches me glancing up at the 'no smoking' sign (a big cigarette with a cross through it) and pulls a face.

'Oh, nobody is around,' she says. 'They just put those signs up to look good.' She shakes the pack towards me and I take one, feeling a giggle tickle up my body.

'So, Harriet,' she continues, her lips clenched as she holds onto her unlit cigarette and searches for her lighter, 'I think we've got some catching-up to do. You seem quite important in Zoe's life, and we barely know each other.'

I smile, taking the lighter. Zoe and Angie are peering up at the departures board, so it's just me and Fanny surrounded by bubbling Italians and other tourists on the platform.

'Yeah,' I agree. 'So what have you been doing in Liverpool? Did you remarry?'

She bats a hand at me. 'God, Harriet, we're not talking about me. I'm far too dull.'

I glance at her. Her lips are immaculately drawn on, pillar-box red, and her jawline is so defined it's as if she takes a sheet of sandpaper and files it down each morning. I don't think I've ever met anyone less dull in my life.

'I don't believe that,' I laugh, trying not to choke on the billow of smoke that fills my lungs.

She raises her eyebrows at me, and I shake my head, trying to convince her that this isn't the first time I've ever had a cigarette even though I'm acting like a sixteen-year-old.

'Well, it's true,' she says matter-of-factly. 'So let's talk about you.'

My smile stays in place, but my stomach slides around slightly. I hate this topic. I never have anything to say. No job, no partner, no ambition, no talent. Those are the things people really want to talk about, aren't they? 'Okay.'

'What's this all about?'

I blink at her. 'This?'

I step out of the way of a lady in a red hat who storms past me. A train slides by and I gape at it. Wow, two floors! I didn't even know trains like that existed.

'This,' Fanny repeats, waving her arms. 'This trip. What's it about?'

I take another drag of my cigarette to try and play for time. God, what type of question is that? I feel like I'm back at a university interview.

'Er . . .' I start. 'Well, finding the ring for Zoe.'

She dismisses me. 'For *Zoe*.'

'Obviously her mum needs to be here. Zoe thinks it'll help her.'

She shakes her head. 'Yes, and that's about Ange. What about you? Why are *you* here?'

A flock of pigeons fly through the station, ducking down between the platforms before flapping away again. My heart picks up pace as I start to get the horrible feeling that Fanny doesn't want me here. As though she can read my mind, she starts speaking in a softer voice.

'I know you're being a good friend and are here to help my Zoe. But I hope that's not the only reason you came.'

I shift my weight from one foot to the other. 'Why?'

She pauses, sucking on her cigarette. When she pulls it away, it leaves a sticky crimson ring.

'Zoe said you quit your job.'

Ah.

'I hated it anyway,' I say honestly. 'And me and Zoe have talked about going travelling for ages.' I laugh. 'I was hardly going to stay behind.'

She smiles, her eyes fixed on a couple on the far side of the platform. 'Why haven't you gone sooner?'

I bite my lip. It's not my place to tell Fanny the real reason: because Zoe doesn't want to leave her mum. But she reads my silence and nods.

'Zoe is very lucky to have you,' she says, 'and I'm glad you're here.'

My heart lifts. 'I'm really glad I'm here too.'

Zoe and Ange reappear beside us as the train chugs into the station. The doors ping open and Zoe turns to me.

'Have you seen who's over there?' she mutters under her breath. I turn my head and spot the Ron Weasley lookalike with his friends climbing into the carriage.

I grin. 'No way.'

'What's that?' Fanny says, craning her head and following our eyeline. 'Oh! Pick yourself up a boyfriend last night, did you, Zoe?'

Zoe scowls. 'No.'

We all climb into the train and fold ourselves into a group of seats facing each other.

Fanny flashes me a wink. 'Next stop, Bugnara.'

Chapter Twenty-Seven

Zoe

We fall silent as the train chugs out of Rome. For the first time since we arrived, everyone else seems quite relaxed, either looking out the window or tapping at their phones, but I can't stop my mind from whirring. I'm concocting a plan.

I can't confront Aunt Fanny about the credit card without more evidence. I've watched enough *Line of Duty* to know that you need to have a solid case before you show your cards. If I bring it up now, she'll shrug it off as some sort of mistake and everyone will think I'm being paranoid. But I need to work out the real reason she's here, and to do that, I need to find out where she's been all this time.

Fourteen years ago, I was able to reel off everything there was to know about Aunt Fanny, with Mum filling in the gaps about those years before I was born. My dad left before I was born, and Mum always told me that Fanny moved in to pick up the pieces (and slag off my dad to high heaven, Aunt Fanny took great pleasure in adding when I was older). But now, even though she's still got the exact same ice-blonde bob and pillar-box-red lipstick, I don't know anything about her at all. She might as well be a stranger. Well, that's what she wanted. Why else would you vanish without a word if not to rebuild yourself as a brand-new person, shedding the skin of your old life and leaving it in cosy, boring Cornwall. Along with her cosy, boring life with us.

It wasn't much of a secret that we loved Aunt Fanny in a different way to my uncle. He didn't understand us like she did. For as long as I can remember, he's always been the same. Nose to the ground, finding the scent of the latest must-have or fashionable party. He's always been desperate to be a part of something bigger and brighter, and never tried to hide the fact that we weren't it. Mum in her Next sale clothes, and me, awkward and scruffy, hiding behind Mum's legs whenever he tried to introduce me to someone he deemed important. But Aunt Fanny wasn't like that; she didn't try to change us. She still wore her sparkly necklaces and pointed boots, but she would proudly stride alongside us in our trainers and dungarees. We didn't look like we went together, but we did. That was the best part.

Uncle Reggie came to all the important things, like birthdays and Christmas, but even then he tried to turn it into something it wasn't. He brought bottles of champagne along to my fifth birthday party, which was a quiet afternoon of pass-the-parcel with a few of my friends. For my first day of secondary school he bought me a designer handbag and took loads of photos of us together with me holding it. 'Make sure you tell everyone your Uncle Reggie bought it for you, okay, Zoe?' he said, squeezing my shoulder as the camera flashed. But Aunt Fanny was there weeks before, calming me down when I felt nervous, and she drove me in on my first day. She was waiting for me at the end of the day too, ready to hear all about how it had gone over my favourite dinner. She said Uncle Reggie was busy. She always made excuses for him, but she was like my second parent. Between her and Mum, I didn't need a dad. I barely noticed that I didn't have one.

That's why it made no sense when she left. My uncle always had his flaws – and he seems to have collected more as he's got older, like badges of honour – but she loved him. She always told me he was the great love of her life, and that they had a good time together. He whisked her away on surprise mini breaks to Prague and secured invites to flashy launch parties in London. Every birthday or Christmas she would show off another piece of jewellery that glittered on her neck. And then one day she was gone and we never heard from her again.

I don't really let myself think about the day she left, though I remember it clearly. The memory instantly makes me feel like the eleven-year-old who shrivelled into Mum's arms when she told me.

It was a Monday. I'd only seen her two days before, when she dragged me shopping with her. Something eleven-year-old me pretended to hate.

When I got home from school, I pushed open the front door and shouted hello, dancing around Georgio the cat, who weaved in and out of my legs. For the first time in my life, I was met with silence. The house wasn't that silent again until Grandma died.

Mum worked in admin for the local hospital. To be honest, I was never really sure what she did, but I knew it involved a computer and a lot of filing cabinets. Aunt Fanny had never worked, claiming the nail file she had invented and sold for millions in

China made her quite enough money. Usually I'd come home and they'd both be in the kitchen, chatting away, with Aunt Fanny sipping a coffee and Mum stirring a pot of something she was stewing for dinner. The silence that day was eerie, and in a second the happy bubble swelling inside my stomach popped.

'Mum?' I called again, pushing the door shut behind me.

When she didn't answer, I walked into the kitchen and saw her sitting at the table, her hands locked together. It was like she'd seen a ghost.

'Oh!' she cried, quickly pushing a smile onto her face and looking at the clock. 'Gosh, I'm so sorry. You're home already.'

I hovered in front of her. 'Yeah.'

She stared back at me wordlessly, and I started to feel a knot forming in my throat. I'd never seen her like this before. She was always so happy and calm, her persona as soft as her pillowy arms. The only thing I could think was that maybe she'd lost her job. That had happened to my friend Jenny's mum the year before, and she had told me that her mum had spent days crying at the dinner table.

'Mum,' I said, 'are you okay?'

She opened her mouth, but no words came out. As I stood there waiting, the downstairs toilet flushed and the door clicked open. I turned, expecting to see Aunt Fanny and hear her loud voice echo through the kitchen, demanding Mum to get up and screw whatever was upsetting her as she was taking us all out for dinner. But instead I saw the sallow face of Uncle Reggie slump through the door. Incredibly, he looked even worse than my mum.

'Hiya, Zo,' he said, slipping past me and dropping into a kitchen chair. I copied him and sat in the chair opposite as he pulled a bottle of something dark out of his bag and began to swig it, wincing slightly each time, as though he was drinking cough medicine.

He looked at Mum gravely. 'Have you told her?'

'Told me what?' I asked. I was starting to panic now. This was the type of scene you saw in *EastEnders* or *Coronation Street*, not something I ever imagined taking place around our kitchen table. Our kitchen table where Mum and Aunt Fanny sat laughing and eating pasta. Uncle Reggie spent at least half the week at some form of party or networking event in London, so it was the three of us for most of the week. We'd always been safe in this house, in our little bubble. Bad stuff didn't happen here.

Mum didn't speak, although I could tell a thousand thoughts were shooting through her mind. A kinder man might have let her find the words to tell her daughter as gently as possible that one of the key people in her life had left without a word. But even in this moment, Uncle Reggie couldn't resist a scene.

'She's left,' he said. 'Your aunt has left.'

I was only eleven; I didn't understand what he meant. Looking back, perhaps I should have realised from the looks on their faces, the way Mum's shoulders were hunched forward and Uncle Reggie's eyes were bloodshot and sunken.

'Where has she gone?' I said.

Uncle Reggie laughed bitterly. 'Who knows? But she's left me. Us. She's left *us*.'

These words were harder to misunderstand. Even my naïve, romantic, childish mind couldn't spin this sentence into something hopeful.

'Left us?' I repeated.

At this, Uncle Reggie slammed his fist on the table, making us all jump.

'What is it you don't understand?' he shouted. 'She's gone! Left in the middle of the night! Run off with another man, that bloke Jon who she always said was just a friend. She doesn't want anything to do with us any more, Zoe. She's sick of us. She wanted to get away.'

My throat started to burn as I turned to look at Mum, who was glaring at her brother. 'She's gone?' I said stupidly, my voice cracking. 'But she didn't say goodbye.'

Mum spotted the shine in my eyes and grabbed my hand.

'She still loves us, Zoe,' she said.

Uncle Reggie laughed again. 'Oh come on, Ange,' he snarled. 'You don't just leave without saying goodbye. You don't do that to people you love.'

Not long after that, Uncle Reggie left. Mum said he'd had too much to drink, so he left his sports car in our drive and stormed down the road on foot, no doubt straight to the pub that sat on the corner of our street. As soon as the door closed behind him, I turned to Mum, hope filling me back up as she wrapped her arms around me.

'She hasn't gone properly, though, Mum? She'll come back?' I said, my words muffled by her thick jumper.

She held me tight and took a deep breath.

'We'll phone her, love,' she said. 'And we'll write to her. I'm sure she'll still want to see us. She just needs some space right now, but I'm sure she'll get back in touch when she's ready.'

At the time, I believed her. I believed her for years, every time I wrote Aunt Fanny a letter or sat next to Mum as she dialled that number we both knew so well and waited for her to answer. But she never did. She never answered a single call or message. Eventually, we just gave up and accepted the fact that Uncle Reggie was right. She didn't love us. Perhaps she never had.

'Want some?' Harriet wafts a bottle of Diet Coke under my nose. I take a sip and look at Mum. She's staring out of the window, her fingers gripped so tightly around her bottle of water it looks as if the lid is moments away from pinging off.

I take a deep breath, pushing the memories to the back of my mind.

'We're almost there.' I smile at her. 'In a couple of hours' time, we'll be back at Grandma's house, having dinner at her kitchen table.'

My words hang in the air as Mum nods silently, keeping her gaze fixed on the flashing blurs of green passing by outside.

Aunt Fanny cranes her head to look at Sam and his friends, who are laughing loudly at the other end of the carriage. She slowly raises her eyebrows at me, and I feel my body tense. She always gives me this look when she's about to quiz me on something very embarrassing. The first time she did it, I was about ten and she'd caught me trying on Mum's bra.

'So,' Aunt Fanny says, leaning forward in her seat. 'No boy-friend then, Zo? What happened? Bad break-up?'

'Nope,' I say.

'Dating anyone nice?'

'Nope.'

'There isn't anybody nice in Truro,' Harriet quips.

'Well,' I say, 'there is. But they're all engaged or have moved away. Or are gay.'

'Or one of us has dated them or they're into something weird.'

'Like the guy who was obsessed with tomatoes.'

'Exactly.'

'I know the type,' Aunt Fanny says wistfully. 'I once dated a man who was obsessed with hot fudge, and God, it was a *nightmare* to get it out of your—'

'Aunt Fanny!' I blurt, my face bright red. 'We were talking about eating them! This guy loved eating them!'

She shrugs at me, a faux innocence playing on her face. 'I was going to say teeth.' She takes a sip of her water, then looks at us both. 'So you're telling me neither of you girls is dating anyone? Why not? You're both beautiful women! Your mum has told me all about your job, Zoe, and how well you're doing. You're great fun and have a gorgeous pair of legs on you. What's going on?'

I try and hide my smile as I am transported back to being ten years old again. I used to get this type of pep talk from Aunt Fanny almost weekly, about anything. Going to a dance class, wearing a dress I liked, inviting someone for a sleepover. If there was anything I was unsure about, she was there, ready with one of her famous pep talks. She did exactly the same thing to Mum. It was thanks to her that Mum got a perm.

'Nothing,' I say.

'If there's nobody in Truro, go on an adventure! Pack your bags, move to the big smoke!'

'Follow a red-headed man onto a European train,' Harriet says under her breath. I give her a swift kick.

'Speaking of men,' I say, finally seeing a window I can jump through, 'how are things going with Jon?'

The bright smile plastered across Aunt Fanny's face fades a little, and she touches her stiff hair. 'I don't want to talk about him.'

I'm about to challenge her when the train jolts and me and Harriet rock forward. Mum, who has been in a daze since we boarded, jerks to attention and looks around.

'Whoops,' says Aunt Fanny. 'Looks like the driver dropped his drink.'

Mum's fingers clench tighter around her water bottle as a slightly terse Italian voice spills through the carriage. I immediately stare at Aunt Fanny, desperate for her to translate, but she's back playing Candy Crush on her phone and doesn't even seem to register the announcement.

'Aunt Fanny!' I cry. 'What did he say?'

She doesn't look up. 'Who?'

'The train guy!'

'Oh.' She shrugs. 'Not sure, lovey. I wasn't listening.' She catches my exasperated look and rolls her eyes at me. 'Relax, pet, they'll do it in English in a minute.'

'But what if they—'

'Ladies and gentlemen, due to an unforeseen issue with the track, this train will be terminating at our next stop, Carsoli.'

Harriet turns to face me. 'Where is Carsoli?'

My heart sinks. 'I have no idea.'

★

'This is a bad omen,' Mum mutters as we pile onto the platform twenty minutes later. 'And it's the third bad omen we've had since we started this trip. I've tried to ignore them, but it's too much. She doesn't want us going! I was right!'

'Bad omen?' I repeat. 'What do you mean?'

But she ignores me, storming off the platform. We trail after her, Harriet lugging her heavy bag and Aunt Fanny eagerly lighting up another cigarette, her designer sunglasses pushed up onto her head. The mid-afternoon sun beats down on us, and I try

145

to manoeuvre us away from the rest of the disgruntled passengers and into a quiet corner where we can gather our thoughts.

As I push my way through a group of people, I look up and meet Sam's eyes. He shoots me a happy-go-lucky smile as he bounds after his friends, and my heart turns over. Then he disappears into the crowd, and the panic simmering under my skin returns.

Mum practically exploded when they announced that the train was going to be terminating earlier than she'd planned, and has been manically muttering to herself since, her face getting redder and redder with each word, her wispy hair wilder and wilder. We all stop in a corner outside the station.

'We shouldn't be here!' she screeches. 'She doesn't want us here!'

'Who doesn't?' Aunt Fanny asks, tilting her head back and puffing smoke into the air.

I flinch as Mum whirls round to face us, as though Aunt Fanny's question has given her a fresh injection of fury.

'Mum! I *knew* it was a bad idea to come here, and I *never* wanted to!' She shoots a look at me. 'Your grandmother clearly doesn't want us to be here either. Reggie is dealing with things, and we should be at home, not lying to him and racing across Italy hoping we don't get caught!'

She breaks off, sucking in a great intake of breath. As I stare into her desperate brown eyes, I can feel them pleading with me, begging for us to agree and let her go home.

'Ange,' Aunt Fanny says, pulling out her phone, 'I know this is stressful, but you need to calm down. Your mum is not sending us signals from above telling us not to do this. She'd probably love the idea.'

I nod at Mum, desperate for her to agree.

'You have no idea what she'd want,' Mum snaps. I flinch.

After a moment, she brushes her hair off her face and tries to compose herself.

'We have to go home,' she says firmly.

'We can't,' Aunt Fanny says, holding a hand up.

I scowl at her. She can be so *rude*.

'Yes we can,' Mum says, her voice shaking. 'We can, and we should have done this right at the beginning. We should never have left Cornwall.'

'No, I mean we literally can't,' Aunt Fanny says, finally lowering her hand as the Italian voice over the tannoy stops. 'They just said they're closing the station. There aren't any more trains going in or out of this place until Tuesday.'

'*Tuesday?*' I echo. But our flight home is on Monday! I need to be back in the office Tuesday morning!'

'That doesn't matter,' Mum says briskly. 'We can get a taxi back to Rome, and just stay there until our flight home.'

Aunt Fanny rustles in her bag and pulls out her cigarettes. She flicks the pack open and angles it towards Mum.

'Ange,' she says, 'we're over halfway there. We can't turn back now. These aren't signs, they're just bad luck.'

For the briefest second, Mum's eyes flicker down at the open cigarette packet.

'It'll be okay,' Fanny continues. 'Everything is going to be fine.'

And then one by one, we each pull out a cigarette from the packet. We pass round Aunt Fanny's lurid pink lighter, and we stand and smoke without saying a word.

★

Carsoli, as it turns out, is a tiny ancient town, surrounded by beautiful rolling hills stacked high with little houses. Many of them have the same teal-blue shutters and terracotta roofs. It's a world away from the bustling city centre of Rome. The locals stroll through the cobbled streets, chatting rapidly to each other, shooting us the odd look. I hold my arms around my body in an attempt to hide my hideous I HEART ROME T-shirt as the four of us wander aimlessly. We have barely spoken since Mum's outburst, and apart from Harriet gasping and cooing at the buildings and offering us suncream every five seconds, we're walking in silence.

'Zoe, look!' Harriet nudges me in the ribs. 'Is that a castle over there?'

'I'm not sure,' I mumble, not looking up.

'Wow. I think it is. I wonder who lived there.' She looks at me. 'Are you okay?'

'Yeah.'

'What's wrong?'

I can't help but smile. I will forever be grateful for the universal language between best friends. They are the only people who listen to what you say but hear what you mean.

'I just don't like seeing Mum upset,' I mumble, glancing over my shoulder at Mum who is a few paces behind us with Aunt Fanny. 'And I feel bad. This trip was my idea, and things keep going wrong.'

'You don't really think it's all an omen, though, do you?' Harriet says.

'Well,' I give a forced laugh, 'it's hard not to.'

'I don't think your grandma would have disrupted the entire train schedule or lost your bag if she didn't want you to come,' Harriet says. 'She was an artist.'

'So?'

'So I reckon she would have done something a bit more creative.' She tucks her hands into the straps of her backpack and gives me a look.

'What, like rearranging the stars to write a message?' I say sarcastically.

Harriet laughs, nodding in agreement. 'Exactly. Or, like, possessing a bunch of birds to sing a song for us.'

I laugh. 'Very Disney princess.'

She grins. 'Exactly.'

'I don't know,' I sigh. 'Sorry, I think I'm just stressed. This trip was meant to be fun and a way to make Mum feel better about everything, and it just seems to be making her feel worse.'

'This is a nightmare,' Mum says, right on cue. 'Does anybody know where we're going? We can't just walk for ever. How are we going to get home?'

'Just relax, Ange,' Aunt Fanny says airily, her head swivelling around.

'Don't tell me to relax.'

'Would you like another cigarette?'

'No,' Mum says shortly, quickly adding, 'thank you,' as she catches herself.

'We just need to find a nice café or bar,' Aunt Fanny continues in the calming, spa-like tone she's adopted since Mum's outburst. 'Then we can sit down and work out one of your brilliant plans.' She hooks her arm in Mum's and gives her a shake. 'We're still in Italy, remember? It's not as if they've dropped us in Timbuktu. Ah!' She stops walking and turns to face a little café. It is barely noticeable, only a little sun umbrella out front

149

giving it away. It looks about the size of our front room, but it's the only café we've seen since we started walking, and a tight band of pain has started to snake its way across my forehead.

A bell rings as Aunt Fanny pushes on the door, and the floor underneath me moves as I feel a strange sense that I've been here before. This is exactly the type of place Grandma would have taken us. She'd fling open the door and hold an arm in the air, greeting the owners as if they were long-lost friends.

My eyes are immediately drawn to the vivid blood-orange colour of the walls and the lime-green panelling that skirts around the middle. A string of fairy lights bends into each curve and corner of the room, illuminating a glass counter that boasts flaky pastries and an enormous focaccia with sprigs of herbs and fat bulbs of garlic sprouting from its surface. As soon as I step inside, the smell of warm bread and that smooth, rich scent of coffee blend together, awakening my taste buds and pushing my stress away as though I've had a shoulder massage. I close my eyes and for a moment allow myself to take it all in.

Then a friendly, romantic voice fills the room, and I open my eyes to see a large dark-haired man standing behind the counter in a chef's apron. He has bushy eyebrows and a huge smile that beams back at us. '*Ciao belle, signore! Vieni a sederti, cosa possiamo portarti?*'

This is why we came here. This smell. These people.

Aunt Fanny tips her sunglasses towards the end of her nose and flashes him a dazzling smile. He gestures to the table right in front of the counter and we sit down.

'Actually, I think I'll just pop to the ladies,' Harriet says.

I get to my feet. 'Me too.'

CHAPTER TWENTY-EIGHT

ANGIE

Harriet and Zoe skip off towards the toilets and I sink into my seat. I can feel my neck drop into my shoulders, like the muscles in my body, which have been so tight with emotion, are giving up. All the anger and hurt I've been dragging around with me burst out of my mouth as soon as the train stopped in Carsoli. I suddenly felt like I couldn't do it any more.

I once heard someone say that when you lose your parents, you revert to being a child, and it's true. It's like a cruel trick of fate. It's only when they're gone that you're presented with this stark, sobering reminder that *of course* you're not ready for them to leave you. You still need them. You can't live without them, you don't know how.

So you stamp your feet and scream at the sky, you cry uncontrollably when your favourite TV show is on half an hour late because of the football, and you push the broccoli to the side of

151

your plate in disgust. Or that's what I wanted to do. But I couldn't, I couldn't fall apart like that. So I squashed it down and tried to wrangle it into a quiet box in the pit of my stomach. Which was working right up until the train chugged to an unexpected halt and something within me snapped.

And then there's Fanny, the person who knows me better than anyone else. If I believe in signs (which apparently I do), she's the biggest one of them all. Having her pop up at my front door, fresh from a time capsule. I mean, it's been fourteen years and not even a strand of hair has changed. Her smile is the same, her air of importance. It's like the time without her never even happened.

And I don't know what to do with that. I'm only just managing to wrestle my burning emotions back into their box. I can't ask Fanny where she's been, what happened, what she's really doing here. I don't have the resilience any more. I don't have the strength.

Opposite me, she flicks open a wine menu and flashes the waiter a dazzling smile.

'Oh no,' I say, 'no wine for me. I need a clear head, and we need to come up with a plan. I need to calm down.'

She eyes me over the menu. 'Darling, what you *need* more than anything is a glass of wine.' She gushes something in Italian to the waiter, then turns back to me. 'And don't you dare calm down. That screaming woman who stormed down the platform and practically ate her cigarette was the closest I've seen to the real Ange since I got here.'

I flush. 'I am not a screaming woman, thanks very much.'

'You're not this wind-up all-smiles robot either.' She hooks one leg over the other and I look down at the table.

She's right. But I quite like the idea of being a wind-up smiling robot. Everything in order, everything where it's supposed to be. That sounds quite nice.

'Aunt Fanny,' Zoe says as she and Harriet reappear at the table to see the waiter pouring wine into our glasses, 'we can't have wine. We need to plan this trip with clear heads.' She glances at me and I avoid her eyes, heat flaming up my body. 'We need to try and make this situation better.'

Fanny picks up her glass and gestures at us all to do the same. Reluctantly, I copy her.

'Darling,' she says, giving Zoe a knowing look as she clinks her glass against mine, 'wine makes everything better.'

Chapter Twenty-Nine

Fanny

Rip off the plaster. That was always my father's motto in life. Anything you're dreading, it's best to get it over with quickly in one swift motion. Don't dwell on it. It's how I've tried to live my life. It's how I dealt with my grief when he died – I ripped the plaster off. There was nothing I could do about it, so I decided I might as well get on with it. A psychiatrist might say that it isn't the best way to cope with things, but it's always done me fine. It's how I left Reggie. I packed my bags, booked a train and ripped that wretched plaster off.

It's been harder to do in the last twelve months, but I've still bloody done it. I'm made of strong stuff, that's what my mother always said to me. She's dead too. Another plaster gone. Rip, rip, rip. All of them ripped off.

I thought this trip would be good for Angie. I had hoped that it would take her mind off things and help her realise that

Clarice would want her to live her life and be happy. But it doesn't seem to be working, and if it doesn't work, then nothing I have planned out will, and then why am I even here? Why don't I just let Angie go home and give it all up?

But Angie has always been different from me. You can rip the plaster off her, but then she starts to bleed.

Chapter Thirty

Zoe

I shut my eyes, willing my brain to stop swimming as 'Murder on the Dancefloor' plays through the speakers. We've been in the café for hours. Or at least it feels like hours. We've been here for as long as it has taken us to drink three bottles of wine and have the same conversation eight times. Mum's pocket map is spread out in front of us on the table, and Aunt Fanny has been peering down at it for the past five minutes.

Mum cranes her neck to take a look, eyeing Aunt Fanny's scrunched-up face. 'Fanny, do you need my glasses?'

Aunt Fanny looks at her as if she's asked her to join a cult. 'No!' she cries. 'I do not need *glasses*.'

'The quickest way to get to Sulmona from here is to drive,' Mum says: the opening line of the never-ending conversation.

'Apart from the train,' Aunt Fanny quips, smirking.

'Will you stop saying that!' Mum retorts. She's trying to

scowl, but a small laugh manages to escape before she quickly composes herself. 'The trains are *cancelled*. That isn't an option.'

Harriet giggles next to me as Aunt Fanny pulls a funny face at us.

'Right,' I say, trying to steer the conversation back on track. 'So we need to drive.'

'How about a Vespa?' Fanny says, her eyes brightening. 'That's pretty Italian, isn't it?'

'No offence, but I don't trust you driving a moped,' I say drily.

She puts her wine to her lips and raises her eyebrows at me knowingly. 'I'll have you know I'm an excellent ride.'

Gross.

Mum ignores us and presses on. 'We need to hire a car.'

'What about a taxi?' Harriet suggests.

Mum shakes her head. 'We won't be able to find one this last-minute to drive us that far, love. I don't suppose there are many taxis around here either.'

'We could hitch-hike?' Aunt Fanny pipes up.

'No,' we all say in unison.

'So, we just need to find somewhere to hire a car,' Mum says, pushing her hand through her hair and leaning her forehead against her palm. 'And we'd have to go first thing in the morning,' she adds, looking at the empty wine bottles sitting in between us.

'Well, in that case . . . Gino!' Aunt Fanny calls over her shoulder. '*Dove andiamo a cena?*'

'You didn't just order another bottle, did you?' I mutter. She bats her hand at me as Gino plucks the empty bottle from the table and replaces it with a fresh one.

'We need to find somewhere to stay,' Mum mumbles, and I can see the nerves prickling across her face. 'What even is the time?'

'Six o'clock,' Harriet answers, turning her phone in her hand. I glance down at mine and my stomach contracts.

Shit. A message from Kitty.

Hey! How's it going? What's your grandma's house like?! I need pictures!!!! Could you give me a call when you get five mins? Oh, and do you want dinner when you get back on Monday? Let me know, I can make us tacos!!!! Xxxxxx

I lock my phone and slip it in my pocket.

Our flight home is at 4.30 on Monday afternoon. We'd planned to leave Grandma's on Monday morning to get there in time. But without the trains running, how is that even possible?

'Where are we going to find a car at this hour?' Mum muses into her wine glass.

'Is it a long drive?' Harriet asks.

Mum shakes her head. 'An hour, I'd say.'

Aunt Fanny takes this as her cue and swivels round in her seat to face Gino.

'*Gino, puòi aiutarci? Dobiamo noleggiare un auto,*' she says.

'Could we walk?' Harriet suggests.

'No,' Aunt Fanny says at once, turning back quickly to give her a look. Harriet smiles and takes a big swig of wine.

Gino leans his arms on the counter. '*Dove vai?*'

'Sulmona.'

I arch my back and try to catch Mum's eye. 'What is she saying?' I mouth. Mum shrugs back at me.

'*Posso aiutarti,*' Gino continues.

'*Grazie di cuore*,' Aunt Fanny gushes, linking her fingers over her heart. Then she turns back to the table and claps her hands. 'Sorted.'

I raise my eyebrows sceptically at her. 'Sorted?'

'Gino is going to help us. Now, who's hungry?'

Chapter Thirty-One

Harriet

I hook one leg over the other and hold the phone to my ear. I snuck out of the café when Zoe and Fanny started bickering about whether a carbonara is actually Italian. I know Zoe needs me here, and obviously I wasn't going to be left behind, but I try to slip away every couple of hours just to give them some time on their own. Alarmingly, I seem to be the one who is the most sane on this trip. And this is me! I can't hold down a job, I sprint from any adult responsibility, and I still live at home with my mum, even though I'm certain that I have outstayed my welcome.

But I don't have to worry about any of that now. Where Zoe seems to have picked up her problems and taken them on a nice holiday to Italy, I left mine firmly at home. I have absolutely no idea what I'm going to do when I go back, but that's for Future Harriet to worry about. And she's always sorted me out so far, just about.

The September sun is still high in the sky, beaming down on me, and I close my eyes as the dialling tone sounds in my ear.

'Hello?' I open my eyes as my mum's stretched voice shoots down the phone, carried by a wave of noise, which immediately pops my happy bubble. I can hear Daniel whining in the background and the chirpy babble of children's cartoons.

'Hi, Mum,' I say. 'It's me.'

'Hang on, darling.' There is a scuffle of noise and I gently bat away a bug that has landed on my arm. 'Okay, I'm back. Are you still at work? Are you doing a night shift?'

My heart turns over.

So, here's the thing. Like I said, it's always been just me and Mum. We did everything together, and we had a routine. I felt safe, I was happy, and it never really crossed my mind that she wasn't. Until one day when I came home from university for the weekend and noticed her cheeks were pinker than usual and she'd had her hair done. She was all sparkly and giggly and she told me that she'd met someone and it was getting quite serious. The next weekend, she brought Darren home for me to meet. He was fine. Quite funny, very caring, and always opened the door for her. Really, he was everything you'd want of your mum's boyfriend. But that wasn't the point, he wasn't part of the deal.

And yes, I know that makes me sound like a terrible person, but when he was suddenly sitting on our sofa every Saturday night and making us cups of tea and parking his car on the drive, I started to feel like I didn't have a place any more. And then Mum told me that they were expecting a baby, and I had this horrible feeling that I didn't fit in this new picture at all.

I've never said any of this to my mum, obviously. But when

the opportunity came for me to run away for a few days, a small part of me saw it as an opportunity to put my theory to the test. Would she actually miss me if I was gone? Could I just slip away without her noticing? I don't want to worry her, so I haven't dropped off the face of the earth without any contact at all. But if I can go a whole weekend without her realising I'm not in the country, then I will have been right. She doesn't need me any more, she has a new life.

And the part that makes me feel equal parts terrified and horrified with myself is I don't like how all this makes me feel. I was so used to me and Mum floating through life together, making it up as we went along, I had no idea that one day she'd suddenly have it all. She'd have the nice boyfriend and the gorgeous baby, the perfect pram and the Farrow & Ball Elephant's Breath walls. Suddenly it wasn't so funny and quirky that I had absolutely no idea what I was doing with my life. It was like my mum picking up this new life was a horrible, stark invitation for me to grow the hell up and start mine. A reminder that I couldn't live for ever in my childhood bedroom, hopping from job to job with no real idea what I was doing or who I was meant to be. And yes, deep down I did know that. I didn't picture myself aged fifty still living with my mum. But I didn't think I'd have to figure all these things out *quite yet*. I still feel like a child myself.

Mum hasn't said any of this, but she doesn't have to. I don't know if she even notices how I'm feeling, she's so wrapped up with the baby. Which is how it should be. I'm twenty-five, for God's sake. But I don't know where I fit. I feel a bit like I'm being pushed from the nest and I still don't know how to fly.

If she doesn't miss me this weekend, maybe it'll be the final shove I need. I won't have a choice. I've already quit my job, with no idea what to do next. What would there be to go back to if Mum doesn't need me any more?

'Sorry, darling,' she says as Daniel starts screaming. 'Can I call you back?'

I open my purse and look at the stash of scratch cards shoved in there.

I'd have to learn how to use my wings and pray to God I don't get eaten alive.

'Sure, Mum. Love you.'

'Harriet?'

I hang up the phone as Zoe steps out of the café. Her face is flushed and I hide a smile at the indignation in her eyes. I don't want her to be upset, obviously, but there is something quite funny about how wound up she gets at almost everything Fanny says. Maybe it's a good thing Fanny wasn't around when Zoe hit puberty. I think they would have murdered each other.

'Hey,' I say, pushing a chair out for her with my foot. 'You okay?'

'Yeah.' She slumps down and takes a cigarette from the packet on the table.

I raise my eyebrows. 'That bad?'

She cocks her head as the flame flicks towards her cupped hands. 'Worse. God, she's so annoying. Are you all right? What are you doing out here?'

I take a cigarette too and lean my head back. 'Just enjoying the sights.'

'Yeah?'

'I thought I'd give Mum a call, but it wasn't a great time.'

I push my sunglasses to the top of my head and try to ignore Zoe's worried face. Zoe loves talking about feelings. I'd rather chuck my feelings in the air and run off into the sunset like the footloose and fancy-free woman of chaos I like to pretend to be.

'Actually,' she says, handing me back my lighter, 'I've been thinking about your job situation.'

'Mmm?'

'When we get back, why don't you come and work with me? You'd be so great, and I'm sure Heidi would take you on. You can put me as a reference.' She shoots me a toothy grin.

'Is that allowed? We've never worked together.'

'We handed out flyers for that local builder in town when we were sixteen, remember?'

'We threw those in the bin,' I say, catching the eye of a muscular dark-skinned man who strolls past us.

Ding dong.

'*You* threw yours in the bin,' Zoe says indignantly. 'I handed out all of mine.'

I pull a face at her and she laughs.

'A character reference then,' she says. 'I could totally give you one of those.'

I wave a hand. 'Thanks, but I can't think about work. Right now, we're in Italy, smoking cigarettes and half drunk on wine.' I take a glorious drag. 'And that's all I will be thinking about for the foreseeable future.'

A motorbike skirts past us, and I look up as a woman throws open her shutters, yelling something in Italian.

This is how I imagined travelling would be. Not the tourist sites that everyone else goes to, but places like this. Being shoulder to shoulder with the locals, wrapping yourself up in the language, eating in tiny restaurants that have been in the family for years. We never would have found this place if our train hadn't broken down.

'How's your mum getting on with the baby?'

Zoe pops my bubble and I fall back down to earth with a thud.

'Fine,' I say. 'She's happy. Tired, but I think that's quite normal.'

She pushes her hair off her face, her fringe sticking up. 'And what about you? Have you got used to it yet?'

I scoff. 'God, no. I'm sure I never cried this much when I was a baby.'

She raises her eyebrows at me and we both laugh.

'I don't want to get used to it,' I say, taking a deep breath, 'because that would mean living in that house with them for ever. There's only so long I can cling onto my bedroom before they turn it into a playroom.'

I grin at Zoe, but her eyes are wide and worried.

'Anyway,' I say quickly, before she can probe further and make me face my feelings, 'these Italians are pretty hot, aren't they?'

CHAPTER THIRTY-TWO

ZOE

An hour later, we're sitting in another tiny restaurant, on Gino's recommendation. This one has floor-to-ceiling shelves stacked high with bottles of wine, each with a hand-written tag tied around its neck stating the price and the date it was created.

A slick, petite waitress slipped menus in front of us about five minutes ago, and I'm trying not to dribble on mine as I stare down at the options.

Clams and mussels.

Baked pork with porcini mushrooms.

Grilled beef with rosemary and potatoes.

Carbonara.

I lean forward as Harriet flashes me a picture of her baby brother that her mum has just sent through.

'Look,' she says.

'He's so cute.'

'He's much cuter now I can't hear him screaming.' She grins at me and takes a slug of her wine.

I smile, tuning into Aunt Fanny, who is chatting busily at Mum and fluffing the back of her hair.

'I just think you need some more oomph, Ange,' she says. 'You've let it get so flat.'

'Really?' Mum says, trying to smooth down her thin hair.

'You know, I have this incredible hairdryer, but I left it in Cornwall. Let me have a go when we get back.'

Mum tucks her hair behind her ears and I feel myself bristle. I don't like it when Fanny talks to her like this.

'I know you don't like change, but I think this would really suit you. You liked it when I did it before, remember? Then maybe we could look at setting you up on a date! I mean, when was the last time you had—'

'Aunt Fanny!' I cry, desperate for her not to finish that sentence. 'What do you want to eat?'

Fanny turns to me and Mum pushes back her chair. 'Actually, I think I'll just nip to the loo. If the waitress comes over, can you ask her for a few more minutes?'

'I'll come with you,' Harriet says, getting to her feet.

As they disappear through the restaurant, Aunt Fanny angles her body to face me. She flashes me a smile and then immediately rolls her eyes when I don't return it.

'God, I thought by missing the teenage years I might have missed the *moodiness*.'

'I don't like the way you talk to Mum. You keep trying to improve her or make her feel like she needs to change, but she doesn't. She's happy as she is.'

Aunt Fanny sighs and touches her hair, the bravado that she

constantly carries with her momentarily disappearing. 'Zoe, if I didn't push your mum to change, then she never would.'

'What's wrong with that?' I say hotly. 'She doesn't need to change. She's perfect how she is.'

'She's not happy, Zo. I know her like a sister.'

I can't help it, the words fire out of me. 'How can you say that? You haven't been here! You don't know anything!'

'I know when she's not happy.'

'And you think giving her a blow-dry is going to change that?' I snap. 'I've been trying to get her to talk to me about Grandma and how she feels, but she *won't*, and you being here isn't going to make it any better. You don't know anything about us any more.'

I can feel my heartbeat in my throat as I force myself to keep my eyes fixed on her. I'm expecting her to retaliate, to call me a child or say I don't know what I'm talking about, but to my surprise, her shoulders soften.

'Yes,' she says quietly, 'I suppose you're right.'

We slip into silence, and the back of my neck begins to prickle with guilt. When I glance up at her, she's gazing out of the window, and I realise it's the first time since she came back that I'm looking at her with her guard dropped. Her face is sallow and tight from Botox, but it's etched with lines that collect in the corner of each eye, as though a crow has landed in fresh cement. Her lips are plump and stretched with filler, but they sag at the sides. I notice with a jolt that her eyes are shining. She looks sad.

Maybe she's just tired and hung-over from all the wine we've had. We've barely eaten all day.

She turns to face me, linking her bony fingers together. 'I am only trying to help, Zo. I know that I'm sometimes a bit unorthodox, but I love your mum very much. And I love you,' she adds pointedly. 'I'm back here to make amends. I want to be part of your family again.'

'And that's the only reason you're here?' I retort spitefully. As soon as I say the words, I wish I could shove them back in my mouth. Aunt Fanny looks as if she's been slapped.

'What do you mean?'

'I've just seen the steak and it looks incredible!'

I jump as Harriet reappears, my face burning as I break Aunt Fanny's gaze.

'I'm totally getting it, I'm so hungry.' She drops back into her seat and pulls the menu closer to her. 'Is anyone getting starters?'

Chapter Thirty-Three

Zoe

After dinner, we let Aunt Fanny lead us to a tiny B&B tucked down a side street. A concrete spiral staircase took us up to our rooms. There were only two rooms available, but Aunt Fanny refused to share with anyone, which meant me, Mum and Harriet had to squeeze into a double bed. I thought she was joking at first, and tried to argue with her, but she stalked up the stairs in her towering heels without so much as a backwards glance.

Honestly, if I thought I felt rough before, it was nothing compared to how I felt after a night lying between Mum and Harriet. At one point I considered getting up and sleeping in the bath, but they were both gripping their sides of the duvet with such vigour that you would have had to saw me out of the bed. So instead I spent the night sweating like a pig and staring up at the ceiling.

One of the things keeping me awake was guilt. It pecked away at my skin like a persistent bird and every time I felt like

I was finally drifting off it would peck peck peck me awake. I felt guilty about Mum, about dragging her here when it was clearly making her unhappier than she was at home (something I didn't think was possible). I felt guilty about Kitty, leaving her to deal with this wedding on her own. I felt guilty about lying to Heidi. And most surprisingly, I felt guilty about Aunt Fanny. When she appeared at our doorstep earlier this week, I didn't think I'd be able to feel anything but rage towards her. I was so angry with her. How dare she turn up, after all this time? But last night, when I snapped at her, she looked vulnerable. It was the first time I'd seen her like that since she came back. It was like I was looking at the real Aunt Fanny: the kind, sensitive, but fierce woman who would move a mountain to keep me and Mum safe. I don't know where she's been these past fourteen years, but that part of her hasn't changed. It's still in there.

At some point, I must have fallen asleep, though, because at 6 a.m. Mum is shaking me awake. My brain is aching from the many glasses of rich red wine and my eyes stay firmly scrunched shut.

'Zo?' I pull an eye open as Harriet nudges me. She's holding a steaming cup of coffee under my nose. I take it gratefully as I hear the shower click on.

'Thank you so much,' I mutter, my voice coming out as more of a growl.

'Do you need to borrow a top today?'

To my alarm, my eyes prick with tears.

'What's wrong?' Harriet says, sitting down on the bed. I push myself up to a sitting position and wipe my eyes quickly.

'God,' I mutter. 'Sorry. I just feel like this whole trip has been a disaster. I can't believe I dragged you here.'

She blinks at me. 'Are you joking? I'm having the time of my

171

life! When else would we visit a tiny historical town like this? And meet Gino, and drink real Italian wine? And today I'm going to get to see your grandma's house!' She grips my leg and gives it a shake. 'It's all part of the adventure, Zo. Honestly, if I wasn't here, I'd be hiding in the toilets at work or cleaning up some arsehole's sick.'

I take a sip of the coffee, blinking the tears away.

'Sorry. God, I don't know what's wrong with me.'

She cocks her head. 'You're allowed to be sad,' she says kindly. 'I know you want to be strong for your mum and you don't really trust your aunt, but this is me. You don't have to pretend with me.'

She hops off the bed as a loud rap on the door vibrates through the room, and pulls it open to reveal an effortlessly glamorous Aunt Fanny. Once again, her skinny legs are commanding full attention in a pale green mini dress. She pulls her sunglasses off her head and purses her shiny red lips.

'How did you fit all these outfits into that tiny bag?' I ask, gaping at her.

She ignores my question. 'We're not hung-over, are we, Miss Zoe?' She strides into the room and drops onto the end of the bed.

I push my hair out of my face. 'No. Think I'm just hormonal.'

'Did you sleep okay?' Harriet asks, turning to Fanny whilst pulling a brush through her long red hair.

Aunt Fanny smiles. 'As well as I can these days.'

'Do you still go to bed at like two in the morning?' I ask.

When I was little and had a nightmare, it was always Aunt Fanny's room I'd run into. Mum would be fast asleep by eleven, but Aunt Fanny would be lounging around her room, pushing expensive creams into her skin and foams into her hair. She'd scoop me up and talk me through her beauty routine. It wasn't the calming goodnight story most six-year-olds got, but it worked for us.

'Nobody needs more than five hours' sleep,' she says knowingly. 'It's a waste of time otherwise.'

We look round as Mum emerges from the bathroom. She's surrounded by a cloud of steam, as though she's about to appear on *Stars in Their Eyes*.

'Oh look at you!' Aunt Fanny coos. 'You're like a little cherub.'

Mum slaps her arm as she walks past. 'That was a lovely shower. Do either of you girls want one?'

'Oh I do,' Harriet says, turning to me.

I wave my hand at her. 'You go first. I need to finish my coffee.'

She skips into the bathroom as Mum sits down and starts brushing her hair.

'What time do we need to go?' I ask.

Aunt Fanny exhales. 'Gino said he'd be here at eight.'

'Is he driving us?'

She makes herself comfortable on the bed. 'Oh the darling, I'm sure he would have done, but he has the shop to manage, so he's lending us his car.'

Mum starts rubbing cream on her face. 'So one of us has to drive?'

'Don't give it a second thought, Ange. I'll drive,' Aunt Fanny says, looking at us both in a saintly way. I try to ignore my stomach flipping.

'Have you ever driven an Italian car before?' I say carefully.

She shrugs and pulls out her phone. 'All the pedals are the same.'

Are they?

'I'm not sure how . . .' Mum begins, but she trails off as her phone starts to ring next to her. Her face pales. 'Ah,' she says, picking it up. 'It's Reggie. He wants me to call him.'

'No!'

I jolt upwards, looking round at Aunt Fanny as we shout in unison.

Mum puffs out her chest. 'I can't ignore him. He might be worried about us.'

Aunt Fanny rolls her eyes.

'Or something might have happened to him,' Mum continues. 'He might need my help.'

'That's more like it,' Fanny mutters.

'What are you going to say to him?' I ask, shuffling forward in the bed. She can't tell him where we're going, not when we're so close. He might be nearby, and I have no doubt he would do his best to beat us to the house if he knew we were in Italy. I know it sounds awful, but I don't trust him not to hide the ring. I *have* to get there before he does.

'I'm just going to let him know that we're okay,' Mum says calmly.

'What if he asks where you are?' I press.

Aunt Fanny scoffs. 'He won't care where you are.'

Mum shoots her a look and holds the phone to her ear. My whole body tenses.

'Hello? . . . Hi, Reg. Sorry about earlier, my phone has been playing up . . . Yeah, I know . . . Oh, sure. Are you back from France then? . . . Yes, of course. You know where my spare is, don't you? . . . Yeah, that's right . . . Of course, help yourself to whatever . . .'

Aunt Fanny gets to her feet and walks towards the window, tripping over a stray shoe as she goes.

'Oh fuck!' she cries, as I reach forward to catch her.

Mum presses her hand to the phone, attempting to block out Fanny's outburst. She pushes a finger into her free ear.

'Sure,' she says, increasing her volume. 'That's fine, Reg . . . Okay . . . Sure. Okay, bye then.'

I don't realise I'm holding my breath until she ends the call. Aunt Fanny lets go of my hand and examines her heeled foot.

'What did he want?' she asks.

'Oh, he was just asking if he could pop into the house. He came back from France early; his business trip was cut short or something.' Mum pauses, turning to Aunt Fanny. 'Are you okay?'

An unlit cigarette is hanging from Aunt Fanny's lips. 'Oh yeah. Hand me the lighter, will you?'

'You can't smoke in here,' Mum says.

'We're in Italy, Ange!'

'Didn't he ask why you're not at home?' I ask.

Mum contemplates my question for a second. 'No, he didn't.'

'See,' Aunt Fanny says, taking the cigarette out of her mouth as Mum points to the 'No Smoking' sign. 'I told you. He doesn't care.'

*

Today I am wearing one of Mum's shirts, which falls just above my knees thanks to my lack of a double-G-sized chest. (My boobs are big, but thankfully I only inherited half of Mum's. Although God knows what will happen if I ever have a baby.) My short hair is pulled back into a low ponytail, which sits at the nape of my neck, and every time I think my fringe is lying in a sexy, slightly ruffled I-just-got-out-of-bed-and-I-look-this-effortlessly-cool way, another bead of sweat licks across my forehead and glues it back to my skin.

Harriet is wearing her shortest denim shorts and a white cami, her pale skin reflecting the rays of Italian sunlight with such vigour it's a wonder she isn't stopping traffic. Mum is in camel–coloured linen trousers and a baggy shirt. Even though it is about twenty-five degrees, she'd rather pass out than show even a whisper of skin. The only thing to rival Harriet's pale legs is the gloss of Aunt Fanny's bob, which is shimmering in the sunlight, perfect as always. Honestly, it's like she's smuggled a miniature hairdresser into her suitcase. Nothing I do could make my hair look that good.

On Mum's orders, we filed out of our room like misbehaving sheep and stepped outside into the Italian heat just before eight, ready for Gino's prompt arrival. But now it's 8.15 and he's not here, and I'm starting to question why we trusted a man we'd never met before just because he was in charge of the parmesan.

A gaggle of Italians walk past us on the opposite side of the road, their lyrical chat floating across the street and wrapping around us like a hug. I have absolutely no idea what they're saying, but the rhythm of it, the smoothness of the language and the laughter that is laced through each word reminds me of Grandma.

I turn to face Mum and find that her eyes are shut. I give her a gentle nudge.

'Don't you just love that?'

She opens her eyes. 'What?'

I gesture to the group of people, who are now snaking their way inside a coffee shop. 'Hearing them all speak. I find it so relaxing being here. It just reminds me of Grandma.'

I smile at her, hoping she'll respond, but she keeps her eyes fixed forward. I feel a pang in my chest. Why won't she talk to me?

'Oh!' Harriet cries. 'Is that him?'

I follow her finger to an original Mini that is speeding down the road towards us. My heart turns over. Please tell me that's not for us, I pray silently as I weigh up the likelihood of the car having working air conditioning.

It races past us, and I breathe a sigh of relief. Thank God. That is *not* a car made for several passengers. It looked like a clown car.

As the relief leaves my body, concern returns. 'Is he definitely coming? How long should we wait?'

Aunt Fanny sighs. 'It's only quarter past, I'm sure he'll be here soon.'

'But what if he doesn't come? Do we even have his number?'

'He'll be here.'

Her phone starts to ring, and I glance at it, expecting to see Gino's name pop up on the screen.

Jon.

She looks down and rejects the call immediately.

Harriet shrugs at me, but I keep looking at Aunt Fanny. Her shoulders are slightly rolled forward today, her head dipped a little lower than before. She looks exhausted.

How can she be tired? She's the only one who had a whole bed to herself last night!

Maybe she's more hung-over than I thought.

I check the time, trying to stay calm. But at that moment, my phone starts vibrating in my hand and Kitty's name flashes up on the screen. Panic shoots through me as I take a deep breath and answer.

'Hey, Kitty!' I say, trying to sound nonchalant. 'How are you? I hope you're not working on a Sunday!'

Even as I say it, I feel my insides coil with guilt.

Of course she'll be working on a Sunday. You've left her on her own and gone gallivanting across Europe to find a ring, dragging your grieving mother with you against her will.

'Oh, it's hardly work!' she says, and I can almost feel her beaming down the phone. 'I love doing it! I've spent the entire morning looking for biodegradable personalised confetti and I've just found some with glitter!'

What did I do in a past life to deserve Kitty? I mean, Jesus, I must have been Gandhi. Or, like, Maria von Trapp.

'That's amazing.' I instantly feel myself relax a little. 'Is everything all right?'

'Oh yes!' she sings. 'How are you? How's Italy? Did you find the ring?'

I chew on my lip, manically weighing up the pros and cons of lying to her.

Pros: I won't have to face the music quite yet and can continue living in ignorant bliss. La la la, maybe everything will be just fine.

Cons: if I lie to Kitty, aka the nicest person ever, I'll go straight to hell, where I'll spend eternity trying to unblock a never-ending plughole. Anyone who tries to claim that there is anything worse than picking out someone else's hair from a slimy drain hasn't lived with my eight university roommates, each of whom shaved their legs daily and shed hair like badly groomed yetis. No arguments please, or I'll meet you there.

'No,' I answer after a moment, 'not yet. We haven't actually got to the house,' I force myself to add, before Kitty can ask more innocent questions and accidentally tip me into a panic attack.

'Oh? Where are you?'

I look around the desolate street. Bloody Gino.

'Well, I'm not entirely sure. Our train broke down yesterday on our way to the house, so we had to stay overnight in this little town.'

'How lovely!' Kitty chirps, and despite my worry, I smile.

I step out of earshot of Mum. 'Yes, but it's been a bit stressful as our travels keep going wrong and we're running out of time.'

'Ah. Yes, I can see why that's stressful.' There's a pause before Kitty continues. 'Do you reckon you'll make your flight?'

I chew the corner of my thumb. 'I don't know.'

'Do you think you'll be in the office for Tuesday?'

My stomach turns over. 'I don't know,' I say again. 'Probably . . . I mean, yeah.'

Surely I will be?

The line goes silent, and without Kitty's calming optimism, I feel as though I might be sick.

'Okay! How's this? I'll keep working on what I'm doing, and you focus on finding this ring and getting home, and then we'll regroup later?' Her happy, sing-song voice trills down the phone and I suddenly feel as though I could burst into tears.

'Thank you, you really are the—'

'But can I talk to you quickly about Libby?' Her voice gabbles across mine and I take a deep breath.

Oh no. That doesn't sound good.

'Yeah, of course. Is she okay?'

I hear Kitty take a breath. 'I'm not sure. She's not making much sense and won't tell me what the problem is, but she's called me three times in the last twenty-four hours, crying down the phone. I think it has something to do with the table settings, because every time I ask her about them, she changes the subject.'

My heart rate quickens. Fuck. Her wedding is on Thursday.

'Okay.' I try to stay calm. 'She's probably just really stressed, and it's our job to keep her calm and make this process as smooth as possible.'

Well, it's supposed to be our job. However, *I'm* hundreds of miles away, drinking wine and eating gelato, so fat lot of good I am.

'Yeah,' Kitty says after a pause. 'I'm sure you're right.'

'Just keep doing what you're doing, Kitty, and keep me posted. I'm always at the end of the phone, and do feel free to email anything over to me that I can help with. I'll be back in the UK tomorrow and in the office on Tuesday.'

I force myself to say this, even though I know that at this rate it is highly unlikely that we'll be going home tomorrow. But I can't think about that now. Everything will be fine.

We say goodbye and I slip my phone back into my pocket and look over my shoulder. Mum, Harriet and Aunt Fanny are still standing in a sad line, with Harriet peering about every couple of seconds as if Gino is about to race around the corner.

'I'm going to run to that shop and get some water,' I say, pointing to a little corner shop on the opposite side of the street. 'Does anyone want anything?'

They all shake their heads at me wordlessly, and I turn on my heel, trying to shake off the panic that has started to bubble up inside me yet again.

Gino isn't coming, and he was our only way to get to Sulmona from here. The trains still aren't running, and walking would take us *hours*. If we have to stay here another night, we will definitely miss our flight, not to mention hugely increase the likelihood of bumping into Uncle Reggie. The auction is on Tuesday! The whole point of this was to get to the house, find the ring and leave again without Reggie being any the wiser. He can't be here when we are; he'll ruin everything. He'll try and take the ring for himself, and he'll scare Aunt Fanny away so she leaves us again.

The last thought shoots through my brain before I really register it, and I'm surprised to feel my heart clench at the idea.

Where did that come from?

I step into the shop and go to the fridge, where I pick up three bottles of water, closing my eyes for a moment as the cool air wafts over my face and my eyes start to sting.

This trip was supposed to be so straightforward. How has it ended up like this?

'Are you okay?'

I almost drop the water as a familiar voice greets me. To my surprise, Sam is standing next to me, also holding a bottle of water. Before I can stop myself, the tears pooling in the corner of my eyes start to spill out down my cheeks.

Oh my God, I'm *crying* in front of Sam!

'Oh no,' he says, stepping forward as though unsure whether to comfort me. 'I'm so sorry. I just . . . You just looked quite . . . like you were meditating in front of the fridge.'

Stupidly, I glance up into his kind eyes, and the concern I see there makes me cry even harder.

'Please stop crying!' he gabbles. 'I know. I bet I can guess your name in five goes. If I don't, you can throw your drink over me.' He gestures to the bottle of water clenched in my tight fist. 'I know you like doing that,' he adds, laughing awkwardly.

I smile, wiping the tears off my face with my sleeve. 'Fine, but you only get three guesses.'

He nods. 'Deal. Okay, first guess . . . Maureen?'

I laugh. 'Maureen? Do I look like a Maureen to you?'

He holds up his hands in surrender. 'There's no need to be discriminatory towards Maureens. There are plenty of hot Maureens these days.'

My cheeks redden. 'That's one guess gone already.'

He pretends to think. 'Helga?'

This time the laugh that comes out of me is more like a bark. 'Helga?' I repeat. 'What are these guesses? What kind of girls do you hang out with?'

He grins, clearly delighted that he's making me laugh. 'Point taken.'

'You only have one guess left,' I warn.

'Shit.' He looks me up and down, and my stomach turns over. 'I've got it.'

I raise my eyebrows at him, waiting for him to suggest Gertrude or Agnes.

He pauses, now looking me dead in the eyes. 'Zoe.'

I gasp, and then catch his grin and thwack him on the arm. 'You cheated! You already knew my name, didn't you?'

He laughs, running his hand through his hair. 'Fine. I heard your friend call you Zoe at the bar the other night.'

'I should really throw the water over you for that.' I pretend to undo the cap.

'To be honest, I'll do anything to get you to stop crying.' He smiles, a single dimple creasing in his cheek. He's picked up more freckles since our first meeting.

My heart lifts as for a moment we just look at each other.

'Well, Zoe,' he says after a beat, 'now that we officially know each other's names and we've both spilt drinks over each other, are you okay? You don't have to tell me,' he adds quickly, 'but I've never seen a girl cry at a water bottle before . . .'

For a second, I feel the panic leave me as a sense of calm takes over and I contemplate the idea that everything will be fine. I look at Sam more closely, his red hair pushed off his forehead into a quiff, revealing more of his soft features, which somehow make me feel as though I could tell him anything.

'No,' I say, surprising myself. 'My grandma used to live in Sulmona, but she died recently. She was an incredible artist, and her work is being auctioned on Tuesday, and I'm supposed to have this ring that she left me but my uncle doesn't seem fussed about finding it, but I think he just wants to sell it at the auction. So I've come here to find it, dragging along my mum, who is so full of grief that she barely speaks to me, and my best friend. Oh, and my aunt, who deserted us fourteen years ago, has also joined us. But our train broke down and the guy who said he would give us a lift to Sulmona hasn't turned up, and we need to get there asap because we're meant to fly home tomorrow afternoon and the longer we're out here the worse my mum seems to be, even though I had hoped that this trip would give her closure and make her feel better.' I break off, realising I've said it all in one strained breath.

Great. I've just word-vomited at a guy who is not only a near-total stranger but also the first guy I've fancied in months. Well done, me. Why couldn't I have said I was fine and commented on the weather?

I finally look up at Sam, giving him an awkward smile. I'm expecting him to shrug and say something like 'that sucks' and walk away, but his face hasn't moved.

'So you need to get to Sulmona?'

'Yeah, so—'

'*Scusa?*'

I turn around to see an Italian woman peering at us over the counter. She gestures to the water bottles and the till, and I quickly turn on my heel and scuttle towards her. We both hand over some coins before stepping out of the shop.

'Sorry for dumping all that on you.' I turn to face Sam, silently cursing myself for using the word 'dumping' and panicking that he might think I want to do a poo on him. 'Have a great trip. I hope nobody else throws a drink at you.'

He gives me a half-smile and holds his hand up in a wave as I almost run back to Harriet, who is finishing a cigarette.

'No Gino yet?' I say quietly as I reach her and open my bottle of water.

She shakes her head. 'Nope, and worse than that, Fanny's lighter has stopped working.'

I tune in to the constant zipping sound of Aunt Fanny's desperate thumb swiping the lighter, her pillowy lips tense against her drooping cigarette.

I glance down at my phone. It's 8.30. Mum is staring into the distance, sipping on a bottle of water, but I can see her hand shaking slightly as she raises it to her mouth.

'Oh my God,' Harriet hisses in my ear as she manically starts to jab me. 'Zoe, Zoe, Zoe, Zoe . . .'

'Zoe?'

I turn around and see Sam walking towards us. His backpack is slung over his shoulder and his hazel eyes are smiling.

'Oh, hi,' I say, oddly surprised considering I saw him literally two minutes ago. 'This is Sam,' I add, noticing Mum and Aunt Fanny peering at him like he's an endangered species.

They all give him a little wave, apart from Fanny, who throws back her head and curses loudly as the flicker of a flame is sucked away by the wind.

Sam returns their waves, then turns back to me. 'Still no sign of your lift then?'

'No.' I try to keep my voice upbeat, willing myself to not burst into tears in front of him for the second time today. 'Not yet.'

He gives a sympathetic smile. 'Listen. What would you say if I said that I think I have a way to get you all to Sulmona?'

At this, Aunt Fanny lets out a guttural moan as her cigarette finally starts to sizzle under the flick of a flame. She turns to face Sam, pulling her sunglasses off to give him a proper look.

'I'd say,' she stops to take a gloriously long drag of her cigarette, tipping her head towards the sky before looking at me, 'Zoe, bloody marry this man.'

'This is my aunt,' I say to Sam.

'Fanny,' Aunt Fanny says, smiling innocently as she watches Sam try not to laugh at her announcing her name is the same as the word for 'vagina'.

Her real name is Fenella, and I'm sure she calls herself Fanny for this exact reason.

She takes another suck of her cigarette. 'Where is this ride then?'

★

The smoky fumes fill my lungs and gradually release the tension coiled around my muscles as I puff the cloud of smoke into the air. My eyes are closed, the sun is beaming down on my face, and if I concentrate on the bitter taste of tobacco, I can pretend that I can't hear Mum, who is muttering frantically to Aunt Fanny about why she can't get in the back of a jeep. I'm also trying to pretend that my phone didn't vibrate five seconds ago with a rather aggressive message from Uncle Reggie:

Zoe, where are you

No hello, not even a simple question mark. I mean, where is the small talk? The pleasantries? If Mum saw this message, she'd probably collapse. That is, if the current situation wasn't keeping her heat racing at four hundred miles per hour.

'What is the problem?' Aunt Fanny whispers, taking Mum by the elbow and steering her away from the jeep that pulled up about twenty minutes ago. 'We need to get to Sulmona, and this nice young man has offered us a lift with his uncle.'

'Not his uncle,' Harriet chips in. 'His friend's uncle.'

Mum smooths down her hair, which is gradually gaining a life of its own under the intense Italian heat.

'We don't know anything about him!' she says under her breath. 'We are four vulnerable women . . .'

'Vulnerable?' Aunt Fanny guffaws.

'. . . and he could drive us anywhere! We would be completely at his mercy.'

'That sounds quite nice,' Fanny murmurs, pulling her sunglasses down to take a better look at Aldo, a man in his mid fifties with shiny dark hair and a stream of tattoos up his tanned arms.

Mum thwacks her on the shoulder, and Fanny yelps.

'Oh will you calm down. I'm joking.'

'We are not getting in that car,' Mum says firmly.

At this Aunt Fanny props her sunglasses on top of her head

and raises her perfect eyebrows. Well, she tries to. She's had a lot of Botox.

'And what is the alternative, Ange? We need to get to Sulmona as soon as possible if we have any hope of catching a flight home tomorrow afternoon.'

'You were happy getting a lift with Gino,' I mumble, immediately wishing I'd stayed silent when Mum flashes me a glare.

'I thought he would be lending us a car,' she snaps. 'Or booking us a taxi.'

'There are no taxis!' Aunt Fanny cries.

'Of course there are taxis,' Mum huffs.

Fanny scoffs. 'Oh really?' She turns on her heel and marches into the middle of the desolate road. 'Where, Ange? I'll just flag one down, shall I? Taxi!' she yells, throwing a bony arm into the air. 'Taxi! Oh shit. Why aren't they stopping, Ange?'

Mum storms into the road and drags Aunt Fanny back. As Fanny stumbles behind Mum's strong grip, her handbag spills onto the floor. I quickly bend down and scoop up the clatter of cards and lipsticks.

Aunt Fanny takes a deep breath. 'Look, we need to get to your mum's—'

'No, we don't.'

Aunt Fanny blinks, the smirk on her face fading away as Mum glares at her fiercely. 'Ange . . .'

'I've just been chatting to Aldo,' Harriet says, bouncing back over to us. 'He's really nice. He's a hairdresser! He works in a salon on the other side of town. Apparently it's only an hour's drive or so to Sulmona.'

I frown at her. 'I didn't know you could speak Italian.'

'His nephew, Harry, translated.' Harriet winks at me. I grin, rolling my eyes, then turn back to Mum, but she is already stalking towards the jeep. I watch as she climbs into the front seat and slams the door.

Next to me, Aunt Fanny sighs. I hold the handful of credit cards towards her, my eyes flicking down at them as she takes them back.

Mr Reginald Winters.

My stomach drops.

★

The jeep has been rattling along the near-empty road for about ten minutes, and I haven't heard a peep from Mum, though Aldo did turn up the radio shortly after she climbed in. Aunt Fanny climbed into the back seat with Sam's friend Harry (send thoughts and prayers to the poor boy), which leaves me and Harriet in the open back with Sam and his other friend James. We're slouched on the floor, trying not to squeal whenever we go over a pothole.

Thankfully Mum hasn't seen how we're travelling. I don't know where she thinks we are, but I'm sure she'd ram her feet into the ground and stop the car herself if she knew we were bouncing around in the back like kernels of corn in a frying pan.

'Do you want some suncream?'

I catch Sam's worried eyes flitting down to my crisping legs.

'Yes!' Harriet cries, snatching the cream from him. 'Thank God. Knew I could count on a fellow ginger to pack some. I used pretty much all of mine on the first day.'

'Did you not pack any?' He turns to me.

I shrug. 'We weren't planning on staying long enough to really catch the sun.'

Harriet passes me the bottle and I squirt some onto my hands. 'Thank you.'

'So, where are you guys meant to be?' she asks, leaning on her elbows and stretching her legs out in front of her.

Sam frowns. 'What do you mean?'

'With the train breaking down at Carsoli,' she explains. 'Where were you going?'

'Oh,' James replies. 'We were always going to Carsoli. We're travelling around Europe and wanted to visit Harry's uncle so he could show us around.'

'Ah, lucky you.'

'How long are you travelling for?' I ask.

'We're not sure,' Sam says, flicking open a pair of sunglasses and slipping them on. 'Until we get bored,' he adds, flashing me a grin.

'What about your jobs?' I say, and then immediately want to kick myself.

Great. Well done for making yourself sound like their mum, Zoe.

'We quit,' James says. 'Well, Harry is a graphic designer, so he's got some freelance stuff on the road.'

'We'll just do fruit picking or something.' Sam shrugs. 'Or, you know, stripping.' He shoots me a look and I immediately flame red. 'I'm joking,' he adds, giving me a nudge.

At this point I feel as though I'm about to burst into flames. I quickly push my sunglasses over my eyes to try and avoid Harriet, who is practically mouthing 'Shag him!' at me.

'What about you girls?' James asks. 'Have you done any travelling?'

Harriet snorts. 'I wish. I've just quit my job, but Zoe has a wedding to plan.'

'Not mine,' I add, a bit too quickly.

Urgh. Why does she have to always say it like that? Why can't she just say I work in weddings instead of lumping me with a fictional fiancé?

'I'm a wedding planner,' I explain. 'So yeah. This is just a flying trip, or it's meant to be. Our flight home is at four thirty tomorrow.' I laugh far too loudly at this and suddenly feel as though I'm about to pop a blood vessel.

'We've had a bit of a difficult journey,' Harriet sighs. 'And we're on a deadline.'

'So we really appreciate you guys helping us out,' I continue, smiling at Sam.

'Of course,' he replies, smiling back and making my heart flutter in my chest. 'I'm excited to see Sulmona too,' he adds. 'What do the bright sights have to offer us?'

The jeep pulls round a sharp corner and we all lean awkwardly into each other. To my alarm, Sam has squashed up so closely that his face is now dangerously near my armpit.

Harriet smirks at me as we all reposition ourselves. 'I don't know, I've never been.'

'My grandma lived there,' I say, 'so I've spent a lot of my life visiting her. It has great food, and the people are really nice.'

'She was an artist,' Harriet says, her face lighting up. 'She lived in this huge house in the mountains and painted every day right up until she was . . . what was it, Zo? Ninety?'

'Ninety-one.'

'Wow,' Sam says, 'she sounds amazing.'

I smile, feeling a small pang behind my heart.

'Yeah,' I say, 'she really was.'

Chapter Thirty-Four

Angie

I lock my fingers together and place them on my lap as the jeep judders through the countryside. We're surrounded by green. Florets of tall trees are huddled together in packs on either side of the road. They skim past us in a blur. I haven't seen a single car on the road since we started driving.

Aldo is what I would describe as burly. He's tall and wide, with dark hair that is pulled into a low ponytail at the nape of his neck. He has a defined jaw and small dark eyes that have been squashed in concentration since we left Carsoli, but I'm not going to offer him my glasses. I've learnt from Fanny that that is the worst insult you can apparently give someone over the age of fifty.

The radio has been blaring out a mixture of Italian and English songs, providing the only sound between us. I'm quite grateful for it. My entire body is reeling.

They were right then, as it goes. Losing a parent does turn you back into a child. I haven't had a toddler tantrum since I was pregnant with Zoe (although I was tempted many times when I was being dragged backwards through the menopause), and now in less than a week, I've had two. Two! But they're different to usual tantrums; they don't leave you with the sense of relief you have when you swear at the door frame you've stubbed your toe on or mutter something cutting under your breath when another driver sidles in front of you as if you don't even exist. These tantrums are leaving me exhausted. All I want to do is go home and go to bed. I feel like a shell, and nobody seems to be listening to me.

'Oh, I like this one.' Aldo reaches forward to the radio and fiddles with one of the buttons until the Black Eyed Peas sing louder round the car, asking us where the love is.

I give him a small smile. 'Thank you so much for driving us.'

He nods. 'Sam said you were in trouble.'

I'm about to retort that we weren't in trouble; that my daughter and my friend were just too stubborn to admit defeat and go home, but I stop myself. I cannot have my third tantrum of this trip. But honestly, how Zoe ever got so stubborn is beyond me.

'It's really kind of you,' I say instead.

He glances over at me and then back to the road.

'What do you want to see in Sulmona? You'll be there for the markets.'

Despite myself, I smile. I love the markets. It became a little tradition of mine whenever I stayed with Mum. I'd get up early and get a taxi down the mountain. I loved watching the same people each week setting up their stalls. Fresh loaves and pastries, cheeses and wines. And so much confetti – the sugared almonds in the shape of bouquets of flowers. I'd pick up some coffee, fill my arms with whatever I could carry, and then return to Mum's to make breakfast.

'Your English is very good,' I say, swerving the question about Sulmona. I can't face the awkward sincerity of someone telling me how sorry they are for my loss. I can't bear it.

He smiles and cocks his head. 'My sister married an Englishman. So if I didn't learn, I would not be able to speak to my nephews or new brother.'

I hear Fanny bark a laugh from the back seat. I hope she's behaving herself back there.

'Your nephew is one of these boys?' I gesture behind me. 'Sorry, I didn't catch his name.' I was too busy royally throwing my toys out of the pram and trying to stop my head from flying off my shoulders.

'Harry.' He smiles. 'I love having him here. He and his friends want to explore Italy.'

'That sounds lovely.'

He raises his eyebrows at me, catching my tone. 'But not for you?'

'Oh,' I laugh and shake my head, 'I don't think so. I'm too old. I need to get back home. I've got responsibilities and things.'

He clicks his tongue. 'Too old? You're about forty-three.'

I snort. 'Add ten years!'

'Still younger than me, and look!' He briefly lets go of the steering wheel. 'I'm driving lovely ladies round Italy. *Exploring.*'

I laugh. 'That's a good point.'

We drift back into silence as the Black Eyed Peas peter out and Shania Twain rockets through the speakers.

He catches my eye and smiles. 'I don't think you have

responsibilities to get home to. I think they can wait. Nothing is that important.'

I flush. 'No, I do need to get back.'

He raises his eyebrows. 'Well, once you've seen to your responsibilities, you can come back to Carsoli and give me a call. I'll show you around.'

Fuck it.

I throw my arms in the air as it gets to the chorus. He laughs and shakes his shoulders too. It feels much better than another toddler tantrum.

For the moment, anyway.

Chapter Thirty-Five

Zoe

Harriet throws back her head and laughs as she triumphs against James in the final round of rock paper scissors and wins the last sip of his Diet Coke.

'What's Cornwall like then?' Sam says, turning to face me.

I push my sunglasses to the top of my head. 'Have you never been?'

He shakes his head. 'It's miles away for me. We flew from there as we were in Devon for a wedding, but I only saw the inside of the airport.'

We both look round as my mum's deep, earthy laugh sounds from the front of the car. I try to peer through the tinted back window, but I can't make much out. She's laughing, though, and that has to be a good sign.

'Where are you guys from?' I ask.

'Leeds.'

I nod, pleased to finally be able to place the accent in his low voice.

'Cornwall is nice,' I say. 'Really beautiful. It's such a lovely place to live.'

'Boring,' Harriet blurts. 'She means it's boring.'

I give Sam a look. 'It's somewhere people come for a holiday. Or people come back after living in London, for a quieter life. It's lovely, but there isn't that much to do.'

'Is that what you did?' He looks at me innocently, and I have to stop myself from snorting.

'Er, no,' I manage, 'no. I've always lived there. I've never moved away, apart from to go to uni, neither of us have.'

'How come?'

'Well, I—'

I break off as the jeep hits another pothole and suddenly the entire car starts to judder. Without quite meaning to, I grip onto Sam's hand, but he doesn't pull away.

'Shit,' James mutters, craning his neck to look at the back wheel. 'I think we've just popped a tyre. Harry!' he calls, banging on the back window. 'I think we've just popped a tyre!'

The car rolls to a stop and I quickly let go of Sam's hand.

'God, that really made me jump!' I laugh, trying to distract him from my awful damsel-in-distress impression. I stupidly look at Harriet, who is smirking. I'm not fooling anyone.

The driver's door opens and Aldo climbs out, muttering to himself in Italian. A second later, a red-faced Harry hops out to help, giving Sam a withering look on his way. Poor guy. God only knows what Aunt Fanny has been talking to him about for the past half an hour.

'What is it?' Sam asks, leaning over the side of the jeep. 'A flat?'

Harry nods, and my stomach turns over. Aldo is still muttering to himself in Italian, but from the speed and intensity of his words, I'm pretty sure he's swearing.

Mum and Aunt Fanny climb out of the car. 'Well,' Fanny says lightly, 'at least we know the roads are just as bad here as they are in England.'

Mum pushes her fingers through her hair. 'Oh no,' she mumbles. 'Aldo, I am so sorry.'

For a second, Aldo stops swearing; then, to my astonishment, he takes Mum's hand and *kisses it*.

'*Bella signora*,' he says in a low, gravelly voice. '*Non scusarti.*'

I stare open-mouthed as Mum lets out a high-pitched giggle and pulls her hand away.

Well! She's had a change of tune! Not looking so much like a serial killer now, is he?

'How far are we from Sulmona?' I ask, pulling out my phone to check the time. It's 11.30.

'It's just over there,' Harry says, pointing at the green hills in the distance. 'We're probably about ten minutes away by car.'

'So, like, an hour's walk?' I say, catching sight of Aunt Fanny's ridiculous shoes. 'Two?'

She follows my gaze and shoots me a look. 'I could run circles around you, missy.'

'How long do you think it will take to get the tyre fixed?' I ask Harry. He turns to Aldo and they start mumbling in quick Italian. He looks at me and shrugs.

'It's hard to say. He's got a friend who can help, but he'll be at work. It could be hours.'

My heart sinks. Hours?

'Are you in a hurry?' Harry adds, reading my expression, as Mum turns around and starts breathing deeply again.

'Yeah,' I say, 'a bit.'

'It sounds like this trip of yours is cursed,' Sam says.

'Please don't say that,' I mutter, eyeing Mum.

Harriet and I climb out of the jeep.

'Well, that's it then, we're going to miss our flight!' Mum suddenly cries. 'There is no way we'll be able to get there in time now.'

Sam passes me Harriet's bag and I smile gratefully.

'Mum, it's okay. We'll work something out.'

Even as I say it, I know I'm lying.

'We need to get home!' she says. 'Three days, that was the deal; we'd be here for three days and that was it!'

She stops abruptly, as though suddenly remembering that we've got company.

'Aldo, thank you so much for your kindness,' she says.

'I think we'd better start walking,' I mutter to Sam, who jumps off the jeep to face me. 'Thank you for everything.'

'Will she be okay?' He gestures to Mum, who has started squabbling with Aunt Fanny.

I shrug. 'Have a great time travelling. And if you end up stripping, make sure they tip well.'

I hold up a hand in a goodbye, but he pulls me into a hug. For a moment, I sink into his firm chest, the smell of suncream and his earthy aftershave filling my nose.

'It was great meeting you,' I say when he finally lets me go.

The assured smile is back. 'Don't go throwing drinks on anyone else, okay?'

I smile. 'Deal.'

'It was great meeting *you*, Helga.'

I pull a face at him, and he laughs, giving my hand a squeeze.

'Right!' Aunt Fanny calls, making me jump. 'Let's walk and have a breakdown, shall we? Come on! Is it this direction, Aldo?' she calls over her shoulder as she links her arm in Mum's and starts dragging her down the road.

Aldo nods and points. '*Ciao, bella!*'

I start to turn away from Sam, but he grabs my arm and hands me his phone.

'Put your number in, just in case my travels ever take me to Cornwall and I need a lift.'

'I don't have a jeep, I'm afraid.'

'I can get over that.'

I feel my cheeks pinch as I jab my number in; then, giving Sam a final smile, I turn away and fold my arm into Harriet's. As we set off after Mum and Aunt Fanny, I feel a bit like I've left more than my only mode of transport behind.

CHAPTER THIRTY-SIX

ZOE

'What do we think about hitch-hiking then?' Aunt Fanny asks, lolloping an arm with her thumb in the air towards the road as a lorry skirts past.

'Don't be absurd,' Mum hisses. Next to me, I feel Harriet flinch.

We've been walking for about twenty minutes, and although Sam and the jeep have faded into nothing more than a speck, it feels like we've been powering through on a treadmill, with the same scenery rolling past, trying to fool us into thinking we're making progress when really all we're doing is stamping uselessly on the spot.

Mum gave in and carried on walking, but I think that was mainly thanks to us having literally no other option. Whether she likes it or not – and she's certainly made it clear that it's the latter – we have to walk in the direction of Grandma's house.

'Well, you quite liked the last fella we hitched a ride with,' Aunt Fanny continues airily. 'He turned out to be not so bad.' She gives Mum a cheeky grin, but Mum keeps staring ahead. Her frown doesn't move an inch.

Harriet shifts her backpack further onto her shoulders and sighs.

'Do you want me to carry it for a bit?' I ask.

She shakes her head. 'No, I'm fine. It's just a bit hot.'

'Okay. Let me know if you change your mind.'

'You think this is hard for you? What about me?' Aunt Fanny says.

'Well, nobody asked you to wear those stupid shoes,' I say, glancing down at her towering stilettos.

'Who said anything about my shoes?'

'Is it your age then?' I grin.

She turns around and slaps my arm. 'No.'

'What is it then?'

She doesn't answer, and we drift into silence, until suddenly she throws her arms in the air in excitement. 'Shall we play a game?' She swings round to face me and Harriet, who are trailing behind.

Harriet grins. 'Go on then.'

Aunt Fanny winks. 'So it's a take on "I can see the sea". First one to spot Clarice's house.'

'Well, that's not fair!' Harriet laughs. 'I don't know what her house looks like!'

'You can be on my team,' I say.

'It doesn't matter. Nobody will beat Ange at this,' Aunt Fanny says, giving Mum a nudge. She ignores her and we all fall into silence.

'How does it feel to be back?' she presses on, her voice softer.

'I told you, I don't want to talk about it,' Mum says, but this time she doesn't sound angry, just tired. 'Stop asking me questions.'

'You need to talk about your feelings, Ange.'

But Mum ignores her, focusing solely on putting one foot in front of the other.

Aunt Fanny pulls out her phone and scowls down at the screen.

'We're walking in the right direction, I think . . .'

I peer over her shoulder at the arrow on Google Maps, which is angling to the right as though we're all walking sideways.

'Yeah, it sometimes does that. I'm not sure—'

But I break off as a call buzzes through.

It only lasts a second before she hurriedly switches it off, though not before I catch the name.

Jon.

That's the second time he's rung her today. He's meant to be her partner. Why is she rejecting his calls?

'You can answer,' I say lightly. 'I don't mind.'

'What?' Aunt Fanny's head snaps up, a startled look on her face.

'Jon.' I nod towards her phone. 'If you want to speak to him, I don't mind.' I stop myself from adding: *You know, Jon, your partner? The one you left us for?*

I feel myself blush as Aunt Fanny looks back at me as though I've caught her doing something private.

'It won't be important,' she says, stuffing her phone into her bag. She looks around, then suddenly takes a sharp left and hooks one leg over a wooden gate, hopping over and miraculously landing on her towering heels like she's just performed a backflip at the Olympics.

'Right!' she says. 'This won't take long, just a quick detour. This way, ladies.'

We all stagger to a halt.

'What?' I say. 'Why? We don't have time for a detour. We need to keep moving.'

She gives me a challenging look.

'This is important, Zo. Come on. It'll take ten minutes. Fifteen tops.'

Harriet gives in first, shrugging limply and swinging one long leg after the other over the gate. I turn to Mum, but she gives me a defeatist look and follows Harriet.

'Are we meeting someone here?' I ask, landing on the other side with a thud.

Aunt Fanny's eyes are fixed ahead. She hoists her bag further up her shoulder and snaps her fingers at us.

'This way. We're going for a walk.'

Chapter Thirty-Seven

Fanny

For the second time this week, I am sweating. Pools of it are gathering under my arms and making my forehead prickle. I don't like it one bit. It's not demure to sweat. I'm sure Coco Chanel never did.

One thing's for sure, I'm back leading the pack. It's the one part of our old dynamic that I've slipped back into. Every time I look at Angie, I see less of her there, but she's getting closer to sticking her middle finger up at me and telling the world to go fuck itself. So that's something.

But my legs are aching. My heart is throbbing under my ribcage and my muscles are screaming for a break.

Zoe was right when she said I couldn't walk this far.

But I've never been a quitter. Not unless I've had to be. And I'm sure as hell not going to start now.

It's incredible how far anger can take you.

Chapter Thirty-Eight

Zoe

Aunt Fanny's iPhone is now firmly tucked inside her bag, and she's striding through the field like a bloodhound fresh on the scent of a fox. How she's marching up this hill so quickly is beyond me. I mean, I'm sure the Grand Old Duke of York wasn't wearing four-inch heels.

Shortly after hopping over the gate, we started to climb a steep incline. I'm trying to ignore the niggling fear of *why* there was a gate. Are we about to come face to face with a goat? Or worse, a bear? Or what about an angry farmer with a shotgun? It's one thing to question my ability to outrun a bear (very unlikely), but there is absolutely no way I could outrun a *bullet*.

All of a sudden, Aunt Fanny disappears over the top of the hill.

Harriet, who has powered ahead, disappears moments after her.

I take the opportunity and give Mum's arm a squeeze. 'Are you okay?'

I wait for her usual chirpy reply, but she just sighs. 'I'm tired, Zo. I want to go home.'

'Nearly there, ladies!' Fanny shouts, her Scouse accent echoing through the trees. I hear the scampering of an animal nearby and flinch.

I heave myself up the final part of the hill, tugging Mum behind me, my hand digging into the crook of her moist elbow. As we reach the top, Aunt Fanny's arms are spread like the proud ringleader of a circus.

I let go of Mum and look around. Aunt Fanny has brought us to the top of a hill. I try not to gape at her. This is why she's detoured us and wasted even more time? For a nice view?

'What are we doing here?' I demand.

She marches over to us, taking us both by the arm and placing us on either side of her. She gestures at Harriet to stand next to me.

'Right. I think we've all got some emotion that we need to get rid of.'

My eyes widen. Is she about to launch into a t'ai chi session? We really don't have time for this!

'So we're going to let it out,' she continues. She takes a deep breath and closes her eyes. I try not to gawp at her as she stands there and breathes, her chest rising and falling rhythmically, her skinny arms hanging by her side.

What on earth is she doing? Is this what she wants us to do? Just stand here and breathe? We could have breathed while we were walking! Why did we need to—

'ARGHHHHHHHHHH!'

I almost jump out of my skin as she lets out an enormous yell. With her eyes still clamped shut, she bellows until all the breath in her lungs has been used up and she peters off like a balloon that's run out of air.

I stare at her, flabbergasted.

'What the hell was that?' I blurt before I can stop myself.

'See,' she says, ignoring me as she takes another deep breath. 'This is what we need. To let it out.'

'You want us to stand here and yell into the air?' I say dubiously.

'Not just into the air,' she replies. 'At life, the universe, whatever. Life isn't always fair, Zo. We're allowed to be mad about it. Go on,' she says when I don't reply. 'I know you're angry. You have a right to be. Let it out.'

I stare at her, watching her breathe as though she's in a deep meditation. I try and catch Mum's eyes to confirm that Aunt Fanny is crazy, but to my surprise, her eyes are also shut.

Following suit, I close my eyes and take a deep breath. As I try to search my mind, another scream rings out next to me. My eyes snap open as Harriet's head launches backwards, her mouth opening wide so she can yell at the sky.

When she breaks off, she takes a deep breath and sits on the floor. I look down at her, worried that she might be crying, but she's hiding her face.

I close my eyes again. What am I angry about?

I'm angry at Aunt Fanny for showing up as though nothing ever happened. For not apologising to Mum. For acting as though nothing has changed between us, as though she didn't completely turn our lives upside down and leave without so much as a word of explanation. I'm angry at Mum for not confronting her; for letting her get away with it and allowing her to just slot back into our lives. I'm angry at Mum for never sticking up for herself and letting Uncle Reggie walk all over her. I'm angry that she won't talk to me and tell me how she's really feeling. That she won't let me in. I'm angry at Uncle Reggie for the way he has always treated us. I'm angry that Harriet and I have never been able to go travelling and I constantly feel like I'm waiting for my life to start. I'm angry at the universe for making it so difficult to get here. I'm angry at my grandma for dying and leaving us. I'm angry.

As each new thought comes into my mind, anger bubbles up inside me like fire, ripping through my body until I can't contain it any more. I open my mouth and a scream comes out. Once it starts, I can't stop it. It's as though the anger I have pushed down inside is finally being set free. Eventually I break off and gasp for air. I open my eyes, suddenly feeling self-conscious, but Aunt Fanny reaches for my hand and grabs it fiercely, and I close them again.

Her hand is gripped onto mine and I firmly clasp her back. She's not going to let me go.

'Your turn, Ange.'

Mum stays silent, and a cold feeling of panic starts to curl up inside me. But then a low, harrowing roar echoes across the hills. My eyes snap open to see Mum, bent in two, bellowing at the wind, the deafening sound storming from the pit of her stomach and into the sky. She screams the longest. When she runs out of air, she sucks in another lungful and yells again, as though desperate not to stop. The longer she yells, the more painful the sound becomes, until eventually sobs take over and we wrap our arms around her, her shoulders heaving as Aunt Fanny grips onto her tightly. Eventually her breathing slows to its normal pace and Aunt Fanny lets her go, her wet face shining as she looks at us all fiercely.

'You have to let it out.'

Chapter Thirty-Nine

Zoe

'Left, left, I had a good job but I left. I left the job because I thought it was right. LEFT, RIGHT, LEFT, RIGHT, LEFT.'

Aunt Fanny has been parping endless hideous songs about walking for the past twenty minutes. After five minutes of lying in the sun to recuperate from screaming our lungs out, she sprang into action and demanded that we start walking again.

'LEFT, RIGHT, LEFT, RIGHT!'

She's taking the role a little too seriously for my liking.

Harriet, on the other hand, is loving it, and has been marching next to her like her second in command, leaving me and Mum trailing behind.

'I lied to your uncle earlier, Zo.' Mum glances towards Aunt Fanny and Harriet to make sure they aren't in earshot, her small voice breaking through the monotonous chanting.

'What do you mean? No you didn't. When?'

She sighs. 'He called me again when we were in the car and asked where we were. He said that he was worried that you hadn't messaged him back.'

Damn.

'And you lied?'

'Not about that. I told him that we were going to Grandma's.'

My heart drops. 'What did he say?'

'He said he was on his way over for the auction anyway so would see us there.'

I nod, looking at the back of Aunt Fanny's glossy blonde head.

Well that's that then. He knows.

'He asked if Fanny was with us. He said he thought he'd heard her voice down the phone earlier.'

For a reason I can't place, I feel a stab of fear.

'I told him she wasn't,' Mum continues.

I pause. Mum never lies, and she always refuses to admit that there could be anything wrong whatsoever with Uncle Reggie. She never sees the need to lie to him.

'It's nice to have her back,' she whispers. 'If I told him the truth, he'd be angry, so angry, and would make her go away. I like having her here, Zo. I've missed her.'

I stare at her, flabbergasted. 'But . . .' I scramble around for the right words, 'aren't you angry with her? For leaving and then just coming back like nothing happened?'

Mum doesn't say anything, and the heat inside me rises.

'How can you not be angry with her?'

She pushes her hair off her face, and I can almost see my question floating above her head, as though she's decided that it's one she doesn't want to hear.

'Well,' I shrug glumly, 'I guess he'll find out when he gets here.'

Mum tucks her hand into the crook of my elbow just as Aunt Fanny swings around, grinning madly at us.

'I can see her house!' she cries, gesturing wildly towards the mountain. Sure enough, Grandma's white house is smiling down at us. 'I win! Ha ha! Drinks are on you, Ange!'

I feel Mum's grip tighten on my arm.

'We'll deal with that when we have to,' she says quietly. 'I'm just not ready to let her go again yet.'

My heart turns over.

'No,' I say. Fanny's laugh roars through the sky as she jostles with Harriet. 'I don't think I am either.'

Chapter Forty

Harriet

I actually felt a lot better after screaming into the sky. It took me by surprise. I didn't realise I had so much emotion stored inside me. But once I started, I couldn't stop, and I was able to fire out all the emotions that I'm so ashamed of feeling.

I'm angry at my mum for starting a new family without me. I'm angry that I'm not enough for her. I'm angry at myself for being such a loser and having absolutely no direction or idea what I'm going to do with my life. I'm angry that in a day or two I'll be back in my childhood bedroom, back at square one. I'm angry that I haven't got it all figured out yet. I'm angry that it feels like I'm running out of time.

Now that we've all yelled out our feelings, everyone's head is a little lower on their shoulders. It's like the effort of throwing the anger away has drained us. Angie screamed the loudest; it was quite terrifying, actually. I've never heard her so much as raise her voice before this trip, but now she's like a different woman. My own screaming gave me relief for about four seconds, and then the guilt seeped in. What do I really have to be angry about? Nothing. All that's bothering me is the fact that I need to grow up and I don't want to. Or rather, I have no idea how. I don't know which is worse.

Now I'm at the back of the pack, walking with Zoe. Ange and Fanny are slightly ahead, but we're all silent now, apart from the odd shriek from Fanny when she spots a bird or something she finds exciting. None of us really has that much energy left.

One thing is for sure, Zoe wasn't joking when she said Sulmona was beautiful. It's still in the distance, but I can't stop staring at the mountains. I really do feel a million miles away from home. From Mum and Darren and my baby brother.

I glance down at my phone. Mum sent me a photo of Dániel earlier, but that's all the contact we've had today. She hasn't worked out I've gone yet, or if she has, she hasn't asked where I am.

'Shit, Zoe.' I prod her in the arm as I spot an aqueduct. 'Is this it? Are we here?'

I glance at her, and the light behind her eyes brightens. 'Yeah,' she breathes. 'This is Sulmona.'

Chapter Forty-One

Zoe

My feet burn as I drop into a plastic seat, my back throbbing and Mum's thin shirt sticking to my skin.

I would never normally walk across Italy in the middle of summer in *trainers*. My feet are so swollen and hot I'd be amazed if I'm ever able to take my shoes off. Although the smell is probably so intense they might peel themselves off my feet in disgust and be done with it.

I packed cotton shorts and loose T-shirts and cute summer dresses for this trip. I packed sandals!

'Gelato?'

I peel open an eye and look at Harriet, who is twisting her long hair into a bun on top of her head. Her pale face is screaming under a new layer of freckles and her cheeks are flaring pink.

'You need some suncream,' I say.

She touches a cheek with the back of her hand. 'Mine ran out and we left lover boy and his supply behind.'

I close my eyes again. 'Don't call him that.'

'What's that?' Mum pipes up.

'Nothing.'

'Oh gosh, Harriet, you have caught the sun!' she coos. 'We need to get you some suncream.'

I hear Harriet's chair scrape back. 'I'll pop to the shop and get some. Can someone order me a chocolate gelato?'

'Only if you say it in Italian,' Aunt Fanny quips.

Harriet laughs. '*Cioccolato, per favore.*'

Aunt Fanny nods. '*Prego, prego.*'

The smell of cigarette smoke floats under my nose and I open my eyes. Fanny hooks one leg over the other and flicks the packet towards Mum, who shakes her head.

We've finally arrived in Sulmona, the town where Grandma spent the second half of her life. The sun is a glow of white light, smiling down at everyone walking through the streets. The buildings are tall and smooth, made out of a sandy-coloured stone, with slim windows framed by pebble-grey shutters.

The ground is a sea of stones placed in a half-moon pattern, and in front of our café seats, a steeple stretches towards the bright blue sky. But my favourite part is the confetti: sugared almonds in every colour, arranged like bouquets of flowers. They pop and burst out of every shop window and street corner. As I turn my face towards the sun, it is impossible not to think of Grandma. It really is no wonder that she loved living here. It is the personification of her.

She spent so much time cooped up in her house, furiously painting, that when she came down into the town, she'd act like she'd been set free. She'd insist that we go into every shop, and chat to people queuing for coffee. We'd get gelato and sit by the fountain, and she'd close her eyes and turn her face towards the sun. It was as though every time she came here, it was the first time she'd ever seen it. I was always so jealous of her unquenchable thirst for life. Everything was an adventure in her eyes. Whether it be chatting to a couple at the fountain in the piazza about the baby they were expecting, or sneaking off to buy us shots of limoncello at eleven in the morning. She'd laugh her head off at my mum's look of horror, and threaten to drink all three herself, and since she was wobbly on her walking stick as it was, she knew that would be enough for us to snatch them off her.

'What time is it, Ange?' Aunt Fanny asks lazily. Her question pulls me out of my thoughts, and my stomach clenches as I wait for Mum to answer.

I know that it's late, far later than we were supposed to arrive. It ended up taking us about two hours to walk here, so I know we're way behind schedule, but I've been enjoying bathing in the bliss of ignorance.

'It's five o'clock.' I feel my stomach sink.

Mum catches my expression. 'Are you okay, Zo? I'm sure we'll still make our flight. Or, I can see if there is a later one we can catch instead. It just means we'll have to leave quite early tomorrow morning.'

'Leave?' Aunt Fanny repeats. 'We've only just got here!'

I force a smile, trying to conjure up the feeling of calm that I was cradling moments before.

'It's fine,' I say, breathing deeply. 'I have an event at work to get back for, that's all. I'll call Kitty and sort something out.'

'An event?' Aunt Fanny questions. 'What kind of event?'

'Hello, ladies, what can I get you?'

I look round as a waitress appears, her English carried by her thick Italian accent. She has an apron tied around her middle, and her dark hair is long and sleek. Aunt Fanny smiles at her, showing off her dazzling white teeth.

'Please can we have four gelatos, two chocolate, two caramel, and four coffees?'

The waitress nods and ducks back into the café, and Aunt Fanny turns back to face me, waiting for me to answer.

I have told her this at least four times since we left Cornwall, but the woman has the attention span of an olive.

'It's a wedding for work,' I explain. 'I had to pitch for it. It's always between me and my colleague, and whoever wins it works with the client and gets the commission.'

She raises her eyebrows, looking vaguely impressed. 'Blimey, and you're going to miss the wedding?'

I force a laugh. 'Well, hopefully not.'

'Would you like some coaching on how to pitch?' she asks, sitting up straighter in her seat. 'I once pitched my way out of a parking ticket.'

'That's not what pitching is.'

'It is if you're doing it properly.'

Harriet reappears and drops back into her seat. She flicks open the lid of her new suncream and starts slathering it onto her pale skin. 'So, are we nearly there?' she asks.

Mum smiles, looking at our surroundings. For the first time since we left Cornwall, her smile seems genuine, as though she's happy at being back here.

'Oh yes. Her house is just over there.' She leans forward and points towards the mountain, where houses are dotted between the trees.

'Wow,' Harriet muses, following Mum's gaze. 'I love that your grandma lived up a mountain,' she adds, turning to me. 'Did she, like, sing to goats?'

'More like bears,' mutters Mum as the waitress reappears with our coffees and gelato.

I roll my eyes and then realise she's serious. 'Bears?' I repeat, my voice going up an octave. 'I always thought Grandma was joking about the bears.'

'Oh no, love,' Mum says lightly. 'There are lots of them in this part of Italy. And wolves. To be honest, I'm amazed we didn't bump into any while we were walking.'

Well, thank God I didn't know that when we were marching through the fields.

'Yes,' she continues, cradling her coffee cup in her hands, 'I'd say it's about an hour's walk from here up to Grandma's house. We've come at a good time, you know,' she adds. 'If I remember correctly, it's market day tomorrow, and they're always gorgeous.'

'So if we get a move on, we'll be there before the sun goes down!' I say excitedly, picking up my gelato and spooning a creamy scoop of chocolate into my mouth. I jostle Harriet. 'Come on,' I joke, 'get that coffee down you, then we can get going!'

'No, Zoe. We'll stay here tonight and go first thing tomorrow.'

I look round at Aunt Fanny. Her sunglasses are hiding her eyes, so I can't read her expression.

'But why?' I say. 'We're so close, and it would be much better to stay at Grandma's than in a random hotel.'

'I've already booked something.'

I feel a dart of annoyance. 'Why did you do that without checking with us?'

'Because I'm tired.' She says it firmly, taking a long sip of her coffee. There is no laughter in her voice.

Harriet gives me a look. 'I mean, if we're not in so much of a hurry, we may as well enjoy ourselves,' she says, stretching her legs out in front of her.

'Well, we are in a bit of a hurry,' I mutter. 'We need to get there before the auction.'

'When's that again?'

'Tuesday.'

'We'll be long gone by then,' Aunt Fanny says breezily, and Mum gives me a reassuring nod.

My stomach turns over at the thought of not being home by Tuesday, sitting at my desk opposite Kitty.

'Your boss is okay with you having time off, right?' Mum says.

I nod into my coffee. If I told her I was planning to call in sick, she'd give me a lecture so vicious I'd be panicked into ringing Heidi up and telling her all my secrets.

'What about your job, Harriet?' Mum asks as I pull out my phone to update Kitty.

'Oh, I quit my job.' Harriet grins. 'I was hoping this would happen. Not that the trip would go a bit wrong,' she adds as I shoot her a look. 'But, you know, that we'd get a bit more of a holiday. Me and Zo haven't been on holiday in years.'

'We went to Newquay last year,' I respond defensively.

'That doesn't count!'

I laugh and unlock my phone, and a message from an unknown number pops up on the screen.

So, we finally managed to get Aldo's car sorted and have decided to check out Sulmona for ourselves. Anything you recommend?

My heart lifts. It must be Sam. I know I gave him my number, but I wasn't expecting—

'What? What's happened?'

I jump as Harriet leans over my shoulder to peer at my phone. I'm too slow to snatch it away, and her eyes gleam at me.

'Oh my God!' she squeals. 'Weasley!'

'Stop calling him that!' I say. 'His name is Sam.'

'Sam?'

I look round at Mum and Aunt Fanny, who are both blinking at me.

Oh great.

'The guy who helped us get here,' Harriet babbles, singing like a canary as she always does. 'He and Zoe fancy each other, and now he's messaged her saying that he's coming to Sulmona to see her.'

'He did *not* say that!' I say crossly, as Mum and Aunt Fanny exchange looks as though we're about to re-enact the opening scene of *Mamma Mia*.

'Well, what are you going to say back?' Harriet says, practically bouncing on her seat with excitement.

'Nothing.' I pause. 'Well, not with all of you sitting here staring at me,' I add before I can stop myself.

Aunt Fanny sticks out her chest indignantly. 'I think you'll find, Zoe, that I am very good with men.'

'That's what I'm afraid of.'

'Oh, charming.'

'Oh, go on, Zoe,' Mum chimes in unexpectedly. 'He was such a nice boy.'

I stare at her. I can practically hear the undertones of *Shall I buy a hat?*

'Look,' Harriet says, and to my horror, she snatches the phone from my hands and unlocks it with ease.

Urgh! Curse Past Me for giving her my password. This is exactly the type of cyber attack I was afraid of!

'He's asking what he can do here. He obviously wants to see you.' She turns in her seat, pointing her ice cream spoon at me. 'You're replying, and you're going on a date with this guy.'

'Do I get a say in this?'

'No,' they all chorus.

'Well,' Mum adds, 'unless you really don't want to, darling.'

'Of course she wants to!' Harriet cries, as I grab the phone back off her. 'We just need to think of a good reply.'

'I can reply by myself,' I say, my face hot.

Aunt Fanny snorts and then quickly composes herself. 'Sorry, sweetheart, I thought you were joking.'

Great.

'Just say "Hello, handsome, do you fancy a drink tonight?"' Aunt Fanny says matter-of-factly.

I shrivel with embarrassment. I absolutely cannot say *hello, handsome*. I'm not Cilla Black.

'No.'

'Oh!' Mum pipes up. 'Why don't you start with, "Hello, Mr Samuel"?'

I gape at her in horror. *Hello, Mr Samuel?* What is wrong with her?

'That makes me sound like a sex pest.'

'Zoe!' she gasps. 'Don't say that! We're in a café.'

I blink at her.

221

'Just say, Hello, would you like a cheeky drink with me tonight? I know a great place for cocktails, winky face.'

I look at Aunt Fanny, unsure of how many euphemisms she's trying to slip in there.

'Nobody says cheeky any more,' I mutter.

Right next to my ear, Mum begins to parp up again.

'How about, "Hello there you, what's a handsome thing like you doing tonight?"'

My eyes snap up to gawp at her.

What is the matter with her?

'Absolutely not.'

'Look,' Harriet says, 'just say something like "I know a great place for a drink. I'll meet you at eight p.m. by the fountain."'

'Oh!' Aunt Fanny leans towards Mum and slaps her arm. 'Angie, what's that place called where you used to go with Gio?'

I turn to Mum. 'Who's Gio?'

She blushes into her coffee. 'Nobody.'

'He was this gorgeous Italian man who used to take your mum out every time we were here. If you know what I mean.'

'Fanny!' Mum cries.

Aunt Fanny gives me an exaggerated wink, and I stare at her in disgust.

'Please don't wink at me like that,' I mutter.

'He once took you to that vineyard,' she carries on, leaning forward. 'Do you remember? God, it was so romantic. Reggie had pissed off back to the UK and I spent the whole day just waiting for you to come home so I could hear all about it.'

'He was very nice,' Mum reflects.

'Let's give him a call!' Aunt Fanny says, suddenly gripped by the idea. 'I bet he still lives around here.'

Mum shakes her head. 'I don't have his number any more. He's probably married now anyway, and even if he's not there's no way he'd want to see me like this.' She gives a little laugh.

Aunt Fanny pulls out her phone. 'Well maybe not right now, but once you've had a shower and a blow-dry, you'll knock his socks off. I bet I can find him on Facebook. The only thing that ages you is those *glasses,* which I wish you'd just chuck or let me buy you some new ones at the very least.'

'I need them to see!' Mum protests.

'Oh pfft.' Fanny waves an arm dismissively. 'I haven't been able to read a number plate for years. Nobody cares about that stuff any more, Ange.'

Harriet gestures down at my phone, where Sam's message is still staring up at us.

'Go on, reply to him,' she urges. 'What's the worst that can happen? If it all goes terribly, you'll never see him again anyway. It'll just be one night of fun.'

I shrug, trying to ignore Mum and Aunt Fanny, who are now giggling together and peering at Aunt Fanny's phone.

'Okay,' I say, tapping a message back to Sam. 'I've sent it.'

CHAPTER FORTY-TWO

ANGIE

I take a sip of wine and lean back in my chair. The four of us have barrelled into Zoe and Harriet's room. Zoe is sitting on the bed, with Harriet behind her with a pair of hair straighteners and Fanny in front holding various shades of glitter up for her approval. Each seems more offensive than the previous one in Zoe's eyes; she has asked for a simple cat-eye black eyeliner, but Fanny is having none of it. If Zoe leaves the room without a pair of Fanny's false eyelashes, I'll be amazed.

So after all that, we made it to Sulmona, and I have to admit, it is nice to be back. Wonderful, even. Now that I'm here, I can't imagine why Mum would be cursing this trip. She loved it here; it carries her spirit. But I'd be lying if I said that when Aldo's car broke down and I realised we'd have to *walk*, if a bear had strolled round the corner I'd have gladly lain down and let it eat me.

But we have made it, and I can see how much it means to Zoe. She and Harriet have been whispering and giggling together all day, with Fanny demanding to be let in on the joke like she too is twenty-five and about to go on a date. Zoe hasn't been this way around me for years, and Fanny hasn't been here at all.

It's nice. I almost feel happy.

Almost.

'Aunt Fanny, *no!*'

I smile into my wine as Fanny brandishes a peach-coloured blusher in Zoe's face.

'Don't you turn your nose up at Estée Lauder, young lady!'

It's funny, I'd have never expected to get on with Fanny like I did. Reggie and I always had a . . . shall we say *stilted* relationship. We were never close. So when he introduced his tall, leggy girlfriend with her sharp tongue, I thought, *Ah, of course he's ended up with someone like you. Someone so different to me.* But Fanny never even noticed we were different, or if she did, she refused to acknowledge it. She rejected any attempt I made to be shy or formal, and barged her way into my life until we became best friends. I never felt I had a real brother in Reggie, but suddenly I had a sister.

'I just want to look natural,' Zoe pleads. 'Look, it's fine. I'll do my make-up myself.'

'No!' Fanny says at once, and I try not to laugh at the desperation in her voice. 'Please, Zo. Just trust me. I know what I'm doing. I'll tone it down. No more blusher, see?' She chucks it back in her make-up bag, looking like she's cast aside a dear friend.

'You look great, Zoe,' I say. 'Sam won't know what's hit him.'

'And if he doesn't say you look gorgeous, then *I* will hit him,' Fanny says at once. Harriet giggles, and Zoe rolls her eyes, but she's smiling.

'This is so fun,' Harriet says. 'Did you used to do this together when you were younger?'

'We'd be doing it now if I had anything to do with it.' Fanny shoots me a look and I stick my tongue out at her.

'Yeah,' I say. 'Fanny was always in charge of getting me ready for my dates.'

'Did you go on many in Sulmona?' Harriet asks.

'Oh, *loads*,' teases Fanny.

I reach forward and flick her, and the girls laugh.

'You should go to that little wine bar tonight,' I say, cradling my glass. 'It's really tiny and about a five-minute walk from the fountain. Do you know the one I'm talking about?'

Zoe peels open an eye. 'The one we used to go to with Grandma?'

I nod. 'A lady called Valentina runs it with her husband. Or they used to. I assume they're still there.'

She nods. 'Okay, cool. We'll go there.'

She looks at me and I smile. 'Your grandma would absolutely love that.'

Chapter Forty-Three

Zoe

It's later that evening, and I have squeezed myself into one of Harriet's summer dresses. After about ten minutes of constant berating and a solemn promise that she wouldn't make me look like I was about to appear on *Strictly Come Dancing*, I let Aunt Fanny do my make-up. She tutted and rolled her eyes at me a lot, but she did stick to her word. She's dusted my cheeks with pale pink and dotted some serum under my eyebrows so that they glisten in the light. She swept a light layer of eyeshadow across my eyes and managed to negotiate my eyelashes into a smooth fan. Harriet was in charge of my hair, attacking it with her straighteners so that it now falls down my back in a shimmering sheet, and my mum spent the entire time regaling me with stories of Grandma and Sulmona, giving me all the recommendations of where she used to go.

And the entire time I've been sitting here, I've felt relaxed.

A warm balloon has been stretching in the pit of my stomach. This is the sort of thing we used to do all the time. Aunt Fanny was the person who taught me how to put on eyeliner. Mum was there too, but she spent the whole time squealing and hiding her face, as she's weirdly squeamish about eyeballs. Every time Fanny got near my eyes, they would water like Niagara and we'd have to start again. Eventually I'd get the giggles, and we'd all give up and order pizza.

Now we're sitting in the hotel room that Aunt Fanny booked for me and Harriet. It's a small room, with magnolia walls and a sprig of fake flowers in a large vase on the windowsill.

'Your grandma would have loved to be here right now,' Mum sighs. 'To see you going on a date in her town. She loved love.'

I smile sadly. 'I know.'

'Oh, she'd be your tour guide!' Aunt Fanny cries, snapping open a pale pink lipstick. 'She'd want to take you both to all her favourite places.'

'Did you know her well?' Harriet asks. 'Zoe's grandma?'

'Clarice? Oh God, yes, I loved the woman.'

'Fanny was here almost as much as we were. Until she . . . Well, until she split with Reg.' Small patches of pink form on Mum's cheeks, and an awkward silence settles over us.

'Right,' Aunt Fanny says, breaking the silence. 'I think you're ready.'

I take Mum's hand and get to my feet. Harriet steps back and ushers me towards a mirror. I feel my face scrunch up in anticipation. I absolutely hate looking at my reflection, and usually just dust a bit of powder and smear some lip balm on before stuffing my feet into my trainers and leaving for work.

'Stand up straight,' Aunt Fanny says, pushing back my shoulders and tapping under my chin. 'Belly button to spine, shoulders back, chest out.'

'Tits and teeth,' Mum quips, and then immediately flames red as Harriet roars with laughter. 'Sorry,' she says quickly, giggling as she catches Aunt Fanny's eye. 'That's something me and Fanny used to say to each other.'

'It's what the showgirls say,' Aunt Fanny says.

'Were you a showgirl?' Harriet asks, wide-eyed.

Fanny gives her a knowing look. 'Not in the professional sense.'

I don't want to know what that means.

'We used to do this all the time,' she says, leaning back on the bed. 'I'd get your mum ready for a date and then sit at home by myself waiting to hear all the gossip.'

'Where was Uncle Reggie?'

She looks at me from the corner of her eye. 'Good question.'

'I didn't leave you all night!' Mum protests as she starts tidying up around us.

'No, as soon as I heard the code word, I would be down like a shot.' Fanny grins at us. 'Not that I was hoping your dates would go badly, Ange,' she adds.

Mum scoffs, but she is smiling.

'We have a code word too!' Harriet says happily. 'It's "pineapple".'

'Pineapple!' Aunt Fanny laughs. 'How on earth are you supposed to slip that subtly into a sentence?'

'We have WhatsApp now.' I grin. 'We didn't have to contact each other via smoke signals like you.'

Aunt Fanny tries to thwack me, but I dart out of the way. 'Cheeky sod.'

Mum's face softens. 'Ours was "dinner plans".'

'But you didn't have mobiles, did you?' Harriet asks.

Mum taps her nose. 'Fanny was always very protective of me, so she'd call the bar after an hour. If it was going badly, I'd tell her that I had dinner plans, and then she'd arrive to rescue me.'

Aunt Fanny holds up her arms in a 'tah-dah' motion and Harriet laughs.

'Anyway, missus,' she points a make-up brush at me, 'you need to hurry up or you'll be late.' She takes a moment to peer at me. 'And you're sure you don't want the red lipstick?'

'Positive. It'll only end up on my teeth.'

'Have a great time,' Mum beams, as Aunt Fanny gets to her feet and hooks an arm around her shoulders. 'Do you want us to walk you to the fountain?'

I smile, picking up Harriet's clutch bag. 'I think I'll be okay. Don't wait up for me.'

'Oh,' Aunt Fanny says, placing a hand on her hip and flashing me a wink, 'we absolutely will.'

Chapter Forty-Four

Harriet

I lean back on the bed and pick up the remote. An Italian soap opera fills the screen, with a man with a half-open white shirt screaming into the wind. Fanny catches sight of him and laughs.

'God, Ange, look at this,' she calls to Angie, who appears from the bathroom.

'What?' Angie says, glancing around.

'This could be an exact moment from thirty years ago.' Fanny gestures to me. 'I used to do exactly this,' she smiles. 'Sit on the bed and watch crappy Italian TV while Angie was out on her dates.'

Angie scoffs. 'Oh please! My *dates*. I hardly went on any.'

'You went on a lot with Gio,' Fanny quips, giving me a wink.

I smile, leaning up on my elbows. 'Did you find him on Facebook?' I ask.

She pulls a rueful face. 'Yes,' she sighs. 'He's married. Worse luck.'

'Oh, that's a shame,' I say.

Fanny swivels and points a hairbrush at Angie. 'But *Aldo* isn't married, is he, Ange? I swear these Italian men can't get enough of you.'

Angie shakes her head, her cheeks pink. 'Honestly,' she mutters.

'We just need to find one for me and you, Harriet, and then we can all date together,' Fanny says matter-of-factly. 'You quite liked that James boy, didn't you? I guess that leaves me with Harry.'

'*Fanny!*' Ange shrieks. 'You're old enough to be his mother!'

Fanny throws her head back and roars with laughter. 'I'm joking, Ange. But if Aldo has a brother, I wouldn't say no.'

She holds out a compact mirror and admires her reflection. I go back to watching the soap, where the Italian man has grabbed his wife/girlfriend/lover in a passionate embrace.

Gosh, if that's how everyone kisses in Italy, Zoe will be in for a treat.

Chapter Forty-Five

Zoe

The fountain sits in the centre of Piazza Garibaldi. It's enormous, its jets of water tipping and dancing over one another like sheets of silk. On market days, the piazza is bustling with people, the lilting Italian language buzzing in the air. Although it's now coated in the dark sheet of the night, it's still filled with people, strolling off to dinner or wandering into bars. The fountain dates back to the nineteenth century, and I've always loved imagining the people who have sat beside it, chatting and laughing . . . sharing their first kiss.

Sam is waiting for me when I arrive, the moon casting a blanket of light over him. He smiles, spotting me as I cross the cobblestones. 'Hey,' he says, folding his arms round me and enveloping me in a hug. He doesn't smell of suncream any more, but his earthy scent from before is still strong, and it makes my heart lift.

'So, tour guide, where are we going?' He grins as he lets me go.

I reluctantly pull away and we start to walk across the square. 'This way. There's a bar I thought we could go to.'

We head through the archways of the medieval aqueduct, which used to carry water hundreds of years ago. The tall buildings beyond are the colour of orange peel, with rectangular windows and defined canopies in concrete white and rusted amber. Small shops hide at the bottom and apartments are slotted into each floor.

'Sounds good. Have you been there before?' he asks.

'My grandma has. It was one of her favourite places in Sulmona, and she had great taste,' I add.

It was Mum who suggested this place – a tiny wine bar nestled in one of the many side streets. Aunt Fanny almost popped with excitement when she heard about it, and I'm sure she would have tried to come with me if Mum hadn't stopped her. Mum gave me detailed instructions about how to get there, but as I walk with Sam, I feel as though I've done this a hundred times before. Almost as if Grandma is holding my hand and leading the way.

'I have to say, it went against every instinct of mine to let you go.'

I look across at him, my stomach flipping.

'To let you walk here, I mean, when we got the puncture,' he adds, and for a moment I notice his face flush. 'I would have preferred to come with you to make sure you were okay.'

'Ah.' I nod. 'To protect us from the bears.'

'Bears?'

I grin. 'Yup. Apparently there are bears and wolves living in the woods round here.'

He stares at me. 'Shit, really?'

I step back as a gaggle of laughing Italians bustle past us.

'Yup.'

'Did you see any?'

I laugh. 'No, thankfully.'

He runs a hand through his hair. 'Yeah, I'm not sure how much use I would have been against a bear.'

'Aren't you supposed to play dead?' I say, gesturing for us to turn a corner.

'I think it depends what type of bear it is,' he says, furrowing his brow in thought.

'So if it was the wrong type, it would just see you lying on the floor as a convenient lunch?'

I look up as someone shouts from a balcony above our heads. The streets are so narrow, you could probably reach out and touch the occupant of the balcony opposite. Each balcony has flowers and vivid green plants threaded through the bars. We walk past a confetti shop, where a woman with waist-length hair is closing up for the day. It takes all my willpower not to pluck a dewy purple almond from a bouquet and pop it in my mouth.

'It's just here,' I announce as we reach the bar. He leans forward to open the door, gesturing for me to step inside first. The floor is a tiny square, with eight tables squashed together. Seven of them are already occupied. The table in the middle is empty, waiting for us. The walls are lined with shelves, housing hundreds of bottles of wine. They tower up to the ceiling, reflecting the candlelight and winking down at us. As I gaze around, I feel nostalgia wrap itself way around my heart, and for a second I fear I might cry.

'Oh my God!'

I look up as a loud Italian voice booms around the room. Everyone stops and turns to stare at us as an effortlessly glamorous woman steps forward and throws open her arms. She has a long face and bright red lips, with large hoops in her ears and dark hair piled on top of her head.

'It is you, isn't it? You are Clarice's granddaughter? You look just like her. It is so good to see you! Remember me? Valentina! I live near Clarice!'

She throws her arms around me, firmly kissing each of my cheeks and then clasping me tightly. When she finally lets me go, she catches sight of Sam and kisses him too, before leading us to the empty table in the centre of the room. She snaps her fingers, and a man strides over and kisses me on each cheek wholeheartedly, his eyes shining.

'Clarice?' he says, looking at me. Valentina nods, beaming at me and then gabbling to him in Italian.

'She was my grandma,' I say, and to my surprise I realise that my face is wet.

Valentina turns to the man, who I assume is her husband, and starts ordering him about, pointing to the highest shelf and gesturing for us to sit down. I quickly pat my face dry as she places two large wine glasses in front of us before beetling back to the bar.

'Sorry,' I mutter to Sam. 'I wasn't expecting all that. It kind of took me by surprise.'

I glance up at him, half expecting him to look away or shrug it off, but he holds my gaze.

'When did you lose her?'

Valentina reappears, uncorking a bottle and pouring streams of dark red liquid into each of our glasses. She beams at me as I thank her.

'Only a few weeks ago. She was special to a lot of people here.'
I notice that several of the other customers are still looking our
way. 'Anyway, what are we drinking to?' I hold up my glass.

'Our first date, courtesy of your grandma.'

I smile. 'I'm glad you like her recommendation.'

'More importantly, it sounds like we never would have met if
it wasn't for her.'

A warm glow fills my chest as he clinks his glass with mine.
'To our first date.'

★

'Do you have a coin?'

I turn around to face Sam, his warm hand linked in mine as
we walk through the streets of Sulmona. He pulls me to a stop
as we reach the fountain. I let go of his hand and search the
pockets of Harriet's dress, pulling out a rogue two pence piece.

He shoves his hand in his own pocket and digs out a five
pence. 'Brilliant. I have one too.'

'What do we need them for?' I ask as he draws me closer to
the fountain.

'Before we say goodbye, we're going to make a wish.'

I laugh. The red wine we were enjoying moments before has
lit a warm glow inside me. Or maybe it was the shots of limoncello Valentina and her husband presented us with as we tried to
leave. I haven't stopped smiling since we sat down. I feel as
though I'm walking on air.

'A wish? This isn't the Trevi Fountain.'

He gives me a mock-stern look. 'We're in Italy, Zoe. All the
fountains here are magical. Everyone knows that.'

'Are they really?'

He leans in close to me. 'If you believe it,' he says, before quickly pulling away. I laugh again as he takes my hand and spins me round so that we both have our backs to the fountain.

'Okay, okay,' I say. 'I believe.'

Just like Grandma, always believing in magic.

'Are you sure?'

'Yes!'

'Okay.' He holds his five pence in one hand and folds his other hand into mine. Warmth spreads through me. 'We need to make a wish. Have you got one?'

I close my eyes, as everything I want swims in front of my mind.

I wish I could get home in time for Libby's wedding.

I wish my mum would feel happier.

I wish Aunt Fanny would stay with us.

I wish I could stay here.

I open my eyes and smile at him. 'Yes, I have.'

He nods. 'Are you ready?'

'I am.'

I wish this feeling could last for ever.

I toss the coin over my shoulder, and it lands with a splash in the fountain.

'What did you wish for?' I ask, but my words are lost as Sam pulls me to him and kisses me.

This is the feeling. This is the feeling I wish could last for ever.

CHAPTER FORTY-SIX

ZOE

I tap the code into the keypad on the wall and step inside the hotel, my eyes landing on the clock sitting above the desk in reception.

It's almost two in the morning. Where did that time go?

I floated back home, but now that I'm here, I feel a shot of energy. I can't possibly go to sleep now, I'm far too excited. I need to talk to someone, and I know at least one person who will definitely be awake.

I climb the stairs as best I can in Harriet's wedges, until I reach Aunt Fanny's door.

She insisted on having her own room again, but at least this time she treated Mum to her own room too, leaving me and Harriet to bunk together. I know Harriet will be desperate to hear all about my evening, but now that I'm here, there is one person I want to tell first. She left when I was eleven, but before

239

then, she was always my biggest cheerleader. Whether I got full marks in a spelling test or came third in the relay race, she was there and waiting to whisk the three of us off for a celebratory dinner. She made everything feel special. She was gone before I could have these conversations with her about dating and falling in love, but she would have been the first person I'd have told my stories to if she'd been there, and now I get the chance to have that moment with her. I feel like a child again, desperately excited to see her reaction and watch her fling her arms in the air as though I've just won an Oscar.

I gently tap my fingers against the door, although I know she'll be awake. She potters around her room for hours before she goes to bed, always claiming that she doesn't need much sleep, which I find baffling.

There is no reply, but as I knock, the door creaks open, so I slip inside. The aroma of her sweet perfume wafts around me, but the room is empty. I am about to call her name when I notice that there is a balcony at the far end, and that the door is open, swinging slightly in the soft breeze.

She must be having a late-night cigarette.

As I step forward, ready to call her name, my eyes lock on a wig hooked on the end of her bed. The perfect ice-blonde bob I know so well. For a moment I am frozen, unable to pull my eyes away.

Heart racing, I walk out onto the balcony. She is crouched on the floor, body bent over, cigarette hanging from her fingers. As I look at her, I feel as though I may collapse.

'Aunt Fanny,' I manage. 'What's going on?'

Chapter Forty-Seven

Fanny

It's funny how we like to imagine how things will play out, as though we have a say, or any sort of control over, how your life will pan out. Well, whatever world I imagined me and my sweet Zoe would end up in, it wasn't like this.

Just like that, the future I painted for us in my mind vanishes. Finally my secret, my heavy, soul-crushing secret, the one I've been carrying around with me since the moment I arrived on their doorstep, is out there. Laid out in plain sight. I have nowhere to hide any more.

Just like that, she knew.

★

Nine months earlier, I was sitting in a hospital waiting room. It was 28 December, that weird time between Christmas and New

Year where nobody really knows what day it is. Nobody wants to go out and party any more and everyone is wrapped up at home with their families. People like me, sad and alone, just have to hold on a few days until New Year's Eve, when everyone starts going out again.

Jon spends every Christmas with his family in Manchester. He always invites me, but I lie and tell him I'm spending it with my cousin (who doesn't exist). I could never bear the thought of sitting around a table eating turkey with anyone who wasn't Zoe and Ange. I'd got over not spending Christmas with Reg a long time ago, but I found it much harder to let those two go. At some point over the Christmas break, when I was suitably drunk on mulled wine, I would toy with the idea of showing up at their house with my arms full of presents and we'd spend Christmas together like we used to. In this fantasy, Reg would be away with work, so it would only be the three of us. Just like old times. I liked thinking about that, but I knew I'd never do it. I dealt with the loneliness; I just got on with it.

Until now, when I was sitting in a stiff plastic chair listening to Christmas music playing. Some of the nurses still wore sad pieces of tinsel around their necks or festive headbands, in a desperate effort to brighten up the worst place to spend your Christmas.

About eight minutes ago, I'd been told I had cancer. I knew it was coming. They'd found a lump in my breast a few weeks before and carted me off for tests. The doctor called it 'aggressive', which seemed pretty apt for me. I was hardly going to have a passive tumour now, was I?

He said lots of things to me about chemotherapy and having a 'good chance' and plenty of other things that washed over my head. I asked for a glass of water and he said I could take a minute to myself. So I did, and here I was. On this chair, in a hospital, alone.

The weird thing was that I'd always felt I was in limbo, ever since I left Reg. Like this phase of my life with Jon was only a stopgap before I started really living again. But in that moment, as I sat in that chair, me, my glass of water and my tumour, it dawned on me that maybe it wasn't a stopgap. Maybe this was my life, and maybe this was how it was going to end.

I accepted the tumour, I accepted the chemotherapy and I accepted the loneliness.

But no matter how hard I tried, I couldn't accept the idea that I'd die without seeing Ange and Zoe again.

So after years of thinking about it, I finally did it.

I came back.

Chapter Forty-Eight

Zoe

My question hangs in the air, unanswered, though Aunt Fanny's silence tells me everything I need to know. It requires no explanation. I already know why she doesn't have any hair, but I wish I didn't. I want her to tell me that she shaved it all off for charity, or that she's on the run and this is a master disguise. Anything but the answer I know she's going to give me.

She doesn't seem shocked or surprised to see me there. It's as though she's been expecting me, or maybe it's just that she doesn't have the energy to fight with me, or push me out the door. She seems to just accept my presence, and takes a drag of her cigarette, puffing a cloud of smoke into the inky black sky. Her small body is hunched over, huddled under her faux-leopard-skin jacket, and I can see that she's shaking. I want to pick her up, force her back into the warmth. But as I stare at her, I feel paralysed.

244

I look at her scalp, forcing myself to take in the reality. I've always known Aunt Fanny for her perfectly manicured bob. Even if you were to burst into her room in the middle of the night, it would still look flawless, not a hair out of place. It's always been that way. Now, there are just a few small tufts of hair poking up through her scalp, catching the light from the room behind her. Without her hair she looks smaller, frailer, more human somehow.

She hands me a cigarette as the silence grows between us. I take it, sitting down beside her, holding it uselessly until she lights it from hers and gives it back to me.

Now that I'm looking at her, it's all I can see. Her sunken papery skin and her bony, jutting hands, screaming for attention. The defeated, frightened look in her eyes that I've caught at off-guard moments over the past few days. The tiredness in her voice.

She's not well. Of course she's not well.

'How did this happen?' I say eventually, my mouth dry.

She doesn't meet my eye as she blows smoke into the air in one swift motion.

'It can happen to anyone, Zo,' she says finally, breaking the silence. 'It doesn't give a shit who you are. Although this probably didn't help.' She gestures to her cigarette and takes another drag.

'Are you okay?' It's all I can manage.

She folds her legs into her chest and wraps her arms around them. 'I don't know. I find out next week if the chemo has worked.'

My heart races as the word rattles around my skull.

Chemo.

Chemotherapy.

That's what people with cancer have.

'I couldn't just sit at home and wait,' she finishes.

I tap my cigarette, realising it's sizzling away under my weak fingers. I wrap my arms around myself, suddenly freezing.

'Does Mum know?'

She shakes her head. 'No. I wasn't going to tell either of you, I just wanted some time away from it all, a reminder of what my life used to be like.'

'What about Jon?'

'What about him?'

'Well, isn't he—'

'Jon and I are friends,' she interrupts. 'Always have been. I only told your uncle that he was my lover to piss him off. He's ringing because he's worried, that's all. We've lived together for years. I'm a needy old crow, remember.'

'What about his credit card?' I blurt before I can stop myself.

She eyes me, and for a second I think she's going to laugh.

'Nosy.' She takes another drag. 'I picked up his card by mistake before I left. He has mine back at home.'

'And Uncle Reggie's?'

This time she smiles at me, but it's a sad smile, devoid of any fire. 'That was the last card we had together before I left. It expired fifteen years ago, Zo.' She catches my expression. 'I didn't want to let it go. I loved your uncle, you know,' she adds.

I look away, feeling my face prick. 'Then why did you leave?'

She sighs and leans back on her hands. I force myself to look at her, and see a flash of pain on her face.

'It's complicated,' she says. 'There's more to it than you think.'

Salty tears begin to fall down my face as fear snakes up my body.

Cancer. She has cancer.

'I was going to come and see you both for a week and then go home. It was supposed to be a week of fun.' She tilts her chin up towards the night sky. 'I never intended on doing anything like this, but it's been so nice having you both back. Being a team again.'

'You need to tell Mum. She needs to know.'

The words come out colder than I meant, so I reach forward and put my hand on hers. She shakes her head slowly. Her eyes stay locked forward, and in the reflection of the hotel lights, I see them shine.

'I know, and I will. Just give me time. Please.'

CHAPTER FORTY-NINE

ZOE

'Zoe, Zoe, Zoe, Zoe, Zoe!'

I jerk awake as Harriet shakes my shoulder, feeling as if I've just been ripped out of a coma. I didn't stay with Aunt Fanny for long last night; she didn't say much else and shooed me inside claiming that she wanted to go to sleep. I didn't get the chance to ask her what the cancer was and how long she'd had it. As soon as I saw her, my mind turned to a horrible wobbly jelly and I could barely think.

I scrunch up my face. 'What?' I groan, trying to ignore Harriet, who has plonked a steaming cup of coffee next to the bed and quickly jumped in next to me.

'You didn't wake me up!' she cries. 'I want to know about your date! How was it?'

'Can't I tell you in a bit? I've hardly had any sleep.' Harriet screams and I whack her arm. 'Not like that.'

'Come on, then!' she says, giving me another shake. 'Tell me!'

'In a bit.'

She lets go of my arm, catching my expression. 'Are you okay?'

Her words cue a ball of hot emotion in the pit of my stomach. I take a deep breath, quickly pushing it back down.

'Yeah,' I say, opening my eyes and forcing a smile onto my face. 'Sorry. Just tired.'

I push myself up to sitting.

'Aunt Fanny isn't well, that's why she's back.' I bite my lip. 'She told me last night.'

Harriet's mouth falls open.

'Oh my God, what—'

I shake my head, unsure what to say and aware that Mum and Aunt Fanny may appear at any moment. 'Let's talk about it later.'

'That's so shit.'

'Yeah.'

I take the coffee as she squeezes my arm. 'I'm so sorry, Zo.'

I push a smile onto my face, blinking away the tears that are forming under my eyelashes and grabbing my phone to send an email to Heidi, telling her I'm bed bound and can't possibly come in. Then I shove the phone under my pillow before I can think too much about it and turn back to Harriet.

'But the date was amazing,' I say, forcing myself to sound bright. 'Literally the best date I've ever been on.'

She gives me a knowing look, like she knows that we'll talk about Aunt Fanny later. 'Okay,' she says, 'tell me everything.'

'We both made a wish and kissed by the fountain.'

'Oh my God,' she cries. 'And?'

'And what?'

'Well, when are you seeing him again?'

I take a sip of the coffee. 'I'm not, am I? We're going home today – hopefully. It was just a one-off.'

Harriet's face drops. 'The best date of your life was a one-off?' she asks flatly.

I shrug. 'Too much of a good thing and all that jazz.'

She rolls her eyes at me. 'That's bollocks and you know it.'

I laugh as there is a knock at the door. Harriet rolls off the bed to answer it, letting Mum and Aunt Fanny into the room. My heart turns over. Fanny's blonde hair is in place once again, and she's teetering on her pointy shoes, her red lips glistening in the morning sunlight. It's like last night never happened.

'Morning, girls,' Mum smiles. 'How did last night go, Zo?'

'It was really fun. Everyone in the bar recognised me as Clarice's granddaughter!'

Mum beams. 'Was Valentina there?'

I nod. 'And her husband.'

'Enzo.'

'Ah,' I slap the duvet, 'that's it. I couldn't remember his name.'

'I spoke to your uncle this morning and told him that we were in Sulmona,' Mum says, and although she's trying to sound conversational, I can see the tension pull at her face. 'He'd like to meet us later.'

Aunt Fanny catches my eye and laughs. 'Don't worry, I'll make myself scarce,' she says.

'Did he say what time he'd arrive?' I ask. 'Like, will we beat him to the house?'

Mum tries to look annoyed, but fails. 'Yes,' she says, 'providing you get out of bed.'

Right on cue, Aunt Fanny suddenly claps her hands together. 'Okay, we need to get ready. I've managed to book us a taxi to take us up to Clarice's house, so we don't have to deal with any more walking. I'm not sure my shoes could manage it.'

'Or my legs,' Mum adds, laughing.

Harriet plucks a towel from the end of the bed. 'I'll jump in the shower.'

I unlock my phone and fire off a message to Heidi to tell her I'm too sick to come in. As soon as I hit send, I see a message from Sam.

Told you all fountains in Italy were magic. Thanks for a great night, Helga, until next time x

It feels as though a swarm of butterflies have been set free in the pit of my stomach and are fluttering wildly up my body. Sadly, this lovely feeling is short-lived, as moments later a message from Kitty pops through.

Hey, Zoe! Hope you're having an amazing time! Heidi hasn't asked me any questions about where you are, did you call in sick? Do you think you'll be back by Tuesday?? Can you call me when you get a second? Need to fill you in on the wedding, there have been some changes xxxxxx

I force myself to read it again, even though I feel as if I might be sick. Then I tap out a reply.

Hey, sorry, can't talk right now. What's happened? Is everything okay? Xxx

'Aunt Fanny,' I say, 'did you look at flights for tomorrow?'

She nods, pulling out a nail file. 'We could either get a flight tomorrow to Gatwick, or—'

'London?' I cut across her. 'That's miles from Cornwall.'

'Or,' she goes on, 'a flight back to Cornwall on Wednesday. I haven't booked anything yet. When is the auction again, Ange?'

'Tuesday,' Mum says, then quickly corrects herself. 'Tomorrow.'

Aunt Fanny cocks her head at us both thoughtfully. 'Guess it depends if you want to stay for it. Do you still need to get back to work, Zoe?'

I bite my lip and look down at my phone, guilt rushing through me. 'Ideally, yes. Kitty said something is going on with the wedding, which doesn't sound great. But if everything is under control, then I guess I don't *have* to be back until Wednesday, the wedding is on Thursday.'

'So you'll stay for the auction?' Aunt Fanny asks.

I look up at her, unsure what to say. It hadn't really crossed my mind that there was an option to stay longer.

I take a deep breath.

'I just want to find the ring.'

CHAPTER FIFTY

HARRIET

This morning, I left Zoe, Fanny and Angie chatting and packing up. There is something a bit different between the three of them today, a slightly tense atmosphere that I can't quite work out. You couldn't slice it with a knife, but if you stuck the knife in, it would stand upright. That kind of tension. Not that any of them were addressing it; they were all discussing Zoe's date and the ring. But I could tell something was up, so I left them to it.

And that's when I got the message from my mum:

I miss you! Are you coming home today in between shifts? Thought we could take Daniel to the park together and get a coffee x

She's done what I wanted her to do. She'd told me that she missed me. But instead of feeling relief that she'd passed my secret test, I felt anger. It made me want to throw my phone out of the window and scream and cry.

I took a deep breath and closed my eyes. When I opened

them again, I decided to take a quick walk around the town, which was bustling with the market in the piazza. I got back to the hotel to find the taxi ready and waiting for us.

If I'm being really honest, I think the reason I'm so angry is because I wanted my mum to fail the test, which is a terrible thing to say. She didn't even know the test was happening. But if she had failed and hadn't noticed I'd been gone for three days, then it would have somehow validated how I've been feeling for the past year – like a spare part, like I don't really belong any more. I would have been able to confront her about how she's made me feel, with evidence to back me up.

The taxi steers around the mountain and I grip my phone in both hands.

But she does miss me, she does want to see me. So where does that leave me? Does it mean that how I've been feeling these past few months is all to do with . . . me?

I take a deep breath and try to squash the feeling down. The more time we spend in Italy, the more food I eat and the longer I feel the sun on my face, the less I want to leave. But every time I think Zoe is feeling the same, she starts talking to me about work and how bad she feels for leaving her assistant, Kitty.

'How are you feeling?' I ask, turning to her now. She's been staring out of the window since we left.

Her eyes are dewy. 'Nervous,' she says in a small voice.

I grab her hand. 'I'm so excited to see the house,' I say.

This makes her smile. 'You'll love it,' she says. 'It really is amazing.'

CHAPTER FIFTY-ONE

ZOE

Harriet gasps as we step out of the taxi. She offered to stay in town today, to give us some space, but we weren't having any of it. The taxi was practically fuelled by our combined nervous energy as it zigzagged up the mountain towards Grandma's house.

Being here is like stepping back in time. It's a time capsule, it's my favourite place. It's my home.

I've been to Grandma's house so many times in my life that I forget how impressive it is when you first see it. It's like something out of a book. It's huge, with flat walls and rectangular windows nestled between turquoise shutters. The doorway sits in a perfect archway, with dainty lights sticking out on either side. It's a world away from the houses in Truro.

On the porch is a swing, which she asked a neighbour to put up not long after she moved in. It sways delicately in the breeze, beckoning us towards the house.

As we move towards the front door, Mum folds her hand into mine. I pause for a moment before giving her hand a squeeze, linking my other hand with Aunt Fanny's at the same time. She looks down at me, slightly surprised, and then smiles. For a moment, the three of us just stand there and look up at the house, and I feel my heart ache. This would be the moment Grandma would appear at the door. She'd have streaks of paint splattered across her dungarees and a paintbrush sticking out of her hair. She'd gallop over and pull us into a huge hug, before dragging us inside towards her latest painting. There is an eerie emptiness without her, like the house has lost its soul.

I turn to Mum. 'Are you okay?'

Her eyes are closed, and her chin is tilted towards the sky.

'Yes,' she says softly. 'I'm okay.'

'Now, Zoe,' Aunt Fanny says, letting go of my hand as we reach the front door and she pulls out the key. 'You do remember what this ring looks like, don't you?'

I smile, suddenly realising that my eyes are filled with tears.

'I could never forget.'

We're all silent as we step inside the house. It is as light and airy as ever, but it's no secret that it is missing a certain shine. Usually Grandma would usher us inside, chatting excitedly and bombarding us with questions. You'd hear her voice echoing through the house whenever you were here, shouting her love and excitement. Without her, it is very quiet. Too quiet. It's a small farmhouse, with high ceilings and terracotta walls that are covered in Grandma's loud and vivacious art. Some of her pieces are framed, others are just painted freely onto the plaster in bright yellows and cyan blues, raisin purples and rusted oranges.

There's not an inch of wall left bare. Her house was its own piece of artwork and her spirit is everywhere.

I take in a deep lungful of air. The light smell of lavender still sits within the house, mixed with the harsh smell of paint and the sweet notes of coffee. It's been weeks since she died, but I can still smell her. I can feel her here.

I turn as Mum grips my hand tightly.

'Look . . .'

A wave ripples up my body as I follow her gaze to the painting Grandma was working on the last time we were here. It's leaning against a shelf, dominating the room, and I feel tears swell as I take it in. The woman's eyes are closed, her face tilted towards the sun. Strands of hair lie across her face, and her skin is etched with the types of creases you get after years of laughing and the lines you collect from hours of concentrating. The marigold yellows glimmer gold in the sunlight and the strokes of blueberry look darker, and richer. As if you could lean in and take a bite.

It takes me a second to realise I'm crying. I wipe my face, and laugh as I realise I'm mirroring Mum.

'It's really incredible, isn't it?' she says.

I nod. 'One of her best.'

Aunt Fanny stands next to me and lets out a whistle. 'She was pretty bloody talented, your grandma.'

I hear Harriet gasp as she walks towards us, and I lean my head on Mum's shoulder.

'She told us that this was her in the painting,' I say, gesturing to the woman.

The four of us stare at it. Although nobody says anything, I know we are all looking at different parts. It's an explosion of colour. Inky blacks and vibrant jades, periwinkle blues and flashes of apricot.

Gazing at the painting, I barely feel the time skim by, but eventually Aunt Fanny speaks. Only her paintings are still on display, almost everything else seems to have been packed away in a box. Uncle Reggie must have been busy.

'Right, Zo, I think your uncle will probably be here pretty soon, so . . .' She trails off and I take a deep breath.

Right. The ring.

I start to climb the wooden stairs, my heavy footsteps echoing throughout the house. The ceilings up here are high, with exposed grey brick on some of the walls and Grandma's paint strokes on others. A bright floral rug takes centre stage on the landing. I take a quick peek into my bedroom. She once painted an enormous sunflower on the far wall, and opposite the double bed is a set of French doors that lead out to a balcony overlooking the mountains. There is nothing quite like watching an electric thunderstorm crackle and pop across those mountains in the middle of the night.

I push open the door of Grandma's bedroom, and my breath is snatched from my body. These walls were always my favourite. She left them the chalky pink of the plaster, but filled them with life. Her bed, a small single with a light sheet and a magenta quilt, stands in the centre of the room. Although I know I am closer to the ring than I have been in months and I should just grab it, it is as though Grandma is reaching out to me. I lie down on the bed, feeling her arms wrapped around me, and for the first time since she died, I really let myself cry.

★

'Zoe?'

I'm sitting cross-legged on the floor of Grandma's bedroom, with boxes piling up around me. There's her jewellery box, the boxes she kept under her bed and the ones I found at the bottom of her wardrobe. All of them are turned out on the floor, and I have been manically rummaging through them for the past half an hour, with no luck.

I've looked everywhere I can think of, and it's not here.

Mum sits down next to me, dropping to the wooden floorboards with a bit of a thud. I can't help but smile at her 'oof' on the way down.

'Don't you laugh at me; this'll happen to you sooner than you think.' She smiles, hooking her hand over my shoulder and pulling me in.

I try to catch my tears before they splodge onto Mum's cotton tunic. Only the light murmurs of birds can be heard in the background, and as I stare at Grandma's things, strewn across the floor, my vision starts to blur.

'It's not here,' I say in a small voice, admitting defeat. 'I can't find it.'

'You've looked everywhere?'

'I don't know where else it could be,' I say, roughly wiping my face with the back of my hand. 'Unless she gave it to somebody else and didn't tell me.'

'Like who?'

I shrug, my shoulders slumped.

'Do you have any idea where it could be?' I ask. 'Did she say anything to you?'

Mum shakes her head slowly. 'Sorry, love.'

We sink into silence.

'You don't need the ring to remember her,' she says quietly. 'She'll always be in here.' She touches her chest with her hand, and I nestle into her, feeling like a child again. 'And in here,' she adds, pointing to my eyes.

I pull myself away and look at her. 'You think I have her eyes?'

She cups my chin with her hand, wiping a tear away with her thumb. 'We both do. That's where her spirit lived, wasn't it? Behind her eyes.'

'Her magic.'

'You can take whatever you want, love. How about one of her paintings?'

'The ring was special, though,' I say. 'If I'm wearing it, I know I'll feel like she's with me.'

'You don't think she's here with us now?' she asks. 'I think she's been here since we left Truro. Probably a bit before then.'

I pull a face. 'I thought you said this trip was cursed?'

A small laugh escapes her. 'Well, your grandma didn't do things by half, did she?'

'No.'

'She would have been so happy to see you going to her bar last night and meeting her friends,' Mum says. 'She loved you so much, Zo.'

She curls her hand into mine and I smile, more tears dropping out of the corners of my eyes.

'She loved you too.'

Mum cocks her head, her own eyes now brimming with tears. 'She loved everyone. That was one of the best parts of her.'

I wipe my tears away and look up as a shadow falls over us.

Aunt Fanny bends herself in two, carefully lowering herself to the floor on her thin heels.

'Do you ever take your heels off?' I laugh.

She winks at me. 'And admit I'm really five foot four? Never.'

She leans back on her hands and looks at us both. 'How are we doing in here then?'

'I couldn't find the ring,' I say, my voice thickening again.

'But we're okay.' Mum gives my hand a squeeze as I nod back at her. I lean my head against Aunt Fanny's shoulder, closing my eyes until a familiar voice speaks behind us.

'Hello, Fanny.'

CHAPTER FIFTY-TWO

ZOE

It only lasts a moment, but it's like watching two lions that are about to fight. Aunt Fanny gets to her feet slowly, her chin lifted as she meets Uncle Reggie's steely glare with ice, and they just stare at each other. Like they're trying to kill each other with just that one look. Their lips are thin lines, and I can feel the anger between them sparking as though it's about to set alight. I'm not sure how long we all stay there, silent, barely moving, but suddenly Harriet is bounding into the room, coming to a halt behind Uncle Reggie. We all turn and face her, the tension breaking just enough. She gives Reggie an awkward wave and then carefully moves past him so she's standing in the centre of the room.

'Any luck?' she says.

I come back down to earth with a crash as I look at the boxes scattered around me.

'No,' I reply. 'It's not here.'

Shock takes over Uncle Reggie's face.

'The ring?' he guesses. 'That's what you're looking for? I told you I'd keep it aside for you.' He shoots Mum a look, and I spot the guilt crawling up her body. We get to our feet.

'Well, we didn't find it anyway,' I mumble, 'and I wanted to look myself. It's not here.'

'I could have saved you a trip and told you that myself,' he says coldly.

'Sorry.' Mum gestures to the boxes. 'I'll clear all this up.'

'Not to worry,' Uncle Reggie booms, his charm back in place as he ignores Aunt Fanny to give me a hug. 'I need to sort through the last bits and pieces for the auction anyway.'

'And you'll double-check for Zoe's ring?' Fanny says.

He gives her a cold stare. 'Of course I will.'

'Where shall we go for dinner?' Mum says, her voice forcefully bright. 'What was that place Mum always loved?'

She directs her question at Reggie, who rolls his eyes at her and turns away. 'Who knows? I'll find somewhere.'

I try my best not to glower at him. I don't want to go out for dinner with him.

'Will you come?' I say pointedly, turning to Aunt Fanny.

'Yes, why are you here?' Uncle Reggie says, hooking an awkward arm over my shoulder that is too heavy for me to shrug off. 'Hear about Mum's death and want to get your hands on something?'

'Reggie!'

He laughs loudly, jostling Mum.

'It was a joke, Ange. Chill out.'

Small circles of red form on Aunt Fanny's cheeks, but she keeps her chin raised.

'I'll let you all catch up,' she says, picking up her bag.

'No,' I say at once. 'Don't go.'

'No, no.' Uncle Reggie waves his arm airily. 'I need to sort out some final things anyway. Why don't you go and say your goodbyes – I imagine you've got a lot to say, considering you skipped that bit last time – and then we'll go out for a nice dinner later as a family? Harriet, you're more than welcome, of course,' he adds with a sickly smile.

His piggy eyes glower at Aunt Fanny as if loaded with bullets. Fanny stiffens, and for the first time since she's been back, I notice a shine in her eyes that makes my heart drop like a stone.

'Fanny has been an enormous help for this trip,' Mum pipes up, her voice shaking slightly. 'Without her, we wouldn't have been able to come.'

'Well you didn't need to come, did you?' Uncle Reggie says, pulling out his phone. 'The ring isn't even here.'

Mum tucks her arm in the crook of Aunt Fanny's elbow, giving Uncle Reggie a steely glare.

'Come on,' she says. 'Let's go for a drink.'

★

I grip my coffee cup, staring down at the latest message from Kitty.

Zoe, I think something is going to happen with this wedding. Libby is really unhappy.

I know I need to reply. I need to face this head on, it's my *job*. But I can't. I can barely string a sentence together.

I can't believe the ring wasn't there. I was so certain I'd find it. How could I have dragged everyone all this way for nothing?

And the worst part is I can't even blame Uncle Reggie. We beat him here, so there's no way he could have hidden it from us. But where else could it be? I don't understand how it could just *disappear.*

For the first time since we left Truro, Aunt Fanny has allowed us all to be silent. We climbed into another taxi and drove back down the mountain until we reached the town square. The silence doesn't feel awkward; it's just that none of us has anything to say. It's as though we're weighed down by our feelings, what just happened sitting heavily on our minds.

We crossed the square and piled into a coffee shop, each ordering something large and warm with steamed milk, apart from Harriet, who went off to do some exploring and check out the markets. At least, that's what she said, but I'm sure she just wanted to give us some time alone.

Aunt Fanny is staring into space, her eyes glazed over as though she's seen a ghost. Her papery hands haven't moved from their tight grip around her mug. Mum is blinking and staring into her drink. She keeps chewing her lip, as though she's trying to stop words from pouring out of her mouth. But then she voices the question that must be playing on a loop in her mind, and as soon as she does, I wish that she hadn't.

'Why did you leave us?'

It's the question I've been trying to get an answer to since the moment Aunt Fanny turned up on our doorstep, but this time it's different. Mum doesn't say it with anger or agitation. She says it more softly, like she's tired and is finally sitting down after a long day. She can't fight it any more; she just needs to know the truth.

Aunt Fanny reacts differently too, and I watch her intently.

She doesn't roll her eyes or smirk, ready to make a joke. She just stirs her drink, twirling the spoon aimlessly.

She sighs, her shoulders slipping, and it's like she's pulling off a mask. She's finally ready.

'I was mad,' she says simply. 'I had this brilliant life. I was so happy with you girls and with Reg. Then one day he took it all away. We were living this fantastic life together – parties and holidays – and I was so desperately in love. You know he never really worked. I funded our lifestyle with my nail file business, but that didn't matter. Then I came home one day and found all these letters that he'd been hiding. He'd as good as bankrupted us.' She pauses, looking up at Mum, her face white and her eyes shining. 'He never told me. He betrayed me, went behind my back and spent everything I had worked for on stupid, flashy tat. I was so mad, I left. I knew he'd never tell you the truth, and would make up some God-awful story about what a monster I was. I knew he was heartbroken and penniless, and I didn't want to take his family away from him too by telling you what had really happened. So I thought it would be easier if I left for good. I moved in with Jon, up in Liverpool, and I've been there since. Pretty miserable, to be honest.'

She laughs bitterly, turning her coffee cup between her spindly hands, and I feel myself being pulled towards her like we're attached by a piece of string.

So that's it. After all this time, that's why she left.

'That was very selfish of you.'

My head jerks round in shock.

Mum's voice is steely. I feel my insides curl.

Aunt Fanny nods, staring down at her hands.

But Mum hasn't finished. 'We needed you,' she continues. '*I* needed you. Zoe needed you. We were a team, the three of us. You were more of a sister to me than Reg ever was a brother, and you knew that. You could have stayed and told me. I would have helped you. You shouldn't have left us. It was selfish and cowardly.'

I stare at her in shock. I've never heard her speak to anyone like this. Usually it's me sticking out my chest and going into battle for her, while she shuffles behind me and murmurs how it doesn't matter.

Aunt Fanny has just opened her mouth to answer when her phone rings. She looks down at it.

'It's Jon. Sorry, I need to take this. I've been ignoring him for the past two days. I'll be right back.'

She slips out from her chair and steps outside. I look at Mum, who is glowering after her.

'She's got cancer,' I say, but it comes out loaded with fury. As soon as the words leave my mouth, I feel a hot prickle of guilt. I know I promised I wouldn't say anything. But I can't help it. I can't hold it in.

'I know.'

I look at her, but her eyes are fixed forward.

What?

'You *know*?' I exclaim. 'Then why are you being so mean to her?'

'Because it's selfish.' Her voice somehow remains even. 'She's only back because she's ill. Where was she when we were ill? When you had the flu, or I started the menopause?'

I try not to scoff. 'Mum, I don't think that's the same.'

'The hell it's not.' She looks at me now, and I flinch. Her eyes are fierce, but I can see they're prickling with tears, and her cheeks are flushed. 'She's only here now because she thinks she's dying. She let us grieve over her for years, and now she's back to make us do it all over again. It's selfish.'

She takes a sip of her coffee, and I notice that her hands are shaking. I want to say something comforting, or at least helpful, but my brain has stopped working. I can't work out who I'm supposed to defend, or even who I agree with.

At that moment, Aunt Fanny reappears, her heavily made-up eyes skirting around anxiously. She drops into her seat, carefully hooking one long leg over the other. I can tell she's trying to look casual, but her face is ashen.

'Mum knows,' I say in a small voice.

She rolls her eyes. 'For God's sake, Zoe,' she mutters, trying to get comfortable on the chair. 'I asked you not to tell her.'

'I've known for days,' Mum says. 'I heard you on the phone to Jon.'

There is a pause as Aunt Fanny looks at us both.

'Well,' she says eventually. 'You could have asked me how I was feeling.'

Mum glares down at her mug and my whole body burns.

Oh God, this is horrible. What's happening? Why can't we go back to laughing and joking together?

'I get my test results back today,' Aunt Fanny continues flatly. 'That's why Jon was ringing. They're due in about an hour, so he's asked me to call him with an update.'

'Right.'

Silence again.

'Listen, we should go back and see how Reg is getting on. We should be helping him with the auction. I hope the results are what you want them to be,' Mum says, getting to her feet and pulling her bag onto her shoulder. She looks at me and I stand too, my legs feeling like jelly. Aunt Fanny has pulled out her phone and is scrolling aimlessly, but I can see the tightness in her face.

'You girls go without me. I'd like to be alone when I get the results anyway.'

I stare at her. We can't leave her here.

'I hope the auction goes well.'

'You're coming, aren't you?' I blurt. 'To the auction tomorrow?'

'No,' she says quietly. 'I don't think I will, Zoe.' Her eyes flit up at me and I feel as if I'm about to cry. 'It was lovely to see you both again. Let's not leave it so long next time.'

I look at Mum, desperate for her to berate Aunt Fanny for not coming. Or just *something*. But she's already turned on her heel and walked out the door.

CHAPTER FIFTY-THREE

HARRIET

I tuck my legs underneath me, arching my back so the porch swing tips forward, rocking me back and forth. There is something really comforting about the motion of swinging; I can totally understand why Zoe's grandma had this built. I could stay on here for hours.

I called my mum, the first time we've actually spoken in days, and it was one of the most horrible conversations we've ever had. I didn't mean for it to go that way, but when everyone left the house and it was just me, alone, it twanged something deep in my gut. Another example of somewhere I don't quite fit. They invited me along, just like Mum always tries to invite me places with her and the baby, but am I really wanted? Would it be better if I wasn't there?

It was all simmering under my skin when I dialled her number, and when she answered, it sort of just fell out of me.

'Hello!' she said. 'How are you?'

'Fine,' I answered straight away, annoyed that I could already hear Daniel whimpering in the background and knew that I would only be getting a slice of her attention, 'I'm in Italy.'

I'm not really sure what I was expecting her to say, or even what I *wanted* her to say. I just wanted to throw it at her, like a metaphorical middle finger. It was childish, I know. But I am a child, remember? That's my problem.

She stayed silent for a moment before repeating, 'Italy? What do you mean?'

'I've been here for three days.'

She was silent again. Then, 'What? With who? Why didn't you tell me?'

It was then, when she asked such an innocent, bewildered question, that I felt like I might cry. It was like someone holding a mirror up to me. Why hadn't I told her? Because I was pathetic. Because I wanted to blame her for my lack of direction in life, as if it was somehow her fault. Because I wanted to prove that she didn't care about me any more, like that would make anything better.

'I'm here with Zoe and her family,' I said, unable to explain why I hadn't told her.

'Oh,' she said, confused. 'Well, that's nice. Are you having fun?'

'Yeah.'

'How lovely.'

And then we dropped back into silence again. I could almost hear her tired brain trying to pick up all the pieces of weird, random information I had just thrown at her. I was in Italy, I'd been here for days, I hadn't bothered to tell her.

'I better go,' she said, after what felt like a lifetime of silence. 'I'll speak to you later. Tell Zoe and Ange I said hi.'

And then we just said goodbye and the line went dead. I've been sitting on the swing ever since, swaying back and forth and trying not to think too hard about myself.

I look up as a car rounds the corner. I notice Ange sitting in the back seat next to Zoe, and for a second my heart lifts, but when Zoe steps out and I see the look on her face, it drops again. She looks ashen.

'Hey,' I say. 'Where's Fanny?'

'Ah!'

I jump as Reggie barrels out of the front door, arms outstretched. I don't know what he's been doing for the past hour or so, but he's been keeping himself busy with the many boxes inside the house.

'There you are,' he says. 'Are we ready for dinner? I'm starving.'

'Are you okay?' Zoe walks towards me, reading my expression. 'What's wrong?'

I force a bright smile onto my face. 'Nothing! I'm fine!'

'Fancy dinner then, Harriet?' Reggie asks, scrolling on his phone.

I step off the swing and push my fingers through my hair. 'Er . . . no. Thank you. I'm not really hungry.'

Zoe takes my arm. 'What's going on?'

I shake my head. 'Mum stuff,' I mumble. 'I'll just chill here. Enjoy dinner.'

And before she can ask any more questions, I slip inside the house and find a spare bedroom. Then I climb under the sheets, hug my knees and just allow myself to cry.

CHAPTER FIFTY-FOUR

ZOE

The next couple of hours pass in a horribly slow blur. Mum and I went back to the house and found Harriet sitting wordlessly on the swing and staring into the distance. She mumbled something about her mum when I asked if she was okay, but before I could really talk to her, Reggie bustled us down the path to go to a restaurant he'd booked. Harriet smiled and said that she'd leave us to have a catch-up, but I caught the look on her face as she slipped inside. I tried to follow her, but Uncle Reggie threw a weighted arm over my shoulder and steered me towards the waiting taxi. Now I'm sitting at the table alone and my head is spinning. That's two people I love that I've left upset and alone, all to be in the company of a man with the emotional depth of an earwig.

I hook one leg over the other, holding the phone to my ear as it rings. Another factor that's been increasing my heart rate for the past twenty-four hours is Kitty. Well, not Kitty herself, who has been nothing short of an angel, but the fact that I've been ignoring her calls and replying to her messages with non-committal lines every time she's given me an update.

Something is happening with the wedding, and it can't be good. You don't have to be a genius to unpick Kitty's manic use of exclamation points, which has been on a steady incline since we last spoke. But with everything that's been happening, I haven't been able to deal with it. I can't just announce that I'm leaving. How could I do that to Aunt Fanny, who has just told me that she has cancer? Or to Mum, who has finally started opening up to me about how she feels? How could I tell them that work is more important than being here with them?

So instead, I've put work in a nice little box in the back of my mind and have been pretending that the wedding has been moved to next week. Or even better, that it's been cancelled for good. *La la la, everything is going to be fine.*

The phone clicks as Kitty picks up, and I take a deep breath. *La la la, everything's going to be fine.*

'Hi, Kitty,' I say brightly. 'Listen, sorry I've been MIA. It's all been a bit mad here, but I—'

'Zoe!' Kitty's high-pitched voice squeals down the phone, and I jump. 'Where are you? I've been trying to call you. Are you nearly home? I think Libby is about to cancel the wedding!'

My mouth goes dry.

Fuck fuck fuck, everything's going to be shit.

'Have I lost you? Hello? Are you nearly back?' Kitty says again when I don't answer.

I look around the restaurant blindly, the silky Italian accents filling my ears and reminding me that I'm hundreds of miles away from home.

'No,' I admit finally. 'I'm not.'

'How long will you be?' she gabbles. 'I can stay up late and wait for you. Or get up super early tomorrow morning and we can meet then?'

I open and close my mouth, my mind whirring.

I can't lie to her. But oh God, her head is going to explode.

'Kitty,' I say carefully, 'I'm still in Italy.'

I hear her take a sharp intake of breath. 'At the airport? On the plane?' Hope saturates every word.

'Er . . . no.' I put a finger in my ear as the couple next to me start chortling loudly. 'I'm in a restaurant.'

'A restaurant at the . . . airport?'

I bite my lip and force myself to say it. 'No. A restaurant in Sulmona. I'm still at my grandma's. I missed my flight.'

'Zoe!' Kitty breathes. 'You missed your flight? Why didn't you tell me? What's going on?'

I take a deep breath. Her stretched, squeaky voice tips my heart rate into overdrive, everything that I've been putting into that little box in the back of my mind finally exploding.

Oh my God. What am I doing? How could I have come to Italy and not told Heidi? I'm skiving off work! I'm *lying* to my boss! And now I'm sitting in a restaurant, in a different country, with my uncle who I *hate*!

And worst of all, I've left Kitty, the kindest and most loyal colleague you could ask for, completely in the shit. All so I could try and get this bloody ring that I *didn't even find*.

I don't have the ring, Mum and Aunt Fanny aren't speaking, something is going on with Harriet, and Aunt Fanny has cancer.

And now my job is falling apart too, and I've left my assistant to pick up the pieces with absolutely no support.

I hold my head in my hands. It's just me at the table. Mum is in the toilet and Uncle Reggie is busy at the bar lecturing some poor eighteen-year-old about wine, even though I'm sure he knows far more than Reggie does. To make matters worse, he's berating the poor boy in English.

'It's all just gone wrong,' I say eventually, Kitty's silence deafening. 'Everything got delayed and I know I should have turned around and come home earlier, but I was just so desperate to try and find Grandma's ring before the auction.' I take a deep breath, trying to ignore the hot panic that's creeping through my body.

'Oh, Zo.' Kitty's voice softens. 'I can understand that. Did you get it?'

My eyes prick.

'No,' I say. 'And I've let you down and lied to Heidi just to get here. But the trains screwed up and our car broke down and we're still here, and fuck! I've left you to deal with this by yourself. I've been the worst manager ever. Heidi is going to fire me . . .'

I trail off as my throat starts to swell. Oh God, I can't start crying in a restaurant by myself, or people will think I've just been dumped.

'Right!' Kitty says, with such an uncharacteristic air of authority that I almost drop the phone. 'Heidi is not going to fire you. I'm going to deal with this.'

'How? Why does Libby want to cancel? Has the groom done something?'

Kitty pauses. 'I can't get it out of her. But she's sounding more and more stressed every time I've spoken to her. She keeps talking about table plans and flowers and family members not speaking to each other.'

'Right.' I chew my thumb. 'Didn't she want a really simple wedding when she first came to us?'

'Yes, and now it's . . .'

'Massive,' I finish.

I hear Kitty take a deep breath. 'Okay. I know what to do. You can trust me.'

I suddenly feel like I might cry again. 'Honestly, Kitty. I trust you with my life.'

She laughs. 'I could make it pretty fabulous.'

'I know.'

'Don't worry,' she says fiercely. 'You take all the time you need and don't rush home. When is the auction?'

'Tomorrow.'

'And are you staying for it?'

I go to reply, and then stop myself. I wasn't going to. I shouldn't.

'I'm not sure,' I say. 'I hadn't really thought that far. I just wanted to find the ring and leave.'

'Well, you should! These are your grandma's things, Zoe. It's important! Don't even think about work. I'll see you whenever you're back. Just let me know how long I need to cover you for. My cousin had food poisoning once and he was in bed for a *week*!'

'Thank you so much, Kitty. You really are the best.'

I can almost hear her beaming. 'Just leave it with me, Zoe,' she says. 'I've got this!'

After a quick goodbye, she rings off and I check to see if I have any messages from Aunt Fanny. I can't forget her face as we left her in the coffee shop. It felt like leaving a child behind. I don't even really know how it happened.

I look down at my phone and jab a quick message to Harriet.

Is Aunt Fanny with you?

She replies instantly.

Nope, just me here. Why?

'Well, that told him!'

I look up as Uncle Reggie reappears, slapping the table as he falls into his seat. Mum is right behind him and tucks herself into her chair delicately.

'That waiter didn't have the faintest idea about the difference between a Merlot and a Rioja! He was just reading what was on the back of the bottle!' He hoots loudly, looking at Mum as though it's a fabulous inside joke. I stare back at him, and Mum offers up an awkward smile.

'I'm sure he did know,' I say, a tight smile pulling at my face.

'Well, he didn't understand a word I was saying!'

'That's probably because you weren't speaking Italian,' I mutter under my breath, trying to spot the waiter over my shoulder. I shall be leaving him a fat tip.

'What shall we have to eat then?' He flicks open the menu. 'I think I fancy a steak. Zoe?'

'I'm not really hungry.'

'Rubbish, how about some nice pasta?'

I shrug limply as he turns to Mum.

'And risotto for you, Angie?'

'That sounds lovely,' Mum says in a small voice.

I don't know where Aunt Fanny will be. Is she out for dinner by herself? Or curled up on a bench somewhere, waiting for her phone to ring?

She shouldn't be waiting for this news alone. We shouldn't have left her. We should be with her.

'I think I'll have a T-bone steak if they have it. I'll ask the waiter.' Reggie looks over his shoulder and starts snapping his fingers.

'How are things going with the auction?' Mum asks, taking a sip of water and flinching each time his fingers click.

'Yup,' he replies, not looking at her, 'all fine. Think we'll have a good turnout tomorrow. Some people are coming in person, but a lot will be joining us online. It's had a fantastic response, we'll make a fortune.' He grins. 'I'll let you know how it goes. Shame you can't come,' he adds as an afterthought.

'Well,' Mum says, 'Zoe has to get back to work.'

'I don't, actually,' I say quickly. 'I don't have to be back until the end of the week. So we can stay for the auction.'

I see Uncle Reggie's smile stiffen.

'No need!' he says. 'I've got it all under control, so you might as well get on the road.'

I narrow my eyes, but Mum shoots me an imploring look, as if begging me not to argue with him.

'Ah!' Uncle Reggie says, finally getting the attention of the waiter, who has been steadily ignoring his clicks. 'There you are. Do you offer a T-bone steak? Go check, will you? And we'll have a bottle of Merlot, too. Ask the chap behind the bar, he'll know which one!' He guffaws heartily and the waiter slinks off.

'Listen,' Reggie continues, turning in his chair to face us with a sudden look of concern on his face. 'I'm sorry you got caught up in all that nasty business with Fanny. I don't know what she was playing at, showing up like that, but she's gone now.'

My face burns. 'It was lovely seeing her,' I say loyally.

'Well of course it was. But that's the thing with her, none of it's real, is it? Like, where is she now? Poof! Gone! Again!' He throws his arms in the air, like he's resting his case and my hands curl into fists on my lap.

'She only went because you made her feel like she had to,' I mutter.

Reggie tries his best to look offended. 'Zoe, I invited her to dinner.'

I stare at him. *No you did not.*

'Anyway,' he says, leaning forward so his arms are resting on the table, 'I'm glad it's back to being just the three of us. This is what Mum would have wanted. Us together, as a real family.'

Chapter Fifty-Five

Fanny

My fingers curl around the stem of a wine glass. It's a Sauvignon Blanc. Ice cold and dry, with a bite that pinches the back of my throat each time I take a sip.

Now that I'm alone, it's what I need.

Well, I guess I got what I deserve. After years of playing out this fantasy in my head of me running back into the arms of Ange and Zoe, it was only going to go in my favour for so long. Now I'm on my own again. Should I have even bothered doing all of this? Would it have been easier just to stay in Liverpool and carry on alone?

The thought makes my eyes prick.

No. No matter how painful this is now, I wouldn't take away these few days I've had with them. Even though I've only had a sliver of them, with both of them hurting and being so angry with me, it was still the best few days I've had in years. Nothing will ever make me regret these moments we've been back together. Even if I have ended up alone, exactly the same as I was nine months ago in that miserable hospital waiting room. The only difference is at least now I have a glass of wine.

I take another sip, sinking into the woozy oblivion only alcohol seems to give. No more aches, no more worry, no more fucking fear.

It's just me, alone again.

Time to rip that plaster off.

Chapter Fifty-Six

Zoe

I stare down at my phone as the text blinks up at me.

Where are you? How did it go? Did you hear from the doctors?

I sent the message two hours ago, but there's been no reply. I've also called her three times, and each one has gone straight to voicemail. It can't be good news. If it was good news, she would have answered my calls or messaged me back. She would have been excited to tell us, wouldn't she?

I lean against the bath, the hot water filling Grandma's small bathroom with steam. In one of my voicemails, I told Aunt Fanny that we were back at the house, hoping that she'd show up and climb into bed with me, Mum and Harriet and we could all stay up late and watch a film. The fact that I have no idea where she is or what she's doing is starting to make me feel a bit ill. What if she's had terrible news and she's all by herself?

A message from Sam smiles up at me from my phone. It's a

picture of him, James and Harry hiking up one of the surrounding mountains. Sam is grinning at the camera, and James and Harry are smiling behind him. Although James is also swearing.

Looking at his face lifts my heart, though not as much as it would have done yesterday. Before everything changed. Our date feels like a lifetime ago now.

I jump at a knock on the bathroom door.

'Yeah?'

The door creaks open and Harriet's face peeks through the steam. She looks around, before spotting me sitting on the floor.

'What are you doing?'

'Running a bath.'

She hesitates for a moment before joining me on the floor.

'Do you want a tea?' she asks.

'No thanks.'

'Some wine? Vodka? Limoncello?'

I smile at her and shake my head. 'I'm good.'

'Have you heard any more from Sam?'

I turn my phone towards her and show her the picture. 'They're still in Sulmona and planning to stay here for a few more days before travelling south.'

Harriet leans her head on the back of the bath. 'That's so cool.'

I sigh. 'I know.'

We drift into silence for a moment, and I inhale deeply, my nose filling with the scent of Grandma's lavender bubble bath, teasing memories of her out of my mind.

'I'm sorry about the ring,' Harriet says quietly.

I shrug, trying to ignore the instant pang in my chest. 'I really thought it was here,' I manage.

'I know.'

'It's all just shit, isn't it?'

'Mm-hmm.'

'Like, I didn't think things could get much worse than before we came here, and now we don't have the ring, Aunt Fanny is sick, Mum and Fanny are fighting, I'm going to miss this wedding, and . . .'

I stop speaking as Harriet swipes away a tear that has dropped down her freckled face. I turn to her. The shadow I spotted earlier has reappeared on her face.

'What's wrong?' I ask.

She lets out a breath. 'I'm sorry, Zo. I know this is really tough for you, but I think I'd swap with you in a second.'

I put my phone down. 'What do you mean? What's going on?'

She pushes the back of her hands across her face. 'I spoke to my mum today.' She pauses, trying to control her breathing. 'I haven't spoken to her properly since we left. I wanted to see how long it would take her before she noticed I'd gone.'

My heart turns over. 'Harriet, of course she'd have noticed that you'd gone!'

'Oh, she did,' Harriet says, nodding. 'Eventually. She couldn't understand why I didn't tell her where I was going.'

'And why didn't you?'

Her face crumples, and I lean forward and stroke her arm. Harriet is always so happy, but it's so easy to forget that sometimes it's the people with the biggest smiles who need the most help.

'Because I don't fit in there any more,' she says eventually. 'Mum has this new life, with Darren and Daniel. I'm not part of that. I've felt that way for ages.' She leans against the damp tiles and closes her eyes. 'Yeah, I know this is shit for you, Zo, but you have a family who love you, who are willing to drop every-thing and travel to Italy with you. Your grandma loved you so much, and thanks to her you'll be set up financially, I'm sure your mum will give you some of the money made from the auc-tion. You're never going to have to worry about anything. You can do what you want, you can literally do *whatever* you want. But I have to go back to Cornwall and get another shitty job to pay my rent in some tiny flat because my mum wants a second go at having a family. And I don't fit. Like, why do you think I do these all the time?' She pulls out a handful of scratch cards stuffed into her pocket. 'I'd do anything to be in your shoes.'

I stare at her, speechless. She shrugs, giving me a watery smile. I reach forward and grab her hand.

'You do fit,' I say. 'Your mum loves you, of course she does.'

She shakes her head. 'Not like your mum loves you. Or your aunt.'

'They love you too. Everyone loves you. I couldn't live with-out you. You're literally the sister I never had, so my family is your family too.'

She takes a deep breath and shakes her head. 'Sorry. I think it's just the wine and the fact that we have to go home again soon, and I don't even know what the fuck that's going to look like for me. I feel so lost.'

She puts her hands under the running water and rubs them over her face. I reach forward and pull her into a hug.

'I just wish that this was my life instead,' she says, her voice muffled in my shoulder.

'Yeah,' I say, 'I wish that too.'

★

I pull my jumper over my I HEART ROME T-shirt and creep downstairs. It's the middle of the night, and the house is completely silent apart from the gentle ticking of the grandfather clock that stands proudly in the hallway. This time tomorrow, almost everything here might be sold.

Uncle Reggie insisted that he didn't want to stay in the house, and instead booked himself into a local hotel. The more he talked, the less I was able to stop the angry thoughts zipping around my mind. *Why are we with you instead of Aunt Fanny? I would never choose you over her.*

Was that what we had done, though? With Fanny alone somewhere in Sulmona, had we chosen my uncle instead?

The thought makes me feel sick. We don't even know where she is.

I walk into the kitchen and flick the kettle on to make a late-night tea, pulling out the array of herbal teas that Grandma loved and dropping a random one into my mug. As the water starts to boil, I walk back into the living room. The high window casts the light of the pearly white moon across the room, and my eyes are drawn to the painting that is propped above the fireplace. Grandma's last painting.

'Are you okay?'

I spin on the spot to find Mum standing in the doorway, her fluffy dressing gown tightly hugging her soft body.

'Why are you up?' I ask. 'It's, like, the middle of the night.'

She cocks her head. 'I couldn't sleep. All the excitement of the day.'

She comes and stands next to me, and we both look at the painting.

'I didn't like the meal tonight,' I say.

'No,' Mum sighs. 'I didn't much like it either.'

'Have you heard from Aunt Fanny?'

She pauses. 'No, love. Have you?'

I shake my head and we fall silent, both looking up at the painting, which is shimmering in the moonlight, the deep purples and blues dancing on the canvas.

'I can't believe Grandma said this was her,' I say, pointing to the woman in the middle of the painting.

Mum turns to me and frowns. 'Why?'

'It just looks like a sad painting. It's like she's being eaten by all her feelings.'

'Your grandma said this painting was about living in the madness and the magic of life, remember?'

I force a laugh. 'Yeah, but she was dying when she painted it. I don't know if the woman looks sad.'

Mum looks back at the painting. 'I don't think that's what it is at all. I think she's letting go of her feelings and embracing them. I don't think it's a sad picture, and look . . .' She leans forward and gestures to the woman's face. 'She's smiling, see?'

I narrow my eyes. I hadn't spotted it before, but she's right. There is a flicker of a smile there.

'She's happy; she's free,' Mum continues. 'She's saying, yeah, life is colourful and mad and can be a bit messy, but I'm okay with that. That's what your grandma was like.' She gives me a knowing look. 'She never liked to colour inside the lines.'

Chapter Fifty-Seven

Harriet

I pull open my eyes as a mug is placed on the bedside table next to me.

'Hey,' I mumble groggily. 'What time is it?'

'Really, really early.' Zoe grins. 'Hence the coffee. I think my uncle will be here soon, ready to boss us all about. You don't have to come to the auction, by the way,' she adds. 'It'll probably be really boring.'

I push up onto my elbow and pick up the mug. 'Are you joking? Like I'd miss it. I've never been to an auction. I can't wait for the drama.'

Zoe laughs, sinking onto the bed. 'Hopefully there won't be any more drama. I don't think I can take it.'

I sigh. 'Have you heard from Fanny? How is she?'

She shrugs. 'No idea.'

We drift into silence as we both sip our coffee. We're in Zoe's old bedroom. The double bed stretches out to almost six feet wide, with an extravagant upholstered headboard and a dangly light fitting shimmering from the ceiling. The wooden floorboards creak when you walk on them, and you can see the view of the mountains peeking through the shutters. It is spectacular.

'Do you really feel that way about your mum?'

I look round. Zoe's wide eyes are full of concern.

I sigh. 'I just don't feel like I fit in there any more,' I say honestly. 'I don't feel like I fit in anywhere, and it scares the hell out of me. I don't even really know if it's got anything to do with Mum or it's just me trying to find someone to blame it on.'

'Does she know?'

I laugh and shake my head. 'No.'

I take another sip. The bitterness of the black coffee bites the back of my tongue and pinches the roof of my mouth.

'I don't want you to feel lost,' Zoe says. 'That's a horrible way to feel.'

I shrug. 'Ah well. What can you do?'

She nods her head at me, 'organised Zoe' activated. 'Yes,' she says, 'what can we do? What would make you feel less lost? Like, if you could do anything in the world, what would it be?'

Ah, the million-dollar question. The one that invites a little flicker of fear each time somebody asks me.

'I have no idea,' I say quietly.

Zoe raises her eyebrows. 'Harriet, I'm asking what you'd do if you could do *anything*. Not something sensible or something you *should* be doing. Imagine that money isn't an obstacle.'

I close my eyes for a second, leaning my head back on the headboard.

'I'd travel the world,' I say. 'Work it out on the way. Or maybe not work it out. Maybe just see the world, work in bars, pick fruit until I'm old and grey. Who knows?'

I glance at Zoe, whose brow is knitted together. I can almost feel her trying to work out how she can make it all happen for me.

'But I don't have a winning lottery ticket.' I smile. 'I can't do that, so it's back to Cornwall we go.'

She's still frowning in concentration. 'Well, while you figure it out, how about we rent a flat together? I think it's time we both said goodbye to our childhood bedrooms.'

I hold my mug towards her, and she clinks with me.

'Deal,' I say.

Chapter Fifty-Eight

Zoe

There's still no word from Aunt Fanny by the morning. I'm really starting to panic now, but as we get ready to leave for the auction, I can tell that the anger Mum felt towards her yesterday has burnt out. She's quiet.

'Do you think she's still in Sulmona?' I ask, pushing Cheerios around my bowl.

Mum sighs. 'I don't know, love. She may have gone back to Liverpool to be with Jon. We can't take this personally,' she adds, as much for herself as for me, I sense. 'She's going through a terribly hard time, and it has to be her decision how to deal with it.'

'You've changed your tune,' I say before I can stop myself.

She flushes. 'Nobody's perfect, Zoe.'

'Would anybody like a coffee?' Harriet joins us at the kitchen table, her long hair twisted in a French plait. 'I might call a cab and pop down to the town to get us some; we seem to have run out here.'

Mum and I shake our heads, and Harriet nods, pushing on her shoes and waving goodbye.

Almost as soon as she's gone, Uncle Reggie's voice reverberates round the house as he clangs his way through the front door.

'Right this way, Gerald.'

I swallow my last mouthful of cereal and look up. Gerald, who I presume is the auctioneer, looks as though he's spent the night in a coffin.

'Zoe, Ange!' Uncle Reggie calls over his shoulder. 'We'll need your help carrying stuff to the van.'

'I thought you didn't need our help,' I mutter, before turning in my seat. 'Hang on, what van? Where is it going?'

He gives a patronising laugh. 'We can't do the auction here, can we? I've hired a hall for the day. I'll take the cost out of today's earnings,' he adds, giving Gerald a wink. 'We'll start upstairs. Hurry up and finish that so we can get going.'

I groan. Mum leans forward and gives my arm a squeeze.

'Come on,' she says. 'We just need to get through today and then we can go home and get back to normal.'

But even as she says it, I can see a flicker of uncertainty in her eyes, which I can't quite place. I'm not sure we'll ever get back to normal after these last few days, and maybe she's having the same thought as me. Maybe she doesn't want to return to normal.

★

I know it's unrealistic of me, but I'd be lying if I said I wasn't expecting the auction to run exactly as it does on *Antiques*

Roadshow. I feel as though I should be having a little joke with Fiona Bruce.

I'm finding the whole thing quite surreal. Half of me is full of pride watching Grandma's paintings being carried around the room, and the other half wants to slam my credit card on the table and bellow: 'You're not selling any of this! I will take it ALL!' Although I'm not sure they'll be very impressed with my £500 overdraft.

We're in a grand-looking hall. It's filled with wooden pews, which Mum keeps telling me must have been inherited from the church, and there are some locals milling around in pashminas and big sunglasses. At the back of the room, about thirty serious-looking people are sitting behind laptops. I tried smiling at one when we walked in, but was met with a stare so cold that I practically froze on the spot. So now I'm standing in a corner with Mum and Harriet, trying not to get in everyone's way whilst trying even harder to zone out Uncle Reggie, who is loudly bossing everyone around. I can only hope that the translator he hired for the day is softening his rude orders.

'This is really odd, isn't it?' Mum says in a small voice next to me as Gerald starts warming up on the stage. Though calling it a stage is ambitious. In reality, it's just a slightly raised part of the floor, but I swear I saw him stretching his hamstrings a minute ago, so who knows what he's planning on doing up there.

'I know,' I say, waving at Harriet as she slips outside for a cigarette. 'I'm not sure if I really want to be here.'

'We don't have to be.' Mum turns to me. 'If you would rather go for a coffee or something instead?'

I shake my head, determination taking over. 'No. I have to

see this, and besides, it's what Grandma wanted. It'll raise loads of money for her charities.'

Grandma's will stated that we were to auction off anything that we saw fit. Half of the money would go to my mum and Uncle Reggie, and the other half to charity.

Mum smiles, patting my arm. 'You're right. Cancer Research, the MS Society, Mind and the Cornwall Dog and Cat Rescue.'

I laugh. 'Arguably her favourite one.'

She folds her arms across her chest. 'Ah, they all meant a lot to her.'

Uncle Reggie laughs loudly with a group of men and slaps one of them on the back.

'He's in his element here, isn't he?' I mutter.

'He's a showman. Always has been.'

I take out my phone and quickly send another message to Aunt Fanny.

Please call me. It's not the same without you. Uncle Reggie is being unbearable as always. The auction is about to start, but I'll try and call you again later.

I'm about to put my phone back in my pocket when a new message appears on the screen.

Look up.

I scan the room, and for a split second, all my stress and worry about Aunt Fanny, about Mum and Harriet, about my job is gone when I spot Sam smiling at me from the doorway. Mum follows my gaze and gives a little yelp.

'I'll be right back,' I mutter, not taking my eyes off him.

I slip through the crowds towards him, and he scoops me up into a hug. His strong arms lift me into the air with ease and I squeal until he puts me down.

'What are you doing here?' I smile, pushing my hair off my face as my heart flutters up and down my body.

He looks over my shoulder. 'Are you kidding? I'm here to get my hands on the latest Clarice Florentina painting.'

Grandma chose her name when she first started painting, which I totally get. 'Florentina' is way more exciting than 'Winters'.

We step back as a middle-aged couple in floaty white linen skim past us.

'Oh yeah? Do you have thirty grand to spare?'

His eyes widen. 'Thirty grand?'

'I told you. She was a big deal.'

'Clearly it runs in the family.'

A big goofy grin takes over my face. His hazel eyes are creased into a smile, and for some reason, I don't seem to care that I smell of suncream and my hair is all frizzy from the heat. I don't even really care that I've had to squash myself into another one of Harriet's dresses, which is making me look like a Greggs sausage roll. Nothing seems to matter when I'm with him. It's weird. I barely know him. Maybe it's all the sun, or the euphoria of gallivanting off to another country. That'll be it.

Uncle Reggie starts clapping his hands in the middle of the stage, and Sam grabs my arm.

'Listen,' he says as I turn back to him. 'I know today is a big day for you and your family. So I just wanted to stop by to give you this.'

Out of his pocket, he pulls a perfect flower. But it's not a real flower; it's the sugared almond, the confetti, that pop from each corner of Sulmona like beautiful rare plants. This one is in the shape of a daisy, with each petal painted a shade of electric pink.

The centre of the flower smiles up at me, sunshine yellow. He places it in my hand and I look up at him. His smile is now so wide it looks as if it's about to swallow his face.

'What do you think? It's pretty cool, huh?'

Before he can say anything else, I take one of the petals and pop it in his mouth, and then put one in mine.

We both look round as Gerald starts thwacking his mallet down on the lectern. I turn back to Sam, lean forward and kiss him. His lips are soft and sweet from the sugary almond, and he pulls me into him.

'I'll message you once the auction is over,' I say, heat rippling up my body as he lets me go.

He gives my hand a final squeeze before I turn and make my way back through the growing crowd towards Mum. I turn back and return his wave, and then – to my horror – realise he's waving at my mum who is lolloping her arm in the air fiercely like she's waving her only son off to sea.

For goodness sake.

Chapter Fifty-Nine

Ange

I feel a little bit like I've snuck into a party I'm not invited to. Everyone here is so *fancy*, and then there's my brother, who always seems to blend in with an elite crowd effortlessly. All of Mum's things are displayed in this little booklet and nobody is even giving me a second glance. Me and Zoe don't even have a *seat*.

I shift my weight from one foot to the other.

So, I had yet another tantrum yesterday. Although at least I had the good grace just to walk away instead of stamping my feet again and ranting at everyone. But that doesn't mean this wasn't the worst one to date.

It had been bubbling up inside me ever since I overheard Fanny on the phone a few days before. I knew something was going on with her; she would never show up unannounced without a reason. But I ignored it. I knew she'd tell me eventually. I just didn't think it would be this.

I step back, pressing against the wall to make room for a man in a silk scarf to shimmer past me.

I think several people would collapse in shock if they knew I was Clarice Florentina's daughter. This dumpy, sad, middle-aged woman in the corner. I didn't inherit even a whisper of her artistic talent (much to my annoyance growing up), and her carefree spirit didn't even flirt with the idea of passing down to me. We couldn't be more different, but that's why we needed each other.

It's how me and Fanny always worked too. We're two sides of the same coin. It felt so good to have that back.

I steal a glance at Zoe. Her lips are pressed together in concentration as she takes it all in, and there is a line between her eyebrows from where she is frowning. I wanted her to have that ring so badly.

Zoe's dad left before she was even born. He didn't like the idea of having a baby; to be honest, I don't think he liked the idea of me in general very much, but there you go. So in the hospital it was just me and Mum. Fanny kept sticking her head in (she and Reg had been married for two years at this point), but she couldn't stay too long without recoiling in horror at the sight of me or needing a cigarette.

Mum's small hand gripped mine fiercely and she kept repeating wishy-washy, airy-fairy expressions that were no help at all. Nobody wants to hear that you're in the middle of 'nature's greatest miracle' when you're pushing so hard your vagina is turning blue.

But then Zoe was there, and she really was a miracle. All pink and scrunched up and squishy.

'Oh Angie,' Mum breathed as I held my tiny daughter in my arms, 'she is gorgeous. I'm so proud of you.'

Her wild hair was hidden under a hairnet, and her cheeks were flushed with the excitement of it all.

'I'm glad you took the drugs,' she added. 'I would have happily had some too if they'd let me.'

I laughed. 'I think they're only for people in labour.'

She smiled, leaning forward and running a finger across Zoe's tiny pink nose. Her engagement ring caught the light and glistened. She pulled it off her finger.

'Ah, she needs some of this,' she said, taking Zoe's tiny finger and slipping it on. I couldn't help but roll my eyes.

'Mum,' I said, 'she's barely an hour old.'

'She needs the magic that's carried in this ring. I used to put it on your finger when you were a baby.'

'Really?'

'Of course. Every day. How else did you turn out so great?'

She hooked her arm round my shoulders and pulled me into her chest.

'Come on then,' she said. 'Is this little Zoe?'

I looked down at my perfect baby. Zoe had been the name I'd chosen when I was eight years old. All my dolls were called Zoe.

'Yeah,' I sighed. 'I think she has to be, doesn't she?'

'You're not going to call her after your old mum then?' She grinned.

'No,' I replied. 'There's only one of you.'

She laughed at this and squeezed my shoulder. 'Welcome to the team, little Zoe.'

Chapter Sixty

Zoe

I'm not sure why I was worried about the auction dragging. This is one of the most intense, high-pressure events I've ever been to! No wonder poor Gerald looks like he spends his evenings dancing with the dead. Who was I to laugh at him for warming up his muscles before we started? The speed he has to speak, he's like the verbal version of Usain Bolt!

'Aaaand thirty-six, thirty-six, thirty-six, do I have thirty-eight? Yes, thirty-eight! Do I have forty-five? Yes, forty-five in the back, thank you, sir. Anyone for fifty?'

Honestly, it's enough to make your head spin. Every now and then I get a sudden urge to throw up my arms and yell 'BINGO!' but I have to keep reminding myself that one, we're not playing bingo, two, Uncle Reggie would kill me and then auction off my organs, and three, they would probably only go for about eight pound fifty and Mum would be cross.

'And sold! For fifty thousand pounds!'

The weirdest part is that nobody screams or yelps with excitement when they win, nor do they throw their placard on the floor and yell 'I OBJECT!' if they've lost. They all just clap politely like they're watching cricket.

I mean, where is the *drama*?

Uncle Reggie has spent the entire time flouncing around and peacocking right next to Gerald. Every now and then he raises his eyebrows as if to say 'phwoar' when Gerald announces something, and he keeps winking at the women who are bidding and giving small nods to egg them on when they get outdone. It's highly irritating to watch, but to be fair, he's done a pretty good job. The Cornish cats and dogs will be thrilled.

Gerald smacks his hammer on the lectern as another item is sold, and I turn to Mum, who shakes her head.

'I don't think I have the nerve for this,' she whispers. 'It's all very exciting, isn't it? I can understand why Fiona Bruce has been doing it for so long.'

'And the next lot in today's auction is a fairly recent Clarice Florentina painting, painted in the twilight years of her life. This really is Florentina at her finest.'

A gasp skims across the audience. I glance up from the catalogue I'm grasping and see Grandma's self-portrait. Under the stark lighting of the auction hall, I can see new colours glinting. Mustard yellows and watermelon pinks. I feel my heart rise. Mum was right, it's not a painting of sadness at all; it's *full* of colour and joy.

'It looks weird seeing that outside Grandma's house,' I say to her.

'I know,' she says. 'It's so beautiful, isn't it?'

As Gerald starts gabbling numbers, I stare at the painting, feeling myself being pulled towards it as though we're attached by a piece of string. I'm not sure I can bear for it to be hung in someone else's house. It feels like I'm letting a part of her go.

'We've got fifteen thousand from the gentleman at the front, any advance? Somebody online has bid eighteen, that's eighteen thousand pounds. Can I see twenty?'

Mum catches my expression. 'Zoe, are you all right?'

I wrap my arms around myself. 'Yeah . . . I don't know. I feel a bit weird about selling that painting.'

'And we're up to twenty-five, that's twenty-five thousand pounds! Can I see twenty-eight?'

'Do you want to keep it? You should have said something last night.'

But as I open my mouth to reply, Gerald smacks his mallet down.

'And sold! To the gentleman online for thirty thousand pounds.'

A light smattering of applause fills the room, and I shrug.

'It's fine. That's a lot of money for charity, and it's what Grandma wanted.'

Mum tries to catch my eye, but I keep looking forward, ignoring my stomach, which keeps flipping about.

I don't know if I like watching Grandma's things being sold to strangers. Maybe Uncle Reggie was right and I shouldn't have come to the auction.

'And next up we have this one-of-a-kind 1940s engagement ring.'

My stomach drops.

What?

'This beautiful ring holds an emerald stone and is a nineteen-carat-gold original.'

I stare, frozen in horror, as Gerald holds up the ring. My grandma's engagement ring. The one I've been searching for.

Oh my God, it's here. How did it get here?

I jab Mum in the ribs, but she's already staring open-mouthed at Gerald.

'Don't worry,' she whispers. 'Reggie will realise in a second. There must be some mistake.'

But if Uncle Reggie has realised, he's doing a very good job of hiding it. He parades around the room, pointing at the ring and nudging people on the arm.

I can't let him sell it.

I look around madly, but we're stuck at the back. There are rows of chairs blocking our way to where Gerald is standing. Without climbing on the shoulders of the audience, there is no way for us to get to the front.

'Uncle Reggie,' I hiss as he skirts by us. 'Uncle Reggie!'

He ignores me, upping his speed and rushing back towards the stage.

'Right then.' Gerald clears his throat. 'Shall we start the bidding at one thousand pounds?'

My blood runs cold. *One thousand pounds?*

'It's not for sale!' I whisper to Mum. 'We need to stop it! It's meant for me!'

A man's arm flies into the air.

Oh my God, it's started!

'And we're off. We have one thousand pounds, starting on a thousand, anyone for fifteen hundred? Fifteen hundred, anyone? Anyone for fifteen hundred?'

Before I know what I'm doing, I throw my arm into the air. Uncle Reggie catches my eye and glares at me.

'Fifteen hundred pounds!' Mum shrieks in my ear. 'Zoe, you don't have that money, do you?'

'I'm not going to pay it,' I mutter. 'I just need to make sure that nobody else buys it.'

She blinks at me. 'I don't think you can just not pay it.'

'And straight back in, gentleman in the front row for two thousand pounds!'

Just as I am about to throw my arm in the air again, a man sitting behind a computer raises a hand calmly.

'Three thousand.'

I gape at him.

The man in the front row raises his arm again, and I start to feel a bit sick. At that moment, Harriet shuffles in next to me.

'Zoe!' she hisses. 'That's the ring, isn't it? You were right! He did want to sell it!'

'We're on four thousand pounds, can I get five? Five thousand pounds, anyone?'

The man behind the laptop lifts his hand again.

'Five thousand.'

'Six!' the man in the front row shouts.

'Do we have seven thousand from the bidder online?' Gerald calls.

The man at the laptop nods.

'Zoe,' Harriet nudges me, 'we need to stop it! They're going to sell it!'

I blink, suddenly brought back into the room and out of my thoughts. Any second now, the ring could be lost to me for ever.

'Eight thousand,' I squeak, forcing my voice to carry across the room. My heart races in my chest as the people in front turn around to face me. Even as I say it, I feel as though I might pass out. I don't have eight thousand pounds. I can't pay that money.

'Nine,' the man at the laptop says lightly.

I watch wordlessly as the man in the front row and the one behind the laptop start bidding against each other.

Ten thousand.

Fifteen.

Twenty.

'Any advance on twenty?' Gerald calls, his mallet held in the air. 'Do I have twenty-five? Anyone for twenty-five? Going for twenty thousand pounds? Going once, going twice . . .'

He slams the mallet down, and the impact shakes through my body.

Just like that, the ring is gone.

Chapter Sixty-One

Zoe

'That was fantastic!' Uncle Reggie booms, throwing out his arms and pulling me and Mum into a hug. He's practically shaking with excitement, but I guess anyone would be if they were about to pocket thousands of pounds. Harriet glares at him from over her phone.

'Reggie,' Mum snaps at him, pushing herself free of the hug. 'That ring shouldn't have been sold. Didn't you notice us waving? We need to get it back. It was meant for Zoe!'

For a split second I see a look of bemusement cross Uncle Reggie's face, before it's quickly replaced by a sympathetic smile.

'Oh yes, of course. And!' He turns to me, his arms wide in a 'can you believe it?' gesture. 'The bloody ring showed up after all that! Guess we didn't look hard enough in the house what with everything being boxed up, eh?' He nudges me and I bristle.

'We should go up and explain,' Harriet says, craning her neck over the crowds. 'The man who bought it is over there; he was bidding for someone else online. We can just tell him what happened and I'm sure he'll give it back.'

'I don't think so!' Uncle Reggie scoffs. 'Unless you have twenty grand you want to offer him for it.' He raises his eyebrows at me, and I want to slap him.

'Could I use some of the money we get from the auction,' I gabble desperately, turning to Mum.

Uncle Reggie snorts. 'Think you'll be getting twenty grand, do you?'

'We'd have to do the maths,' Mum says, her face scrunched up with concentration. 'But after taxes and things, I'm not sure we'd have enough.'

'But it's Zoe's ring,' Harriet says, pulling herself up to her full height and turning to my uncle. 'Her grandma wanted her to have it.'

'Well I never saw anything about it in the will,' Reggie says, and I see anger flash across his face. 'You had the chance to keep it aside and you didn't.'

'That's only because you hid it,' I mutter under my breath. Thankfully he doesn't hear, but Mum shoots me a look of alarm.

'It's fine,' I force myself to say, even though my eyes are prickling. 'One of those things.'

Harriet turns to me, aghast. 'Zoe!'

'It's fine,' I say again, taking a deep breath and stepping out of the way as a couple try to manoeuvre past me towards the exit.

'I suppose you'll be getting on the road then?' Uncle Reggie says absent-mindedly.

I'm about to reply when my phone vibrates in my hand. I

turn it over, for a second thinking I might finally see Aunt Fanny's name flashing up at me, but the reality makes my heart stop.

Heidi.

As quickly as I can, I push my way through the crowds of people and lock myself in the toilet. After taking a deep breath to calm my nerves, I call her back.

'Hi, Heidi, how are you?'

'Hello, darling!' she coos. 'How are you feeling? Kitty said you've had the worst type of stomach bug. She said the doctors thought it might be norovirus?'

I don't even know what norovirus is.

'I'm okay, thank you,' I say after a beat. 'I think I'm over the worst of it now. I'll be back in the office next Monday for sure.'

'Oh good, we've missed you! Although Kitty really has taken it all in her stride. Guess where I am?'

I bite my lip, trying to fight the thought that Heidi might somehow be in Sulmona about to catch me out.

'Hang on,' she says. 'Let me send you a picture.'

I put her on loudspeaker as I check my messages. A photo comes through of Heidi sitting in a café, looking out onto a beach where a small group of people are gathered. A woman wearing a long white dress is holding hands with a man in a suit. Both are barefoot. I spot Kitty standing next to an older woman.

'Is that . . . Libby's wedding?'

'Yes!' Heidi gushes. 'She was having a terrible time with all the stress of it, so do you know what Kitty did? She told her that the most important thing was simply getting married, and then she organised this super-intimate last-minute beach wedding. Libby cancelled the huge wedding and pulled it forward a few days! Isn't it gorgeous? She just had so many fabulous ideas, they were so unique! Honestly, you two make one hell of a team. Where have you been hiding all these plans?'

I open and close my mouth stupidly.

'It was all Kitty,' I manage. 'She is great.'

'Well!' Heidi gasps. 'Libby was very impressed, as am I. I can't wait to have you back in the office so we can get the next wedding planned. And you'll both be getting a fat commission off the back of this! Plus we have a new bride coming in on Monday that you and Orla will need to pitch for.'

After a brief back and forth of small talk, we say goodbye and the line goes dead. My arm drops to my side as my heart races in my chest, but it's not for the usual reason. I'm relieved the wedding went well, but the idea of going back into the office on Monday and starting another pitch makes me feel quite cold inside. I don't want to do it.

I don't want to go back.

Chapter Sixty-Two

Harriet

I pop a sugared almond in my mouth. This one is buttercup yellow. Honestly, I've never seen anything like it. The streets of Sulmona are *full* of them. Every corner is bright with posies of confetti, the sugared almonds painted in different colours to imitate a bunch of flowers. I think I'd prefer to get a bunch of these over real flowers; these ones taste *great*.

I sit on the side of the fountain, watching as pockets of people bustle across the piazza. Families, couples, young children. The town is buzzing.

I take a deep breath and pull out my phone, finding Mum's name in my contacts and clicking call.

Watching the auction and how upset Zoe and Angie were, it was like someone had marched up to me and given me a slap in the face. Like, *wake up*. You can't waste your life being annoyed at someone over something they have absolutely no idea about, because one day they won't be here any more. Life is too short, nobody is perfect. Get over it.

So soon after the auction finished, I said I was going for a walk and slipped away. I knew I needed to make things right. I couldn't blame my mum for my life any more.

'Hi,' I say when she picks up, 'it's me.'

'Oh, hello, darling.'

I pause, waiting for the sound of Daniel in the background, but it doesn't come.

'How's Daniel?' I ask. 'Is he with you?'

She sighs. 'He's actually with Darren, so I'm having a rare afternoon to myself.'

'That sounds nice.'

'It would be nicer if you were here.'

I feel my heart turn over.

'How is Italy?' she asks. 'Are you near a fountain? I can hear water.'

'Oh.' I get to my feet and walk across the piazza. 'Sorry, yes, I was. I've moved away.'

'Ah,' she says, 'that's better. I can hear you now.'

I start to wander through the streets. I don't really know where I'm going, but I feel like I can't get too lost in Sulmona. The narrow streets seem to weave in and out of each other, and each one has a shop selling confetti, like a mark on a map that I'm going in the right direction.

'Harri,' Mum says, 'why didn't you tell me you were going away, love?'

'I don't have to tell you everything,' I say before I can stop myself. 'I am twenty-five.'

She sighs. 'Yes, but normally you tell me roughly where you're going. You've been in a different country for four days and I had no idea.' To my horror, her voice thickens.

'Wait, Mum,' I gabble. 'I'm sorry. Please don't get upset. This is all my fault. I didn't tell you on purpose.'

'Why?'

I stop walking and lean against a wall, trying to force myself to finally articulate the fear that's been swimming in my mind for the past year. 'Because I wanted to see whether you'd miss me.'

'Miss you?' she repeats, bewildered.

'I haven't really felt part of everything since Daniel was born. I've felt a bit like a spare part, like you don't need me any more. And it's made me feel like I have no idea what I'm doing with my life. Like I've lost my purpose.'

It seems like a lifetime before she speaks.

'Oh,' she says, 'I'm so sorry you've been feeling that way.'

'No,' I say at once, '*I'm* sorry I've been feeling this way! I shouldn't! You're so happy and it's so selfish for me to want you to need me all the time. You have your own life—'

'Darling,' she cuts across me, 'you are one of the biggest parts of my life and always will be. I can't believe you'd ever feel like I didn't need you, let alone that I wouldn't miss you. You're my *child*. And Daniel needs you too.'

I scoff. 'He hates me.'

'He has colic, sweetheart. He hates everyone.'

I laugh, and after a beat Mum laughs too.

'Now,' she says, 'what was that you were saying about how you've lost your purpose?'

I bite my lip. 'Yeah. I have no idea what I'm meant to do.'

I hear her shuffle on the sofa. 'Well, why don't you go find out? And Harriet,' she adds, her voice suddenly stern, 'don't ever think that I won't miss you. I am your mum. I love you more than life itself.'

My eyes prick. 'I love you too.'

Chapter Sixty-Three

Zoe

I link my arm in Mum's, closing my eyes and tilting my head towards the sun, a blanket of warmth spreading over my cheeks. I'm wearing a sundress I bought from a small shop in town, and as the wind blows at the skirt and tousles my hair, I feel miles away from home. My hair isn't pulled off my face, my body isn't squeezed into a pencil skirt. I feel so free. Like, totally at one with the world and just so—

'Zoe, look out!'

My eyes snap open as Mum yanks me backwards as I almost walk straight into a lamppost. Okay, so maybe not totally at one with the world.

I giggle as I loosen my grip on her arm. She looks back at me, alarmed, but my laughter is contagious, and before long she's joining in. For a moment we stand there cackling hysterically, and I realise it's the first time in far too long that the two of us have properly laughed.

We left the auction shortly after it ended. Harriet wanted to stay behind in town, so me and Mum offered to pick up ingredients for dinner before heading back to the house. I'd love to say that Grandma had some magical Italian recipes hidden within the walls of her kitchen, but the woman could barely crack an egg.

'Have you had a nice time then?' I say, wiping a tear from my eye as the giggles finally stop.

Mum sighs. 'For the majority of it, yes. I'll feel better once we hear from Fanny, but I've had a better time than I could have imagined. I was under a cloud in Truro, and now look.' She holds out her free hand and tilts her chin towards the sun. 'I practically need suncream, it's so bright. There are no clouds here.'

I laugh again. 'Is that a metaphor?'

She shrugs, a small smile. 'Maybe. Does it make me sound clever?'

'Not really,' I tease.

She gives me a light tap on the arm. 'I'm just very grateful for you all, and for this trip. And it was lovely having us all back together, while it lasted.'

I hold her arm a little tighter as we drift into silence, listening to the light chatter of Italians laughing and bustling up and down the streets. After a moment, I ask the question that is playing on my mind.

'Have you heard from her yet?'

Mum doesn't even bother to pretend that she doesn't know who I'm talking about. She sighs.

'No. Have you?'

'No.'

'When do you have to be back at work?'

'Not until Monday now,' I reply. 'Heidi thinks I'm sick.'

Mum raises her eyebrows, but she's still smiling. 'Well, I'll look at train times in the morning. Hopefully they'll be running again now. Then we can book flights.'

'What about Aunt Fanny? I don't want to leave her here.'

She sighs. 'Darling, we've called countless times and she hasn't answered. She probably isn't even in Sulmona any more.'

My heart aches. Can she really have left us again?

'Look,' Mum says, nodding towards the coffee shop we visited yesterday. 'Why don't we pick up some bread for tomorrow morning?'

'Good idea. Maybe we could stop and have a coffee too.'

'Perfect.'

We scurry across the road, darting out of the way of a racing moped.

'I just feel bad going home without her,' I mumble as I push open the coffee shop door.

'I know, it isn't the same going home without seeing Grandma, is it?'

The bell dings as we step inside.

'Well, yeah, but I didn't mean Grandma.'

'Fanny?'

'Yeah, exactly.'

'No.' Mum nudges me and I turn around to see Aunt Fanny draped in the exact same spot that we left her, one spindly leg hooked over the other and her shiny red lips pursed on the rim of her coffee cup.

'Fanny.'

A wave of emotions run through me as I take in her nonchalant posture. She's tapping on her phone screen, acting as though it hasn't been buzzing non-stop with calls and messages from me and Mum, desperate to know if she's okay. Relief, excitement, love. But unfortunately, I land on anger.

'There you are!' I cry, storming over to her like she's a child who's been hiding. 'What are you doing here?'

She looks up from her phone idly. 'I'm having a coffee.'

'We've been looking everywhere for you!' I throw my arms in the air and narrowly miss an old man reading a newspaper.

'Well, you haven't been looking very hard,' she says, glancing back down at her phone. 'I stayed exactly where you left me.'

'We didn't leave you!'

'Yes you did.'

'We didn't. I asked you to come, and you said no!' I cry, heat rising up my body.

She shrugs and looks up at Mum, who immediately goes bright pink and walks towards the counter. 'I'll get us a coffee.'

'I'll have a cappuccino, Ange,' Aunt Fanny calls after her.

I shove myself into the seat opposite, frantically trying to get comfortable as my bare legs stick together like sheets of cling film. Logically, I know that she hasn't slept here, but it's like she literally hasn't moved since I last saw her.

'Why didn't you call me back?'

She doesn't answer.

'Have you heard from the doctor?'

'Here we are.' Mum reappears with a tray of three large coffees, and three even larger pastries.

Aunt Fanny puts her phone down. 'Thanks, Ange.'

'I thought we all deserved a treat,' Mum says, and although

318

she is trying to speak in her usual light, upbeat voice, it still carries a slight edge.

'How was the auction?' Aunt Fanny asks, breaking off a piece of the largest pastry and popping it into her mouth.

I clamp my lips together, annoyed at her avoiding my question. I wait for Mum to answer, but she's busy stirring sugar into her drink.

I huff. 'The ring was sold. It was there all along.'

She raises her eyebrows at me. 'Oh really? Well, I told you your uncle would have tried to pocket it to make some money. Did you get it back?'

I tuck my hands under my legs. 'No. It sold for, like, twenty grand.'

She puffs her cheeks out. 'Crikey.'

I look at Mum, waiting for her to chip into our stilted conversation, but she's still stirring her coffee.

Aunt Fanny sits up straight and puts her arms on the table, palms upwards.

'I'm really sorry, Ange.'

'No,' Mum bursts in at once, and to my alarm, I realise she's crying. '*I'm* sorry, I shouldn't have—'

'Angie, let me speak.' Fanny cuts across her. 'You always apologise for everybody, but this is something I need to apologise for. To both of you. You were right, it was selfish of me to leave when the shit hit the fan with Reg, and it was even worse of me not to keep in contact. I came back for selfish reasons too: I knew I needed you both. I've had the best week with you girls. It's made me realise how many years I wasted being mad at your stupid brother when I could have been happy with the two of you.'

She turns to face me, and I feel like I might cry.

'I was really angry at you for leaving,' I say.

'I know.'

'You missed my first day of uni. Mum had to take me by herself.'

'I bet that took years.'

'We got a taxi.'

A small smile plays on her lips, and she looks back at Mum, who is staring down at her hands.

'I shouldn't have said those things to you,' Mum mumbles. 'I was just so happy to have you back, and when I heard that you had cancer and that I might lose you again, I couldn't take it. It just feels so unfair.'

Aunt Fanny takes her hand. 'I know, but life isn't always fair, Ange.'

Mum nods, tears spilling down her face now. 'A lot of the time, she's actually a bit of a bitch.'

CHAPTER SIXTY-FOUR

FANNY

'Jon, I haven't heard from the doctor yet. I promise I will call you as soon as I do . . . Yes, I know they said I'd hear yesterday, but I didn't, all right? . . . Well, how do you think it feels for me? It's not all about you! . . . Yes, fine. I love you too, goodbye.'

I turn to Zoe and roll my eyes. 'Men.'

Harriet laughs, taking a piece of bread and dipping it in the glistening olive oil.

The more we talked earlier in that little coffee shop, the easier I found it to stuff my worries back into the little box in the back of my mind. Afterwards, I looped arms with Ange and Zoe and marched them towards a shop I'd been eyeing up. We bought ribbons of fresh pasta, ripe tomatoes and fat bell peppers, tangy onions and a bulb of garlic the size of a doorknob.

We scooped up Harriet from the porch swing when we arrived, and now the four of us are sitting around Clarice's outdoor table at the back of her house, with a view of the sun setting behind the mountains. It's splattered with paint from over the years, and marked with random dark circles from hot coffee cups and splashes of stray wine. In the middle of the table, we lit a skinny candle that Harriet found slotted in the top of a wine bottle. Dribbles of wax skim down the sides of the bottle from years of illuminating Clarice's nights. I pick up the red wine I bought earlier and slosh some into each glass.

Reggie has gone, hallelujah. He messaged Ange to say he was travelling back to Rome so wouldn't be able to make it for dinner. Like he was invited! Honestly, the cheek of that man.

I lean back in my seat as Ange starts to spoon pasta from the bubbling pot into our mismatched bowls. They're all slightly different sizes. I wonder if Clarice attempted pottery at some point.

'How long did your grandma live here?' Harriet asks Zoe, taking a sip of her wine.

Zoe turns to Ange, eyebrows raised.

'Oh gosh,' Angie says. 'She moved here when my dad died. So thirty-five years ago, I'd say.'

Harriet sighs, turning her face towards the mountains. 'She had this every night for thirty-five years? She had it right.'

'She didn't just do this, though,' Angie adds. 'She travelled around a lot when she was in her twenties. She only settled in Truro when she had me and Reg.'

Zoe frowns. 'I didn't know that. Where did she go?'

'Oh, everywhere. South America, Asia, all across Europe.' She turns to Zoe in surprise. 'You do know this, darling. You don't imagine she stayed in one place, do you? Where do you think she got all her inspiration from?'

Harriet starts plaiting her hair. 'What an absolute rock star.'

Angie laughs, finally sitting down and raising her glass. We all copy and clink our glasses together. It is so nice to hear her laugh again properly. Not the horrible robotic tinkle I heard when I arrived a few days ago. Her real laugh is much more guttural than that. It's like a pelican being sat on.

'I'd like to be Clarice when I grow up,' Harriet says.

Zoe grins. 'Yeah, me too.'

I watch her face. The setting sun is making her dark hair shine. Her high cheekbones are prominent on her face, and her skin is all pink and freckly from the sun. She is so gorgeous. How is she still single?

'So!' I burst out, slapping her leg and making her jump. 'You still haven't told us a single detail about this date of yours.'

'She told me,' Harriet says knowingly. 'And he came to the auction with some of those confetti flowers and *kissed her.*'

Zoe kicks her under the table. I throw my arms in the air, outraged.

'That's even worse! I know I will have missed all the puberty talks, and I assume the revelation of you losing your virginity . . .'

I try to keep a straight face as Zoe almost chokes on her drink. God, she's even more fun to wind up than Angie.

'. . . but I'm back now and I want all the details!'

I lean back in my chair and Angie beams next to me. When Zoe was a toddler, the two of us used to talk about this moment in the future. All of us sitting around a dinner table, probing her on her love life and what she was *really* doing every Saturday night when she claimed to be studying with a friend.

For a second I think she is going to refuse to tell me, but I give her a challenging look. I am not letting this go. I've earned this moment.

'It was really good actually,' she says, a large smile peeling onto her face. 'It was fun, so easy and romantic and spontaneous. I don't know. To be honest, it was nice to go on a date with someone completely new in a different country, not to the same bar me and Harriet seem to go to every weekend.'

Harriet raises her glass and Zoe laughs.

'She said it was the best date of her life,' Harriet adds, and Angie gasps.

'Of your life?' she repeats. 'Zoe, that's wonderful.'

Zoe rolls her eyes, laughing. 'Yeah, but it was a one-time thing, wasn't it? He's travelling around Europe, and we go back to sunny Truro in, what, twenty-four hours or something.'

'Tell them about how it ended,' Harriet prompts.

Angie's eyes light up. 'What happened?'

Two small pink patches form on Zoe's cheeks. 'We went back to the fountain and both threw in a coin and made a wish.'

'That's so romantic!' Angie coos.

I swallow a laugh. She is about to burst into a spritz of wedding confetti.

'Oh Zoe!' she cries. 'You have to see him again!'

'What was your wish?' I ask.

Zoe gives me a knowing grin, and for a second it's like looking into a mirror. 'If I tell you that, it won't come true.'

I tut loudly, but I'm still smiling.

Angie takes a deep breath and clears her throat. 'Now,' she says, 'I'd like to say something, please.'

We all look at her in surprise as she takes mine and Zoe's hands, gesturing for us to take Harriet's too so we look as if we're about to launch into a seance. We all lean in in anticipation as she starts to speak.

'Now,' she says again, 'I'd like to thank you ladies for what you've done for me these past few days. I was stuck under a cloud in Truro, and if it wasn't for the three of you, I think I would have stayed under it for years. Possibly even for the rest of my life. You girls have made me remember what it feels like to really live again, and I will never forget that.'

She turns to me and smiles, and when I catch sight of her mouth, I have to stop myself from bursting out laughing.

I seriously need to teach this woman how to drink a glass of red wine.

'Zoe, I'm so proud of you for the young woman you have become.'

Her face is earnest, but unfortunately the moment is ruined by the horrible squawk that bursts out of Zoe's mouth.

Angie blinks at her, confused.

'It's your teeth, Ange,' I say, trying to stop myself from laughing. 'You look like you've bitten the neck of a cow again.'

She rolls her eyes. 'I'm trying to say something!' She turns away from me, but by this point Harriet and Zoe are laughing too. Tears are squeezing out of the corners of Zoe's eyes and Harriet is turning beetroot.

'I really feel like you and Harriet will go on to do wonderful things, whatever those might be, and I can't wait to see . . . Oh for God's sake, Zoe, pull yourself *together*!'

By this point Zoe is doubled over with giggles, wheezing.

Angie looks at me, bemused. 'Is it really that bad?' She bares her teeth at me. I clap my hands together and let out a hoot of laughter.

'Terrible, Ange,' I laugh. 'Absolutely terrible.'

Her hands fly to her mouth, but then she looks at me and grins madly.

'What do you mean?' she says. 'Is there something in my teeth?' She turns to Zoe and wraps an arm around her shoulder. 'Am I beautiful, Zoe?' She looks deranged as she opens her mouth wide. 'Do you hope you look just like me one day?'

Zoe can barely breathe at this point. I pull out my phone.

'Come on,' I say. 'Everyone show your best red wine mouth. I want a picture of this.'

Chapter Sixty-Five

Angie

Once we'd all calmed down after the red wine incident, we sat and ate and laughed. We chatted and teased each other and found Mum's old blankets when it got cold and wrapped them around ourselves. And it was like the future I had imagined when Zoe was a baby and Fanny was trying to buy her designer trainers as I pushed her around Mothercare had actually happened.

For the first time in years, I just sat in the moment, bathed in its warmth, and let myself believe that this life could actually last for ever. A life where I'm happy.

Where all of us are happy.

★

Later that night, I creep down the hall and into Fanny's room. I know she'll be awake; she's always awake until the early hours.

'Fanny?'

She jerks round as I walk in, her hands flying up to try and cover her bald head. She's wrapped it in a silk scarf, hiding the bumps and shadows of her skull.

'You could have knocked,' she says after a beat as I push the door shut.

'So you could put your wig on?'

She eyes me. 'So I could put my *hair* on. Yes. I've read in some magazines that after you have chemotherapy, your hair comes back *curly*. I'm going to look like a cockapoo.'

She drops down onto the chair at the dressing table and starts scooping cream out of a pot with her fingers.

'Curly hair is lovely! Or you could straighten it?' I offer, sitting down on the bed.

'Well, maybe I won't have to worry about my hair anyway.' She catches my shocked expression. 'Because I'll keep the wig.'

Ah.

'Listen,' I say, taking a deep breath. 'I want you to come back to Truro with me and Zoe. No matter what the results say, I want to look after you.'

'No thank you.'

'Fanny,' I say sternly, 'it's an order.'

She swivels round in her seat to face me. 'Angie, if the chemo hasn't worked, I am absolutely not having you give up your life to be my carer. I'll just slink off into the woods and disappear like a cat.'

I open my mouth to argue, but she gets there first.

'So, that's what you'll be doing, is it?' she asks, turning back to the mirror.

'What do you mean?'

'Going back to Truro?'

I shift on the bed, trying to get comfortable. 'What else would I do?'

'Stay here?' She shrugs.

I shake my head. 'No. I need to get back. I have responsibilities, and Zoe needs me.'

'I'm not sure she'll go back either.'

'She has work.'

'And what's your excuse?' She raises her eyebrows at me.

'Fanny,' I say after a pause, 'I just came in here to say that whatever happens, I'll be here. I'm not going anywhere.'

She lifts her chin, unwinding the silk scarf and staring at her reflection defiantly.

'With any luck, Ange, neither am I.'

Chapter Sixty-Six

Zoe

'I've had such a great time.'

Harriet's voice echoes in the dark, and I fold my arms around my body. Grandma's house is more than big enough for us all to have our own rooms, but me and Harriet wanted to stay together, like we do when we're at Mum's. Her voice is light, floating on the happy waves of wine. I smile into the darkness.

'Yeah,' I say. 'So have I. I just—'

I stop as my phone starts ringing next to me, shooting a blast of white light into the room. Harriet throws an arm over her eyes, and I lean forward, grabbing the phone.

'Sorry,' I mutter. As I go to switch it off, though, I see the name flashing on the screen.

'Why aren't you hanging up?' Harriet moans.

'It's Sam,' I say. 'He's calling me.'

She immediately sits up. 'Answer it!'

'But why is he calling me? It's late!'

'You won't know unless you answer it! Go on! Answer it or I will!' She goes to snatch the phone from my hand, and I quickly slam it to my ear, scrambling off the bed and out of Harriet's reach.

'Hello?'

I glance back at Harriet, who is goggling at me.

'Oh.' Sam sounds surprised. 'Hey, Zoe.'

I quickly slip out onto the balcony, pulling the doors shut behind me.

'Hey, sorry. I've just stepped outside. I'm sharing a room with Harriet. Are you okay?'

I can hear him smiling down the phone. 'I'm good. Sorry, I know it's late. I was thinking about you and just wanted to see how you are.'

'I'm good too. Where are you guys?'

'We're back in Carsoli. We're staying with Aldo for a few days.'

I feel a pang in my chest. 'You didn't say goodbye.'

I can hear the smile in his voice. 'Well, I was hoping it wouldn't be a goodbye. You owe me a second date, remember?'

I laugh. 'I remember.'

'How did the auction go?' he asks.

I lean against the metal railings of the balcony, a shiver prickling up my back.

'Yeah, it was okay.'

'Did you get your ring?'

I sigh. 'No. Someone else did. It's a long story.'

'Ah, I'm sorry.'

I look out into the inky darkness, where a smattering of stars are winking down at me and an aeroplane is slowly skimming across the sky. I wonder where it's going.

'I was hoping I could see you again,' Sam says, and my heart lifts and drops at the same time. 'Are you coming back via Carsoli? Aldo has some great recommendations for places to go.'

'I don't think I can. We go home tomorrow. I need to get back.'

His voice dips. 'Do you have to go?'

I laugh. 'Well, yeah. I can't just, you know . . .'

'What?'

I run my fingers through my hair. I don't even know.

'I need to go home,' I say after a beat. 'But maybe when you're back in England . . .'

I can hear the defeat in his voice. 'Yeah, sure, or if you have a change of heart and stay, you can give me a call, how about that?'

I smile as I ring off and crawl back into bed with Harriet.

'Well?' she says at once. 'What did he say?'

I smile into the pillow. 'He thinks we should stay here.'

'He's right,' she sighs sleepily, pulling the duvet up to her chin. 'Good old Ron. I've always liked him.'

Chapter Sixty-Seven

Zoe

The next day, the four of us are sitting around the kitchen table as Mum fusses over a coffee pot and Aunt Fanny scowls down at her phone. Mum didn't dare offer her glasses this time.

'So,' Fanny begins, 'the good news is that the trains are running again and there is one that leaves tomorrow morning. If we catch that train,' she continues, 'we can get the six o'clock flight from Rome back to Cornwall. We'd get in at about nine. So we'd miss *Corrie*, I'm afraid, Ange.'

Mum laughs, pouring streams of black coffee into four mugs.

'I can live with that,' she says.

'Shall I book it then?'

I keep my eyes firmly on my hands, my stomach flipping when nobody answers. After a moment, Fanny puts her phone down.

'Oh,' Aunt Fanny says. 'I almost forgot, come with me a sec, will you?'

I look up. 'Me?'

'Everyone.' She gets to her feet and gestures for us to follow her. As we troop after her out of the kitchen, I give Harriet a dubious look.

'Right. Close your eyes, all of you.'

'Fanny,' Mum laughs, 'what's going on?'

'You'll find out in a second!' she barks. 'Just shut them.'

We all close our eyes and hover in the hallway. I hear a grunt, and then Aunt Fanny says, 'Surprise, Ange.'

'What do you . . .' Mum trails off, and I open my eyes. Aunt Fanny is standing next to a painting. Not *a* painting, *the* painting. Grandma's painting of the woman. The painting of Grandma.

'I'll tell you what, it was a tough auction!' Aunt Fanny says, slapping her hands together. 'There were a lot of bidders! I only wanted to spend about ten grand, but then I really got into it. I ended up spending an absolute fortune. You can pay for our next holiday, Ange.'

I gape at her.

'It was you?' I manage. 'You bought this?'

'Yup.'

'But how can you afford it?'

To my surprise, Mum scoffs. 'Zoe, how do you think we afforded to go on all those holidays when you were little? Your Aunt Fanny isn't just a pretty face.'

Fanny shoots me a look of triumph.

'But . . . you don't work.'

'Excuse me! I'm an inventor.'

I stare at her. 'What?'

'You know your aunt invented the genie nail file.'

'It's huge in China,' Aunt Fanny quips. 'They can't get enough of me.'

I stare at Mum, my mouth open.

'I have told you this, Zo,' Mum insists.

'I know, but I didn't believe you. I thought it was just, I don't know, an urban myth or something.'

Aunt Fanny clicks her tongue, and Mum steps forward.

'I can't believe you bought this,' she says.

Fanny beams. 'I think it's the message Clarice would have wanted to leave us all. Embrace the colour and the madness and all that jazz.'

Mum's eyes are glistening. 'Thank you so much, Fanny,' she says, enveloping her in a hug.

'It's so lovely,' I say, looking at the painting. Aunt Fanny's eyes snap towards me, and I feel as though I've been jabbed by a cattle prod.

'What are you doing?' she snaps.

'What?'

'Your eyes!' she cries. 'Shut them! I'm not finished!'

I open and close my mouth stupidly, but I do as I'm told. I hear Mum gasp next to me, and then I feel something cold slide onto my finger. I know what it is before I've even opened my eyes.

This is going to sound mad, but straight away I feel as though sparks ignite across my body. Little pops of hope and excitement. Snatches of glitter. Grandma used to tell me how wearing this ring would fill you with magic, and I always believed her, no matter how old I was or how much I wanted her to talk to me like I was a grown-up. And now it's back with me; I've got it for ever.

Finally I have my grandma's ring.

*

I fold my legs into my body and stare out at Sulmona. From Grandma's balcony I can see stretches of green fields, treetops scattered throughout, popping up like florets of broccoli. The white sun is high in the sky, sending shards of light across the pale blue canvas of the sky, the occasional swoop of a bird and the faint echo of Aunt Fanny and Mum laughing in the kitchen reminding me that I'm not the only person in the world.

Grandma painted here, on this terrace. She used to say that she did a lot of her work in the shadow of the sun, craning towards it each day like a sunflower.

I pull out my phone and dial Kitty's number, shutting my eyes as I listen to it ring.

'Hello? Kitty?'

'Zoe, hi! It's so good to hear from you! How are you feeling?'

I grin. 'Yeah, fine. I'm not actually ill, remember?'

'Yes, but I am in the office.'

Shit.

'I'm not on loudspeaker, am I?'

'Of course not!' she cries, her voice reducing to a whisper. 'I would never do that to you! Are you on your way home? I can't wait to see you!'

I take a deep breath and decide to skirt past her question.

'How was the wedding? Tell me everything.'

She gives a little squeal. 'Oh, it was so great!' she gushes. 'So romantic. I knew something wasn't right with Libby, so I went round and saw her. And then she told me everything! Apparently her family had been a *nightmare*, some of her friends were getting competitive about weddings, and it was all too much for her! So I was like, look, you want to get married because you're in love, right? So let's do just that. I've never seen a couple more in love than Libby and her husband, it was perfect.'

'You did an amazing job, Kitty.'

'I loved it! And Heidi is so impressed with us.'

'Yeah, about that . . . This was all you, Kitty. Without you, who knows what would have happened. And I've told Heidi that, and we've agreed that you're taking all the commission.'

'What?' She gasps. 'But I'm your assistant!'

'Only on paper. Let's face it, without you, there wouldn't have been a wedding at all.'

'That's so kind of you,' she breathes. 'You really don't have to do that.'

'Yes I do,' I say. 'And I want to. You deserve it.'

She gives a nervous laugh down the phone. 'Do you think you'll be back on Monday?'

'Yeah,' I say after a pause. 'We're getting a flight tomorrow.'

'Amazing! I can't wait to see you and hear all about it! Did you get the ring?'

I turn my hand towards the light. The emerald glistens as it catches the sun, and I smile down at it.

'Yeah. I've got it.'

'Send me a picture!'

★

Later that night, we all venture down the mountain and into the town. I lead the way to the little restaurant that Sam and I went to on our date, and Valentina bursts into tears as soon as she sees us, setting off Mum. Aunt Fanny acts as translator as they gush to each other about how much they loved Grandma. Valentina shows us a painting that Grandma did for her, which is hanging behind the counter. It demands attention in the small, dark restaurant. Like all Grandma's work, it is a careful mix of colours, which snake around a proud but delicate sunflower. I can't believe I didn't notice it before.

Aunt Fanny insists that we order anything we want from the menu. So we have bruschetta and burrata, antipasti and fat, shiny olives. We demolish bowls of creamy pasta, bolognese and fresh lasagne, and a stretched pizza peppered with strips of pancetta. Then we share rich tiramisu, bowls of thick gelato, and tart citrus panna cotta. We drink glasses of deep red wine and finish with shots of sharp limoncello. We don't talk about the cancer, we don't talk about our lives outside the little bubble we're floating in. We laugh with each other and drink in stories of Grandma.

And then Aunt Fanny books our flights home.

Chapter Sixty-Eight

Fanny

I go to sleep knowing that tomorrow will be the day the phone rings with the news I have been bracing myself for all week. There are some things you just know, deep in your gut. Like the universe, or God, or whatever you believe in, is trying to give you a heads-up. So you can prepare yourself, get ready. Like, 'Hey, enjoy tonight, okay? It'll all be different tomorrow.'

And although I have this feeling in my belly, I don't go to sleep afraid. I go to sleep assured. I lay my head on the pillow knowing that really, out of all this shit, I have been given a gift.

Because if this feeling is right and tonight is my last night of ignorance, I know I am so incredibly lucky to have had a night so perfect and so surrounded by love. If this is how my last night of freedom looks, then quite frankly, I fucking thank my lucky stars.

Chapter Sixty-Nine

Zoe

'Okay,' Mum says, looking around her. 'I'm just going to do another sweep of the house to make sure we have everything.'

I nod as she bustles away, and feel my shoulders droop.

It's eleven in the morning, and with heads slightly fuzzy from a night of rich food and drink, Harriet and I are standing in Grandma's hallway next to the suitcases, waiting to leave. Mum and Aunt Fanny have spoken about coming back here in a few weeks. They're pretending that this doesn't depend on Aunt Fanny's news, like there isn't a rain cloud hovering over her head, ready to break any second. Fanny keeps trying to persuade Mum to track down Aldo.

I take a deep breath. I feel like I'm about to be sick, and I can't work out if it's because of the hangover or if it's the reality that we're about to leave.

340

'I bet you'll be happy to be reunited with your stuff,' Harriet grins, gesturing at my outfit.

I'm back in my I HEART ROME T-shirt and a pair of shorts that Harriet has lent me. Thankfully, staying at Grandma's meant I could at least wash the clothes I had, though let's just say I was ready to burn my pants.

I roll my eyes. 'If they've managed to find it. You know, I was so desperate to get that stuff back and felt really naked without it . . .'

'You *would* have been naked if it wasn't for me,' she quips.

'. . . but now I can't even really remember what was in the bag. It feels like I don't need any of it.'

'That's very profound, Zoe.'

'Thanks very much.'

I look up as Aunt Fanny appears, scratching her head.

'Is it itchy, the wig?' I ask.

She looks at me in horror. 'I'm not about to take it off, if that's what you're suggesting.'

I swallow a laugh as she drops onto a chair.

'What's going to happen to this house?' Harriet asks. 'Are you going to sell it?'

I shrug. 'Guess so. I'm sure Uncle Reggie will be keen to.'

Aunt Fanny scoffs. 'He has enough money from that auction to tide him over for a while. With any luck, you won't hear from him for a few years.'

'Right!' Mum reappears, clapping her hands together. 'I've done a thorough search of the rooms and they're all good. So I think we're ready!' She says the last bit in a forced, upbeat voice and looks round at us all. We avoid her eyes. Nobody moves.

'I should probably call a taxi,' Aunt Fanny says.

'Yeah,' I say quietly. 'Probably.'

We're back in silence as Aunt Fanny mutters Italian into her phone. Harriet is busy scrolling and Mum pretends to be looking at her shoes. I can feel my heart climbing up my body.

'Right,' she says. 'All booked. It will be here in about ten minutes.'

'That's great. Thanks, Fanny.'

'No problem.'

Silence falls, and the quieter we are, the louder my thoughts ring in my brain.

I don't want to leave.

As I open my mouth to speak, Aunt Fanny's phone starts to ring.

'Oh!' Mum jumps. 'That was quick!'

But when Fanny looks at the screen, her face goes pale and my stomach drops. Mum has read her expression too. We all understand why her phone is ringing.

'Answer it.'

She glances up at us, and suddenly she looks like a child. An expression of pure fear has taken over her features, and she's gripping onto the phone so tightly, her fingers have gone white.

'No.'

'We're not leaving until you answer it,' Mum says sternly. 'And if we miss our train, I am not having us walking to Rome.'

My heart races as Aunt Fanny slowly lifts her phone to her ear. I get to my feet and walk to Mum, holding my breath as Fanny speaks, desperately trying to read her facial expression for any hint of what they're saying to her. Next to me, Mum's hands have started to shake as she clings onto my arm, and I can tell that she's trying to hold it together. Aunt Fanny turns away, still on the phone, and I close my eyes.

Treasure these last moments, Zoe. In just a few seconds this could all change and she might go again, this time for good. Hold onto what you have, make it last as long as you can.

Mum gasps next to me, and my eyes snap open as I see that Aunt Fanny has doubled over, cradling her head in her hands. Harriet takes in a sharp breath, and her hands fly to her face. Me and Mum hurry over, and Mum grips Fanny's shoulders fiercely.

'It's okay,' she says, her voice shaking. 'It will be okay. It will all be okay.'

Bile rises up my body as I crouch next to her, my arm clutched desperately round her waist, as though without my support she might fall apart entirely.

No. Please no.

'It's gone.' Her voice is only small. A tiny murmur from under her hands, but it's enough to make my heart stop.

'Gone?' Mum repeats mindlessly. 'What do you mean?'

Aunt Fanny pulls her hands from her face. There are dark smears of mascara under her eyes, but she's laughing.

'It's gone,' she says again. 'It's fucked off. The cancer. I've done it, Ange. I've beaten it.'

'The cancer has gone?'

'Yeah. It's gone.'

Relief storms through my body and a manic laugh bursts out of me. Fanny turns to me and flings her arms around me, knocking me off balance and pulling me to the floor.

'It's gone!' I cry, laughing into her hair as Mum squeals next to us.

'Does this mean you're back then?' I ask, finally pulling

myself away. Aunt Fanny smiles up at me, one hand still covering her face as she lies on the floor.

'Oh yeah,' she says. 'I'm back.'

A car honks outside and Harriet looks round. 'Oh. I think the taxi is here.'

We clamber to our feet and pause, blinking at each other wordlessly. Fanny dabs her eyes, then turns to us.

'Change of plan,' she says. 'We're going for lunch first. The taxi can drop us in town.'

I glance at Mum. 'Have we got time? Won't we miss our flight?'

Mum glances at her watch. 'I think we have time.'

Aunt Fanny grins. 'Live life on the edge, Zo! Also, I bloody need a glass of wine.'

Chapter Seventy

Fanny

I suck on my cigarette, a gloriously long drag. I use all my energy to pull the smoke into my body for as long as I can. When I'm done, I tip back my head and puff it in swirls towards the sky.

'Ahhhhhhh.'

Next to me, I hear Angie wince. 'Should you really be doing that? You've just been cleared of cancer.'

'Exactly,' I say, not moving. 'I'm celebrating, Ange.'

Harriet giggles, and I flash her a wink.

I tap the cigarette against the ashtray. Opposite me, Zoe is concentrating on her phone. She's been looking at it anxiously for the past twenty minutes, and has barely said a word.

'So,' I say, 'what's going to happen when you get back, Zo?'

She jumps as though I've pulled her out of a trance. 'Huh?'

'Straight back to work?' Next to her, Harriet's face falls.

'Yeah,' she mumbles, 'I guess so.'

Ange is busy turning her cappuccino cup in her hands.

'And you, Ange? Back to your errands?'

'Oh yes,' she says in a small voice, not looking up.

'What about you?' Harriet asks me.

A gleeful smile pulls onto my face as she asks the exact question I've been waiting for.

'Oh, I'm not coming,' I say.

All three of them snap their eyes up to stare at me.

I readjust my sunglasses, waving at a man I catch looking at my legs. She's still got it.

'I'm not going back to England,' I say. 'It's too cold. I'm going to stay in Italy. I love it here.'

Zoe's mouth falls open. 'Are you joking?' she splutters. 'What about us? How can you be so selfish as to leave us again?'

I raise my eyebrows at her. 'Selfish?' I say. 'That's one way of looking at it.'

She scoffs. 'It's the *only* way of looking at it!'

'Well, I was hoping you might want to stay here too. Live in Clarice's house for a bit, do some travelling.' I give Ange a look. 'Give Aldo a call.'

She blushes, but she doesn't say no.

'I'll stay.'

I look round in surprise at Harriet, who has sat up a little straighter.

'I don't have a job to go back to, and we've always talked about travelling.' She turns in her seat to look at Zoe. 'Come on, Zo. I know you don't want to go back. We could get jobs on the way like Sam and his mates are doing or something.' She stares at her pleadingly.

Zoe's eyes flit between me and Harriet.

Come on, Zoe. Come on.

'I . . . I don't know.'

I spot her glance at Angie, and my heart thuds. That's why she's not going, not because she doesn't want to.

I turn towards Angie, a fire tickling my belly. 'Angie? What do you say? You want to stay here, don't you?'

She laughs, still looking down at her hands. 'I can't just do that, Fanny!'

I fold my arms. 'Why not? Give me three reasons.'

'Well, I have errands to run,' she says after a pause.

'The garden will survive without you there. That isn't a good reason,' I say at once.

'And Zoe . . .' She gestures towards Zoe, who blushes.

'Zoe wants to go travelling with Harriet, don't you, Zo?' I say. After a pause, Zoe nods. Harriet squeals and grabs her arm.

'I don't think you can give one good reason not to stay,' I say triumphantly.

'Unless you don't want to,' Zoe adds, leaning forward and taking Angie's hand.

Angie looks up at her and laughs. 'Oh,' she says. 'I think I want to, love.'

I feel a rush of excitement. *Yes.* I love winning.

'That's settled then!' I cry. 'Where's that waiter? We need more wine!'

Angie shoots me a look and nudges me in the ribs. 'You're a right bossy cow, Fanny.'

CHAPTER SEVENTY-ONE

ZOE

One month later

'Mum, will you stop crying? Everything is going to be fine.'

Aunt Fanny hands Mum another tissue before turning to me, her hands on her hips as she looks me up and down.

'Right, last-minute emergency checks please. Do you have enough knickers?'

'Yes.'

'A pair of heels?'

'No.'

'A clutch bag?'

'No.'

'Stockings?'

'Of course not.'

'I'm sorry,' Mum chimes in, dabbing her eyes for the third time in the last hour. 'I'm just going to miss you so much.'

I grin at her, unable to stop myself.

After we'd made the decision, Harriet went back home to tell her mum and to pack, leaving the three of us alone in Sulmona for a week. Aunt Fanny insisted on buying me everything brand new, though I wouldn't let her get me a 'staple red lipstick', which she insisted was more important than walking boots.

I had a long, heartfelt conversation with Heidi over FaceTime where I told her that I was quitting to travel the world. She understood and wished me all the best, but not before I insisted that Kitty take my job. I had so much annual leave stacked up that I didn't even have to work my notice period.

Now we're at the train station in Sulmona, and the train to our first stop, Turin, leaves in twenty minutes.

'How's your mum, love?' Mum says tearfully as Harriet bounces towards us wearing a backpack so big it's a wonder she doesn't topple over. 'Is she okay?'

'Oh, she's fine!' Harriet says breezily.

Without a job to go to, Harriet spent an entire week with her mum and the baby. She said that she even made him smile at one point, which felt like nothing short of a miracle.

'We'll be okay,' Aunt Fanny says, putting her arm around Mum's shoulders and giving her a shake. 'I'll keep her company in your absence, Zo.'

'Don't corrupt her too much.' I grin.

'I'll do what I like. If I get my way, by the time you're back she'll be on her third husband.'

Mum shakes her head, laughing. 'Shut up, Fanny.'

Aunt Fanny grins, rolling her eyes at me in a teasing way before turning to Harriet.

'Now, have you packed a pair of heels?'

Harriet laughs. 'No, but I don't need them anyway. I'm tall enough as it is.'

Fanny looks at me as though I've only got half a head. 'Yes, you're so lucky to have such long legs, Harriet. Oh, Zoe, before I forget, what about Sam?'

'What about him?'

She raises her eyebrows at me. 'I want every detail of this next date, right? If I don't hear from you with a full account within three days, I will follow you to Turin and ask him myself.'

I laugh, rolling my eyes.

Sam is now in Milan, but when I told him my plans, he insisted on meeting me in Turin for a second date. Apparently he has a friend who lives there, so he's going to be my tour guide for the evening.

'I think we'd better go to our platform,' Harriet says, looking over my shoulder at the departures board, which is blinking down at us.

I feel my heart leap. Mum throws her arms around me.

'Oh, I will miss you so much!' she cries. 'Please be careful, and don't talk to any strange men.'

'Unless they're offering you dinner.'

'Fanny!'

'I'm joking, I'm joking. These girls will have their wits about them.'

'I'll really miss you both,' I say, looking from Mum to Aunt Fanny.

'Don't worry.' Fanny grins, linking her arm in Mum's. 'We'll be right here when you get back.'

'Promise?'

She winks at me knowingly. 'Promise.'

Chapter Seventy-Two

Fanny

My arm is linked tightly through Angie's as we wave Zoe and Harriet off. They're grinning at each other like toddlers, their enormous backpacks far too big for them. I slipped a red lipstick into both when they weren't looking. I don't care what Zoe says, it's important.

Angie's shoulders shake next to me, and I give them a squeeze.

'Come on, you old tart. Let's go and get a drink. Fancy a red?'

She dabs her eyes. 'Only if you promise to drink at least two bottles with me and tell me if it gets all over my teeth.'

'I always will.'

We both start to wave as Zoe and Harriet's train pulls past. They're pressed up against the window, beaming madly and blowing kisses.

'Always?' Angie asks in a small, slightly wobbly voice.

I blow a final kiss as the train disappears around the corner.

'Always.'

Epilogue

Angie

I step into the bedroom and laugh when I catch sight of Fanny. She's lying on the double bed, eyes glued to the television, where a tousled Italian man in an open shirt is speaking intensely to a very beautiful woman.

'Have you worked out what he's saying yet?'

'Yes,' she mumbles, not breaking eye contact with the actor. 'and it's something not even I can repeat.'

I laugh, rolling my eyes as I clip earrings on. Fanny swings her legs round off the bed and takes a proper look at me.

'I can't believe that thirty years later, you're going on a date and I'm back here watching soaps and waiting for you to come home.'

'You don't have to stay in,' I say. 'I'll be fine. I think Aldo has proved himself to be a gentleman by now.'

She shrugs. 'I'm more interested to know if he has any dashing Italian friends.'

We've been living in Mum's house now for six weeks. During the day, we walk, read, watch terrible soaps and talk. In the evenings, we eat fresh food, drink wine and talk some more. We have fourteen years' worth of talking to catch up on.

'Oh!' I start as my phone begins to vibrate and I see Zoe's name flash onto the screen. 'Good. I was hoping they'd call before I left.'

I drop onto the bed next to Fanny so we can both fit in the frame, and slide my finger across the screen. Zoe and Harriet's happy faces pop up. Harriet's hair is bleached from the sun, her skin barely visible now under the millions of freckles that have sprung up all over her body. Zoe has picked up a gorgeous chestnut tan and her hair is wavy, falling past her shoulders. They've just arrived in France.

'Hi, Mum!' Zoe grins. 'Hi, Aunt Fanny! Oh, you look nice!'

'Thanks, darling,' Fanny says, deadpan.

Zoe gives her a look. 'I was talking to Mum. Are you seeing Aldo tonight?'

I blush. 'Yes. We're going out for dinner.'

'Yes, while I'm here all alone!' Fanny cries, clearly taking acting inspiration from the soap. 'Wasting my prime years cooped up by myself!'

'Fanny,' Harriet says, leaning closer to the phone, 'didn't you go on a date yesterday?'

She bats her eyes innocently. 'Yes.'

'Anyway,' I say, taking back the phone, 'how are you both? What are you doing?'

'We're good!' Zoe grins. 'We've just checked into our Airbnb in Nice. It's really cool here.'

'Yeah,' Harriet says. 'There are so many bars, and the place is full of tourists. I think we might stay here for a bit and get bar jobs to earn some money.'

Next to me, Fanny groans. 'Oh girls, *why*? Let me just *give* you the money, for God's sake.'

Zoe laughs and rolls her eyes.

'I think bar jobs sound like a great idea,' I say. 'Nice is supposed to be amazing.'

'Come out and see us!' Harriet cries. 'Mum, Daniel and Darren are going to meet us in Bordeaux.'

'Hey,' Fanny says, shuffling closer and nudging me. 'Now there's an idea. I love Monaco.'

'That's where Zoe is meeting Sam next week.' Harriet smirks. Fanny makes an 'ooh' sound next to me and Zoe shakes her head.

'Why don't we have a look at flights?' I say. 'Maybe we could pop over for a few days.'

'Pop over!' Fanny slaps my leg. 'Hark at her! A new woman! A few weeks ago you nearly had a stroke at the idea of leaving Cornwall.'

I shoot her a look, but I know she's only teasing.

'We better go, Mum,' Zoe says. 'Enjoy your date with Aldo.'

'And yours with Sam!' I chime.

'And I'll enjoy my date with *Un Posto al Sole*,' Fanny says, brandishing an arm at the TV.

'But you're okay, Mum?' Zoe asks, a look of concern appearing on her face.

I smile at her, warmth filling my body.

'Yes, love,' I say honestly, 'I'm fine. And you?'

She grins at the camera, and I spot Mum's engagement ring sparkling on her finger.

'I'm great.'

Acknowledgements

It really does take a village to write a book. So here are my thanks to everyone in my literary village. And yes, I nearly called them 'my village people' and if you now have the YMCA stuck in your head . . . you're welcome.

I have to start, as always, by thanking my Super-Agent Sarah Hornsley, who has believed in me right from the start. I never know how, but you seem to have the power to know how far to push me and you always make me a better writer. Without you, my books would be pants.

Someone else who has been monumental in making sure my book isn't pants is my glorious editor, Bea Grabowska, who somehow saw through the ninety-thousand-word first-draft warble and found what the book could be. Your patience, kindness and honesty has made this book what it is.

Thank you also to Jess Whitlum-Cooper who gave me the confidence to 'write what you love'. That stayed with me throughout every draft of this book.

Thank you to the incredible team at Headline who work endlessly to make my books a success.

Thank you to my cheerleaders: Hayley, Katy, Libby, Tommy, Becca, Andrew, Jamie, Laura, Anna, Pete, Georgia, Kristie, Lydia, Emily and Loren.

Thank you to the Emeralds girls, for never asking how many words I've written when I turn up for a game when I'm supposed to be writing.

Thank you to Claire for endless inspiration and Arianna for endless laughs.

Thank you to Ziggie and Gemma for all the tea, biscuits, chats and wisdom.

Thank you to Kiera, my soul sister.

Thank you to Tony and Pip for letting me borrow your gorgeous home for Clarice's house and for answering all of my questions. Thank you to Dawn, Simon and Suzy for all of your support.

Being an author can be a lonely business, so I am forever grateful to the authors and book bloggers who pick me up and read my work (especially if it's in the early stages!). You know who you are, thank you!

Thank you to YOU, reader, for picking up this book. I still can't believe that people do that (who aren't my mum), so thank you so much. Before I got my book deals, I would scour the acknowledgements in books I loved for any clue or advice on how to make my dreams of being an author a reality. If that's you, then find me on Instagram and message me.

Thank you to my love, my favourite person in the world, my Chris. Life is much, much better with you by my side and I'll always count my lucky stars that I found you.

Thank you to my family. To my sister, Elle, my brothers, Dominic and Tom, my parents and my grandad. My biggest champions, and perhaps the reason for half my book sales (hi, mum!). There is a piece of each of you in everything I write.

And finally, thank you to both of my grandmas. Neither are here to see this book be published but both were here when I decided I wanted to be an author. You left some magic behind for us all to follow.

Will switching lives bring two sisters together or push them apart for ever?

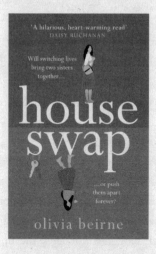

'A hilarious, heart-warming read'
DAISY BUCHANAN

Will switching lives
bring two sisters
together…

house swap

olivia beirne

…or push
them apart
forever?

Twins Katy and Rachel don't know much about
each other's lives any more.

Rachel thinks that Katy is a high-flying event planner in
London, while Katy thinks that Rachel lives in idyllic marital
bliss in the countryside.

Each sister believes the other has created a perfect life – but the
truth is that neither twin has the life she pretends she does.

And when these sisters unexpectedly swap houses for a week,
they're in for a big shock.

But it might just be the wake-up call they've
both been waiting for . . .

Available to order

REVIEW

**Would you open a love letter that
wasn't meant for you?**

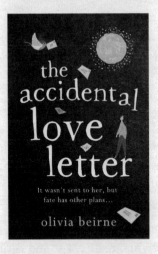

Bea used to feel confident, outgoing and fun, but she's
not sure where that person went.

Over the last few months, she's found herself becoming
reclusive and withdrawn. And despite living with her
two best friends, she's never felt lonelier. To make things
worse, she's become so dependent on her daily routine,
she's started to slip out of everyone else's.

But when a mysterious battered envelope covered in stars
lands on her doormat, Bea wonders if she could find
the courage to open it.

What's written inside might change everything . . .

Available to order

Sometimes all you need is a little push . . .

Georgia loves wine, reality TV and sitting on the sofa
after work. She does not love heights, looking at her bank
account, going on dates, or activities that involve a sports bra.
And she will never, ever take a risk.

That is, until her braver, bolder, big sister finds out that
she won't be able to tick off the things she wanted to do
before turning thirty, and turns to Georgia to help
her finish her list.

With the birthday just months away, Georgia suddenly has a
deadline to learn to grab life with both hands. Could she be
brave enough to take the leap, for her sister?

And how might her own life change if she did?

Available to order

Keep in touch with Olivia Beirne!

www.oliviabeirne.co.uk
olivia.beirne
/Olivia-Beirne